Crown of Hearts

ALSO BY LEANÉ GILIOMEE

THE TWISTED CROWN TRILOGY
Book 1: If The Crown Fits
Book 2: Crown Of Hearts

CROWN OF HEARTS

LEANÉ GILIOMEE

The Twisted Crown Trilogy, Book 2

JOFFE BOOKS

Joffe Books, London

www.joffebooks.com

First published in Great Britain in 2025

Cover design by SeventhStar Art

ISBN: 978-1-83526-979-4

To Dad.
You know why.

THE KINGDOMS OF EVERNESS,
NORRANDALE AND ARGON

Chapter 1

Elara

The crown felt heavy and cold as it rested atop my head.

"I believe it suits you better than it did your predecessor, Your Majesty," Rhen, the captain of my guard, commented. He was standing below the dais, wearing half a smile. I wondered for a moment if my discomfort was that obvious. Who knew crowns could be so impractical?

It was an autumn afternoon in the city of Levernia and the throne room was quiet enough that it gave the illusion of peace and tranquillity.

"You reckon?" I pushed the gem-covered crown a little to the left to keep it from slipping off my head. I had not yet become accustomed to wearing the heavy piece of jewellery. Not just because it often caused the muscles in my neck to strain but also because it represented the unequivocal truth that I was now the Queen of Everness.

"Well, your head is so much bigger than Prince Lance's, so it would make sense that it's a better fit."

Weeks had passed since the rebellious uprising led by my uncle and his clan of thieves, the very rebellion that had placed me on the

1

throne. One of my first orders as queen was to reinstate Rhen as head of the palace guard, with an official pardon from the Crown. Lance had imprisoned him for aiding me and Uncle Arthur during this period of chaos and violence. Instead of helping my wicked brother in his quest to steal heirlooms from the prince of Norrandale, Rhen and his sister, Cordelia, had sided with us.

Lance had me believing he was going to have Rhen executed for treason, when in reality Rhen carried a very precious secret — the knowledge that I was the heir to the throne.

Some days, I still questioned why he hadn't told me the truth earlier. But I couldn't be sure that I would have believed him. I hardly believed I was the lost daughter of King Magnus now, and I'd been living in the palace for more than a month. Nonetheless, it soon became clear that I needed Rhen as more than just my personal guard. He had become a friend and valuable advisor since my coronation. With the aftermath of the rebellion and the death of Uncle Arthur, Rhen was one of the few people left that I could trust. The irony wasn't lost on me. The same person who'd once placed me in a prison cell, so that Lance could blackmail me into stealing from our enemy kingdom, was now my right-hand man.

"Very funny," I muttered. "I rather think I look much better than Lance did, thank you very much." I traced my hands across the velvet armrests of my throne, the material slightly worn from age and faded from the sunlight streaming through the windows.

My throne.

My crown.

It wasn't that long ago that I stood, shackled and chained, facing this very throne. It had looked bigger from below the dais, more intimidating. The throne had housed Evernean kings for centuries.

Powerful men and warlords had perched in this spot as they looked over their subjects. And now, it housed me, perhaps one of the last people in this kingdom who belonged there.

A long time ago, there wasn't a single throne, but two, seated next to each other.

I never saw it in person but there were a few old paintings around the palace that proved this to be true. I couldn't bring myself to ask why there was now only one. Like most parts of Evernean history, I feared an answer that was dark and unwanted.

"Of course, Your Majesty," Rhen responded with a hint of a smile. "Lance could never compete with your beauty, after all." I simply shook my head at him, unable to remain annoyed.

There was a sense of relief at no longer having Lance sit on the throne. And while his only interests now seemed to be finding the bottom of a glass and annoying his prison guards, it didn't stop me from believing that ulterior motives could be at play. No one as self-serving as Lance would simply give up or retreat. He might not have any particular interest in the responsibilities of the monarchy, but he'd been willing to use me as a pawn in his political games, and I would be a fool to think he'd set all his unholy desires aside just because he was momentarily behind bars.

It was harder still to believe that Uncle Arthur was in his grave. Even after everything he'd done and after all the lies, some distant part of me felt guilty that I didn't say goodbye. He was, after all, the only father figure I'd ever known. Even if he didn't tell me the truth about who I really was. Even if he wanted to put me on the throne so that he could control me. I knew it would be for my own benefit to forgive him … and yet … The more I thought about it all, the less I seemed to have anything figured out.

3

Princess Eloisa was still missing. My guess was that she was hiding somewhere in the country. If she'd heard the news that her brother was in prison, she could be waiting to see how things played out. She had no way of knowing if her return would be well received.

But the truth I found most difficult of all was the fact that royal blood ran through my veins. The family I'd been brought up to despise. The family I'd never known. I was the next rightful heir to the throne, burdened with a responsibility I wasn't sure I could carry.

My eyes travelled to the marble floors, worn by centuries of being walked upon. An image entered my mind, of the blood that had coated the floors on the day of the rebellion. Puddles so dark, I'm surprised they didn't leave stains. Weapons clashed as the rebels fought against the palace guards. Fought for what they believed would be their freedom. Fought for what they believed was a better future.

I pushed the images out of my mind. The palace interiors carried tales of horror along every crack and corner. Would that eventually become my fate too? Another crack in the wall, in the history of Everness.

I tried to think of something more light-hearted. "Have you heard anything from your sister recently?"

"The last I heard from Cordelia were those letters from a few weeks ago," Rhen responded.

I'd been both happy and relieved to receive an envelope with Cordelia's handwriting. I couldn't blame my former lady-in-waiting for wanting to leave with Jack, the head of Cai's guard, but I missed her presence and softness, her ability to care like a sister. Cordelia's friendship mattered more to me than I ever allowed myself to admit. Her letters contained stories of Norrandale's beautiful and vibrant towns and people. I had replied to her but kept my responses vague and subtle. More than anything because I feared that whatever news I sent would eventually reach *him*.

The day Rhen informed me Cai had been crowned king of Norrandale, I found myself quite taken by surprise. It was always bound to happen someday, but Cai had left because of his mother's failing health, and instead it was his father who'd passed away. It was difficult to fathom that the once rogue bandit and the charming prince were now the queen and king of neighbouring kingdoms.

I hadn't heard anything from Cai. Not a single word. No letters, no messengers, and certainly no visits. Though I was the one who'd told him to leave, out of anger, I was so sure he would've reached out by now. Instead, I busied myself with anything and everything else to avoid thinking of him. Because I couldn't afford to. Not with my new duties as queen. Cai's silence had told me enough.

There was a soft tapping from above. A crow was outside, pecking against one of the high windows of the throne room. Its dark silhouette shadowed the stained glass, and I frowned in annoyance at the noise. I didn't believe in omens but there was something eerie about the dark-feathered bird. Rhen didn't appear to hear anything.

"Well, as long as Cordelia is safe and happy," I said, matter of fact, and stood up, lifting the hems of my dress so I didn't trip. "Let's go for a walk, shall we?"

The throne room was an enormous hall with high ceilings and large windows, but it now felt stuffy and uncomfortable. It reminded me of the day I was captured and brought to the palace as the Masked Bandit. I could've never imagined that one necklace could bring me so much trouble. A necklace I still held in my possession, even if it didn't truly belong to me. A necklace to serve as a reminder — of what, I wasn't certain.

"Is that jealousy I sense in your tone?" Rhen enquired with a curious grin, following me as I walked away from the dais.

"Of course not," I scoffed, clenching my jaw. "Why would you think me jealous?"

"Because my sister chose love over her friendship with you? And now you're all alone here in Everness, with your kingdom at risk of falling apart."

I halted at the threshold of the throne room. "My kingdom is not falling apart."

Nor would my pride allow me to admit to any kind of jealousy. I really was happy for Cordelia. But coming to terms with how everything had worked out was going to take some time and adjustment.

"Well, it's not falling together, Your Majesty." He said the last part of the sentence with a hint of mockery in his voice and I refrained from rolling my eyes. Rhen had two ways of using my title when he spoke. The first was in public to follow protocol, and the second was with a specific tone when he was trying to get a point across.

"What would you like me to say? I wasn't raised to be a queen." Which we both knew all too well. Most days it was an effort just to remember the little formalities and which damn forks I was supposed to use at the dinner table.

"Don't you see that it can be a good thing? It's because of your past that you have a chance to make better decisions for the kingdom. You understand the lives of the people better than anyone raised in a palace ever could."

What I wanted to say was "How am I going to be responsible for a nation of people when all I wanted to do was run away from it all?"

Instead, I said, "I know you're trying to lure me into talking politics." A subject I wasn't extremely eager to discuss at that moment.

"Can't blame me for trying." He shrugged. "And you can't avoid the subject either."

"Fine. What would you like to discuss?" I hadn't had proper sleep for days and every little thing pricked my temper.

Rhen didn't respond with anything other than two raised eyebrows, annoying me slightly more.

"Why did your sister have to leave me here with you?" I said, more to myself than to him, as we exited the throne room. "Tell me how things are going in the city of Levernia, then."

"Things have settled rather well this side of the kingdom. Most of the aristocrats are pleased you returned the land King Magnus took from them. You've won them over, if nothing else, but as you well know, they can be easily swayed." He paused for a moment. "There are, of course, those who disapprove of your reign."

"Who?"

We continued our walk through the long corridors. We passed the occasional servant with their head bowed, and I cringed inside. I wished they didn't have to do that. I couldn't care less if people bowed for me. It made me feel like some kind of imposter. Couldn't they tell I was nothing more than a bandit wearing a crown?

"The grand dukes of Brett and Creston."

I sighed. "I've already rewarded them for their loyalty and service to the Crown over the past decades. I can't bleed the treasury anymore just because they have an attitude towards me. If I spend any more money, I'm going to run into serious debt." It had been one of my first tasks as queen. I should have been less surprised that loyalty was bought in this place.

"It's more than that," Rhen responded. "They don't believe you to be the true heir of Everness."

"What do they want, some kind of proof?" I asked. "My parents are dead."

"I'm serious."

"As am I. Besides, I look exactly like Eloisa." Or Eloisa looked exactly like me. I didn't want to think about it too much.

"You'd be surprised how little the people actually see of her. I think if Eloisa were to walk the streets, no one would even notice."

I momentarily stopped walking and turned to Rhen. "Magnus and Arthur are dead. Lance is behind bars and Eloisa is who knows where doing who knows what. What exactly do they want me to do? Who do they expect to rule?" Lance may have bought his popularity but only a fool would believe his reign could have lasted very long.

"Your identity as the Masked Bandit hasn't been revealed, but it is known that you were raised as a commoner and then suddenly you show up out of nowhere during Arthur's rebellion and put yourself on the throne."

"I didn't ask for this! The royal council gathered, and it was their vote that put me on the throne."

Everness wasn't the largest kingdom — in fact, in comparison to many kingdoms on the main continent, it was quite small. Across the ocean that separated Norrandale and Everness from the continent lay vast and mighty kingdoms, some almost as old as time itself. Had it not been for the wars they had among themselves, Everness might have been a much bigger target. When it came to our little kingdom, the land was divided among the aristocracy, the most powerful of whom formed part of the royal council. I'd always thought a king had sole authority, but the council was involved with many of the important factors in ruling the kingdom. On the one hand, this could provide assistance with a lot of the decision-making, and with the right people on your side, you could be a very powerful monarch. But I was beginning to learn that this was a double-edged sword. If the council did not approve of you, for whatever reason, the very aristocrats who claimed loyalty could be your downfall.

"Some people still see you as unfit to rule. This is not uncommon for kings and queens, however. We must simply deal with it in the correct manner." Rhen's tone was frank. I never grasped how he approached everything so practically and logically while my emotions went on a rampage with every minor inconvenience.

"Well, it's not like they can just kill me," I grunted, and then remembered Lance was lucky to still be alive.

"Not outright." He shifted his weight, considering his next words. "But these men have influence and there has been unrest in the far east. Country folk in the smaller towns have been rebelling, refusing to pay taxes and spreading words of treason. The people do not know you and therefore they do not trust you to have their best interests at heart. The kingdom is still in turmoil and many of the people live in poverty. Everness is reliant on good crops this year and new trading alliances, the second of which you are responsible for."

"It's not that simple," I retorted. "It's a very isolated kingdom and these things take time."

"You might not have that much time."

I glanced at some of the large paintings and tapestries, depicting scenes of nature, that decorated the corridor walls. Anything to distract me from the anxiety growing inside. "I don't have the strength in me for another rebellion, Rhen."

"Well, it's not entirely out of the question yet, unfortunately." He shrugged. "I'm afraid you don't have many choices."

I clenched my fists, still somewhat in disbelief that I'd got myself into this situation. Two guards opened the glass doors that led out into the gardens. I kept myself from thanking them. They weren't going out of their way. They were merely doing their duty, a duty which was an honour in most eyes. Their uniforms reminded me of Damon and how his eyes would follow me like a hawk when I was still pretending to be Eloisa. I'd never taken any sort of liking towards the guard with the scarred face, but Rhen had told me Damon was one of the many who did not survive the day of the rebellion.

"So, what are my choices, then?" I enquired hesitantly.

"You could marry an Evernean lord who would become king at your side. If it's a suitor the people approve of, it could strengthen your claim to the throne, especially if you have an heir."

This solution appeared to solve only half my problems.

Rhen picked a leaf from one of the hedges we passed.

"And my other choice?"

"You could marry Cai," he said, and my step faltered.

I almost choked out a laugh. "You're kidding, right?"

"On the contrary, I'm being perfectly serious. There was a reason the alliance between Everness and Norrandale was arranged in the first place, even if Lance managed to make an absolute disaster out of it. If you were to align the two kingdoms, the economic and military advantages couldn't be overlooked. It would increase trade and the strength of both kingdoms. Though some conservative Everneans might be opposed because of the kingdoms' past. Of course, Everness isn't an exceptionally powerful kingdom at this stage, being so divided, but we do have a large army that has finally returned from the continent."

"Even *if* I agreed to this …" I entertained the idea for a moment, imagining Cai ruling by my side as king of Everness. The thought only reminded me of his absence. "… we have no guarantee that Cai would do the same. He departed Levernia very abruptly and I haven't heard from him since." I didn't mention that I was the one who'd told him to leave. "I think that sends a pretty clear message."

The hems of my velvet green dress with lace trimming scraped over the cobbled pathway between the hedges. I could hardly remember the last time I'd worn anything but heavy skirts and tight bodices. They were beautiful, of course, but I often forgot how easily the dresses could get damaged or dirty, especially when outside.

The red roses drew my attention, and I picked one from the hedge. It reminded me of the night Cai and I had walked through the gardens of Woodsbrook Manor. I'd lured him from his rooms in the hope that Cordelia would steal his sword so that I could free myself from the deal Lance had blackmailed me into. Instead, I fell victim to his flirtations and charms.

"His mother was dying. He had to leave," Rhen reminded me.

"I heard news that she's recovered. I don't believe it would kill him to reach out."

"And his father has just passed. He was unexpectedly thrust on the throne. My guess is that he has a lot to deal with right now."

As if I didn't know what that felt like.

When I didn't respond, Rhen said, "Why don't you just send a message to him?"

"He's the one who left, why should I write?" I tossed the rose away, watching it tumble into the nearby flower beds, not willing to admit that perhaps my pride was getting in the way of me reaching out to him.

Rhen's expression at my immature comment hinted at mild agitation, though generally his patience with me was applaudable. "I don't understand you sometimes."

"Only sometimes?" I cocked an eyebrow. "Then I suppose you can't complain about the fact that you must obey my every command, as your queen."

"Oh, believe me, I complain. Just not out loud."

We emerged from the rows of hedges, and I looked over the rest of the gardens. There were weeds growing in the flower beds and trees that needed to be trimmed. I realised I had yet to learn who oversaw the maintenance of the palace gardens. It had suffered some damage during the rebellion and there was much work left to be done.

"You know, some days I want to hate my uncle for placing me in this position, but I can never quite bring myself so far."

I had had a small private funeral for Arthur. Only a few of his trusted men were there.

I don't know if he ever told them the truth about my heritage, if that was the reason they supported his cause in the first place. But no one seemed to complain. I wondered how many of them went back to Fairfrith camp or started new lives in the nearby towns. Some had even joined the royal guard. Either way, I hadn't heard anything, which I supposed was a good thing in its own way. The same went for the Baruk clan, which led me to wonder what sort of deal Uncle had made with Olwin. I still hadn't heard news from Ray either, which left me to imagine the worst.

"The man is dead. And we must all move on."

"He made such a mess of things because he couldn't get along with his brother," I said, more to myself than to him.

"Does this mean you intend to do things differently?"

"I mean, I haven't planned Lance's execution yet, which has to count for something." I hadn't seen Lance since he was imprisoned and forced to abdicate. I couldn't bring myself to go down there into the prison cells where I had spent a night myself. In fact, I refused to think about him at all, if possible. No good could come from it, anyway.

"So, you're just going to keep him locked up for ever?"

"I haven't decided yet." I turned to face Rhen. He hadn't shaved in some time but still looked impeccably neat in his royal guard uniform with his hands resting behind his back. Always at attention. Always looking, always watching. Eyes scanning for possible danger. I relaxed a little.

"Let's say I do decide to marry an Evernean lord." I reverted to the previous subject. "Who would my potential suitors be?"

We reached the centre of the garden. "There's the Duke of Dankershire. He's young and rich and owns a considerable stretch of land."

"Only because I gave it back to him." I gave him a sideways glance. "You disapprove of the duke?"

I thought back to our encounter a few weeks prior. There wasn't a big difference in age. But the scrawny duke with hair of snow could never quite meet my eyes. When the duke's father died, he was placed in charge of the estates at a very young age. Making conversation was difficult until we'd heard the horses being exercised outside.

The sound alone made him pipe up and immediately he started to converse about his love for the equine. The only problem … the man didn't stop.

"It's not that I disapprove so much as the fact that he is a complete and utter bore."

"I think that's subjective," Rhen countered.

"Rhen," I huffed. "He showed more interest in my horse's flanks than in me. He wouldn't shut up about the damn fillies, and I like horses as much as the next girl, I really do. But it's the only thing the man talked about all day. All day, Rhen."

He nodded and there was a faint grin on his face. "Okay, so maybe not horse boy." Rhen thought about it for a moment. "There is always the Duke of Darwick's son."

"You mean Edgar Darwick?" I tried to keep my expression neutral but my distaste must have been obvious.

Rhen pressed his lips into a line. "I take it you have something against him as well?"

"He wouldn't stop staring at me the night we stayed at Darwick's estate." The night I got intoxicated on the wine and wanted to kiss Cai outside my bedroom door. The night I drunkenly told him that I was his.

"He was probably just admiring you."

I felt a chill, remembering Lord Edgar's gaze. "There is admiration and then there's what he did. Edgar kind of makes me uncomfortable."

"Even so, the Darwick family is not only incredibly rich, but they are one of the most influential families in the kingdom. You could do much worse than Edgar."

"Still," I protested, "I could also do much better."

"Like whom?" Rhen crossed his arms and tilted his head in taunting question.

"Well." I smirked. "I could always marry you."

His face fell immediately. "Please don't."

I laughed. "Don't worry. We both know that we'd kill each other before the wedding was even over. And then I would lose my right-hand man."

"Yes, how would you ever get along without bossing me around all the time?"

I could tell he was getting frustrated. I wasn't fond of the idea of meeting with the Darwicks, but Rhen was right: they were a powerful family, and if they were not my allies, then I'd better keep my enemies closer.

"Careful now, sir." I turned and started walking back to the palace doors. "It is a queen you're addressing."

"Yes, it is." Rhen replied with mild satisfaction, at what I presumed to be hope that I would finally step into my role.

Chapter 2

Cai

"You're not yourself this morning." Thatcher swung his fist towards my left cheek.

I ducked and barely managed to avoid getting hit.

"You're distracted," my oldest friend and confidant said, with a hint of amusement on his face.

"Am not." I aimed a punch at him, which he blocked before ramming a fist into my stomach. I gasped, stepping back as the air escaped my lungs. Thatcher huffed out a laugh at my rather incompetent defence.

"Yes, you are. You're thinking about *her*, aren't you?" He wiggled his eyebrows, holding up both fists to ready himself for another hit.

There was no proper explanation for why we were throwing punches at each other in a sand ring before ten o'clock in the morning. We had been having breakfast when the topic arose of our training days as two ignorant youths. I had an early start preparing for my role as soldier and king, while Thatcher was only too eager for an excuse to knock me on my behind.

He swore on his honour that he had bested me the majority of the time. I swore he was a liar. Next thing we knew, we were fighting in the dirt, just like the old days. The familiarity of the act held a sense of comfort, which is probably why I didn't want to call it quits just yet, even though I had plenty of responsibilities to attend to today.

I shook off the blow to my torso and put up my fists again. "I'm afraid I don't know who you're talking about," I responded.

"Your lady across the mountains, your forbidden love, the Queen of Everness. What would you like me to call her?" he drawled out, somewhat dramatically, and I looked Thatcher in the eye.

"I'm not thinking about Lara," I said. The mere sound of her name made something in my chest ache.

Thatcher shook his head of curly blond locks and smirked at me. "You should see the way your eyes light up when you say her name."

He was enjoying this way too much.

I kicked behind his knee and tackled him to the ground of the fighting ring, which was just outside the gardens. Though the weather was acceptable, there were few guards on this side of the palace. Usually, they trained during the earlier hours of the morning and then again in the late afternoon. This meant Thatcher and I had the training yard to ourselves, which I had no complaints about. The last thing my men needed to see was their king fighting in the dirt with one of his lords, for no other reason than childish ego.

"Fine, don't talk about her. I know what you're thinking in any case." He shoved me off, hard enough that it caused me to stumble, allowing him to land a kick to my side.

I staggered and pushed myself back into a standing position, just out of his reach. A drop of sweat ran down the side of my brow. I took off my shirt and tossed it outside the ring, needing the distraction to catch my breath. Thatcher used this time to get back up.

"Then you know I'm thinking that I'm about to kick your arse."

He let out another laugh, and then groaned as I punched his nose. It wasn't long before a little blood started to drip. Had it not been for his arrogant expression and the multiple bruises that were likely to cover my body, I might have felt bad. Instead, I was somewhat sleep-deprived, distracted by all my duties and obligations, and trying my best not to think about Elara. Something Thatcher clearly wasn't interested in helping me with.

I didn't want to let him know how much it irked me. Didn't want to let anyone know that I couldn't seem to shake the feeling of being overwhelmed and that this fight in the ring was the only steam I'd let off for days.

"You can say what you like—" he pinched his nose with a grimace — "but I've known you since before we could talk. Don't for a second fool yourself into believing that I don't know what you're thinking."

He sprang at me, taking me by surprise. Thatcher and I shared roughly the same build and height, which is why most of the time there wasn't a definite winner when it came to our sparring. Thatcher feigned left and then dashed right with a lunge. He knocked me to the ground and pinned my neck with his arm. Not hard enough to restrict my breathing, but with enough force to keep me down.

"Just admit that I'm a better fighter than you," he urged. A small line of blood trailed down to his upper lip. I hoped I hadn't fractured anything seriously.

"I might. But it's only because I'm the more mature one out of the two of us," I forced out, tired and slightly sore.

He beamed and sat back in satisfaction, releasing his grip on me. "You know you give up quite easily for someone of your stature."

Thatcher wiped the blood from his face, and I sat up, trying to catch my breath.

"Perhaps I just didn't feel like breaking too many of your bones today."

"Yes, of course, that's what it was."

I reached over to the side of the ring and grabbed my shirt to wipe the sweat and sand from my face. Thatcher picked up a small flask from where his things lay next to the ring and took a sip. I couldn't be sure if it contained water. I was rather parched myself.

"Have you heard anything from Queen Elara at all?" he dared to ask, and I gave him a sideways glance.

"No," I replied curtly, hoping we were done with the topic.

"Have you written to her?"

I sighed. "No."

"Why not?"

I stood up and walked over to him. "It's complicated."

"You mean like the fact that the two of you are engaged?" His tone was teasing but I wasn't exactly in a joking mood anymore.

"We're not engaged. The marital agreement I signed, back when I was supposed to marry Princess Eloisa, was false, in case you forgot. And no one even knows where Princess Eloisa is. She seems to have disappeared off the face of the earth." When I found out Elara had been crowned, I'd thought that news of her sister would soon follow. But rumour had it that Princess Eloisa hadn't been seen in months and that no one was certain of her whereabouts.

"So, what, you're simply going to pretend she doesn't exist now?"

I shrugged. "It's a little difficult to do that. She is the queen of our neighbouring kingdom, after all. I can't ignore her politically."

He handed over the flask and I took a sip. Definitely not water, but maybe I needed it.

"I'm really struggling to see your point here," Thatcher admitted.

I smirked. "I thought you knew everything I was thinking?"

"Clearly I was wrong, because you're an idiot and I don't think like idiots."

"Hey." I handed him back the flask. "Careful now, I could still break one of your bones." I gestured with my head towards the centre of the ring. The idea was growing all the more tempting if he didn't shut up soon. There was a pain to Elara's silence, and it was something I'd rather not think about. Not when there were so many other important things that required my attention.

"Well, the two of you will have to talk to each other eventually. Especially if she's the only woman who has ever loved you." His eyes glinted with mirth.

I shook my head. "She doesn't love me." Saying it out loud was less pleasant than I'd like to admit. Maybe because, deep down, I genuinely believed it to be true. Elara made no promises to me other than to try. And try, I suppose, she did. Neither of us knew just how much things were going to change after the rebellion.

"What do you mean, she doesn't love you? She went back to fight after you told her to run, didn't she?"

"Yes, she went back to fight for her freedom and her family. Not to save me. I made a deal with her that if she didn't want to be with me when the rebellion was over, I would let her go."

"And how do you know she doesn't want to be with you?" Thatcher tilted his head slightly.

Because she told me to leave.

"Rumour has it, she's marrying an Evernean lord," I informed him.

"Rumours are exactly that, rumours. When did you start believing them?"

"It would make sense, wouldn't it? She would strengthen her claim to the throne, which is probably what she needs now more than anything. I can't see why she wouldn't do it." I stepped out of the fighting ring and Thatcher followed.

"Maybe, but would Elara do it? Would the girl you met in the woods do it?"

"The one thing you could count on Lara being is unpredictable. She's reckless but not stupid. Going from the life she lived to being the Queen of Everness could have drastically changed her too. Who knows what she'll do."

"I think you should write to her." We walked over the green lawns, shirts over our shoulders, sweat dripping off our backs. I'd hoped the sparring would ease some of the tension in my gut, but it looked like I'd be carrying those bruises in vain. At least I got to spend some time with Thatcher. Though *this* wasn't exactly panning out to my advantage either, considering he couldn't drop the one topic I'd rather not discuss.

"And say what?" I asked him. "'I'm sorry I didn't tell you the truth about your family but please don't marry another guy even though it would benefit you and your kingdom'?" My tone was more sarcastic than I would have liked.

"Maybe something a little less dramatic?" Thatcher suggested.

"There's nothing I could say without sounding like an utter fool."

"You really do like her, don't you?"

"Just wait, it won't be long before you're in love and miserable." I tried to turn the attention on him and his bachelor lifestyle.

"Aha," he said, walking backwards to face me, pointing with his finger in the air. "So, you do admit that you're in love with her."

"You have a death wish today, don't you?" I followed him through the immaculate gardens. The leaves were turning colour and I would miss the greenery of summer.

"Just calling it like I see it. Though I seriously doubt you'll see me in love with anybody any time soon."

"Still heartbroken over Lady Celia?" I asked with earnest curiosity, but I already had some thoughts as to what the answer would be.

"Celia wasn't like any woman I'd ever met before." He fell into step beside me again. I was thankful to find the garden empty of courtiers, not being in the mood for small talk or to be bombarded with questions. As prince of Norrandale, I used to take for granted all the time I had to myself. Now there was hardly a moment when I was alone.

I refrained from rolling my eyes at Thatcher. "You shared a cup of tea with this woman and a single midday stroll."

"Oh, but, Cai, she was the only one for me," he said dramatically, and I couldn't help but chuckle.

"The only reason you won't be in love with anyone soon is because you have romantic relations with every woman in Norrandale, Thatcher."

"Well, at least then I'm still better off than you, all grumpy and alone."

I shoved him and he swayed slightly. We'd almost reached the doors to the palace when Gwen, Thatch's younger sister, came into view. Gwen, surprisingly, didn't share many of his features. While he, two years her senior, looked like their father, she was the spitting image of their mother. She drew a bowstring, an arrow aimed at a target in the distance.

The intense concentration was visible in Gwen's expression. A light breeze tugged at a lock of hair, blowing it across her face. Despite the obvious irritation, her focus didn't waver for a moment.

"Watch this," Thatcher whispered, picking up a small pebble and pulling back his arm. Yes, I definitely was the mature one, when it came to the two of us. But I knew just as well that there was no point in trying to stop him. One of the very few areas of common ground between Thatcher and his sister was how much they loved to pester each other. He threw it at Gwen and the pebble hit her thigh just as she released the bowstring. The impact of the stone made her jump in surprise and sent the arrow flying in the wrong direction.

Her head swivelled towards us, and I was quick to point a finger in Thatcher's direction, who was bent over with laughter.

"You scoundrel!" Her cheeks reddened.

She might have possessed a sweet and innocent face, but Thatcher and I had attempted too many pranks on her when we were children and I'd suffered enough pain and embarrassing experiences in return to avoid angering her since we'd become young adults. She was certainly the clever one in the family. If Gwen wasn't a lady, she might have even been a valuable royal advisor. But her family had other plans.

"I was this close to improving my tally." She barged over and we instinctively took half a step back.

"You shouldn't take life so seriously, sis. You'll make yourself insane, although it appears you're already halfway there." He turned to throw his arm around her shoulders, but she ducked away and pushed him off.

I quickly stepped between the two of them. "Remember what your mother said," I reprimanded. "No fighting before noon." Which seemed like a silly thing to say, but considering how often they got on each other's nerves, not that surprising. "Shall we call for some dessert when we get back inside?" This seemed to ease Gwen's fury enough that she momentarily calmed down.

"So, you lost against Cai again, huh?" she asked, referring to his bleeding nose, and I'm sure I spotted a hint of pleasure on her face.

"Actually, Cai gave up after a few minutes. These are the battle wounds of my victory."

"Humph." She joined us in our walk back inside, the bow still clutched in her hand.

"And what is it that you have supposedly won?"

"Well, epic bragging rights, of course."

"Yes, having bested His Majesty in hand-to-hand combat really is a victory to brag about." She pushed open the doors to one of the palace's many parlours. We stepped inside the comfortably sized room, decorated with patterned wallpaper and velvet pillows. A few paintings of the palace and surrounding grounds accompanied the chairs and settee.

"You should have seen me, Gwennie." Thatcher started recounting the fight blow by blow, but I could tell Gwen was no longer paying him any attention. She put the bow down and called for a servant. I realised the only reason we still shared her presence was because she'd been promised some dessert. "And then Cai, having realised he could not beat me, finally ceased," Thatcher went on.

"It was good exercise at the very least, and it managed to distract him from Lady Celia." I lightly punched Thatcher on the shoulder. "It was a tough blow for him to see her walking with Lord Leopold the other day."

"I doubt his heart is capable of receiving blows," Gwen retorted, before turning her expression serious. "Cai, I know it's none of my business, but there is a female acquaintance of mine I think you should be introduced to."

"I'm afraid you're too late, Gwen. You know Cai's heart is already set on someone else." Thatcher fell back into one of the chairs and stretched his legs out comfortably. "I, on the other hand, would never say no to another 'female acquaintance'."

Gwen frowned. "I thought Queen Elara was getting married to an Evernean lord?"

I immediately gave Thatcher an "*I told you so*" look.

"Lady Meredette is very intelligent and quite pretty as well," Gwen continued. "I just thought she might be a good fit for you. But what would I know?" Her eyes smiled, all the anger and irritation from before having receded, and I shook my head.

"I'm not meeting any suitors for now, thank you."

"Tell Lady Meredette that he'll see her next week," Thatcher said, and I groaned inwardly.

"Thatcher, I would appreciate it if you didn't meddle whe—"

"I'm not meddling," he said. "I'm doing you a favour. Once Elara hears you're courting women, she'll come crawling back quicker than I crawl to water after a previous night in the tavern."

"How can she not?" Gwen agreed with him. "She'll have no choice but to make him an offer of marriage." She patted my shoulder.

"Could the two of you let this go?" I shook her off without trying to appear rude.

"Oh, he's touchy about it, isn't he?" Gwen looked at her brother and he nodded. One wouldn't think they were fighting only a few minutes earlier. Sometimes I believed it was better when they were. At least then I didn't have this kind of unwanted attention.

My discomfort and irritation regarding the subject growing, I said, "My apologies, but I have duties I must attend to urgently."

"Typical, always leaves when the conversation gets interesting." Gwen crossed her arms and shook her head in disapproval. But a servant entered with a tray of sweet treats and she perked up, the topic of my suitors forgotten. I was surprised she didn't clap her hands as she inspected the selection on the tray before her, deciding which pastry or cake she would like first. There were chocolate truffles, shortcake, caramel tarts and small vanilla cakes to choose from. Even Thatcher appeared to be considering one or two of them. It was an opportunity to take my leave.

I hurried off to my chambers hoping that there was a chance I was already late for some meeting and that Jack was looking for me. Deep down, I knew it did me some good to get into the ring with Thatcher, even if the conversation was less than desirable. He could drive me crazy at times, but he was also my best friend, and I knew he only wanted what was best for me.

My entire world had been shaken when I returned from Everness. Just as my mother finally began to recover from her illness, it was my father who passed away in his sleep. And overnight, I'd become king of Norrandale. Even though I'd always known this day would come, I'd never felt more unprepared for anything in my life. Every morning, I would wake up and wish my father were still alive to guide me and tell me what to do. I was too swamped in my duties to truly grieve him. Most days, it felt like I'd barely had the time to breathe, and worst of all, I just couldn't stop thinking about Elara either. I knew too much of my mental capacity had been taken up by the girl who was a kingdom away. The only bandit I'd ever liked. The only thief I'd ever trusted. Most of the time I tried to push Elara from my mind. Most of the time I was unsuccessful. It drove me positively mad.

I entered my rooms and walked over to the basin to splash my face with some cold water. It felt cool and refreshing against my skin. A servant laid out some clean clothes, while I tried to wash away the dirt from my back, arms and neck. I got dressed in a hurry, not yet certain what awaited me for the day but knowing it was going to have its challenges.

One would think a kingdom so rooted in its traditions, with clear societal roles, would run more smoothly. Instead, every single day, a new problem presented itself. Farmers with feuds about land, distant kingdoms wanting to consider trade agreements, court scandals among the gentry. I found it difficult to comprehend how my father ruled for so many years when I was only about a month in and completely overwhelmed.

The shirt that the servant had laid out for me was neat and oddly decorated with the occasional ruffle. I positively hated the way it clung to my neck and arms. Not to mention I hadn't yet properly cooled down from my spar with Thatcher, or the conversation that followed. I tossed the shirt to the side and riffled through the large wardrobe in the corner of my room. I pulled out one of my older, looser white shirts and threw it on, already relieved at the comfort.

A knock sounded on the door.

"Come in." I pulled down my cuffs while staring at my reflection in the mirror.

Jack entered with Conner trailing behind him like a puppy. He seemed to follow Jack just about everywhere these days. Thankfully, the captain of my guard was the sort of man with the right patience for the job, and I was certain that within a few years Conner was going to be a very good soldier. Although I did have to give it to Conner for sticking it out so long. The kid had been through a lot. Especially in Everness. Still, he didn't waver at the hint of danger.

"I've been looking for you, Your Majesty."

They both did a quick bow. Jack stood up straight, a few inches taller than Conner, who pushed out his shoulders, trying to appear bigger.

"I know." I dipped my hands in the bowl of cold water again and ran my fingers through my hair. There was no saving it, really. I had yet to cut it since I'd returned from Everness. However, my hair was the very least of my worries at this point.

"You're late, Your Majesty." He stood to the side and held open the door for me.

"I know." I sighed and turned towards them. I had no idea what I was late for, but I knew there was someone or something that required my attention. Every matter always labelled as urgent and important, though I hardly thought plans for dances and royal hunts were national crises.

"You've got a bruise on your cheek, Your Majesty," Conner commented, before he could stop himself, and Jack immediately gave him a look to suggest he should shut up if he knew what was good for him.

"I know."

Chapter 3

Elara

The chill morning breeze swept into my chambers through the open window.

Anesta, my lady-in-waiting, noticed the goosebumps form on my skin. The sun chose to remain hidden behind the clouds, casting a shadowy feel over the land of Everness with its dark forests and long winding rivers. The hills rested beneath their cloudy blankets, and the gloominess suited my mood.

"Are you cold, Your Majesty?" she asked.

"Cold, nervous, thinking about jumping out of that window — does it matter?"

She couldn't help but let out a laugh. "You really dread meeting the Darwicks, don't you?" Anesta walked over to the window and closed it.

Of course I dreaded meeting them. I wasn't sure how other royals handled these kinds of situations, but I was never not going to feel awkward discussing the prospect of marriage like I was discussing what to have for dinner. I knew I couldn't exactly avoid them for ever. As Rhen had mentioned, they were a very influential and popular family. And if I wanted to remain Queen of Everness, I needed the strong noble families on my side.

"Have you met the Darwicks before?" I asked, meeting her gaze in the mirror as she placed a pearl necklace around my neck.

I should have been used to wearing expensive jewellery by now. Still, I couldn't help touching a fingertip to one of the pearls. I'd held plenty of expensive jewels in my hand as a thief, but I never wore them. They were a means to an end, not a decoration meant to flatter me. And yet, I couldn't help but like the way it looked on me.

My dress was more comfortable than I'd thought it would be. The light blue silk trailed past my ankles to where my shoes laced up my calves.

"No, I haven't," she admitted. "But I've heard plenty about them."

"Well, once you see them, you might understand my mood."

"I'm sure Lord Edgar's not as horrid as you remember." She tidied up the room by putting the brushes, ribbons and hairpins back into the drawers.

"You should have seen him the first time we met back at the Darwicks' estate. He kept looking at me, and I can promise you now, he wasn't thinking, '*Hey that's a nice dress she's got there*'."

"Well, then go out there and be the queen I know you are. Show him who he's dealing with," she reminded me. "Besides, you should get used to men's eyes falling out at the sight of you. You are now the most desired woman in the kingdom." I could almost have snorted at the preposterous thought. If they knew who I really was underneath all the glamour, they probably wouldn't be that interested.

"You know, sometimes I wish I possessed the confidence you have in me."

Anesta talked like I was fully capable of ruling a kingdom. I wish I could believe it.

She tweaked a few strands of my hair once more. "The more you act like a queen, the more people will learn to respect and even fear you." And then she added, "Your Majesty," with a grin.

I watched her fuss over my hair in the mirror, making sure not a lock was out of place.

Acting. That's exactly what it felt like I was doing. Temporarily filling in a role until someone better came along and replaced me.

I stood up, taking in my reflection. With Anesta's talent, I looked like a blue fairy. And not the childish kind, more like the enchanting, ethereal kind.

"Just remember that you are the prize. The Duke of Darwick is here to make a proposal which you can deny at any time. He cannot force you into marrying his son."

"One thing I've learned," I said, brushing down my dress and taking a final glance at my reflection in the mirror, "is that it's a dangerous game to underestimate people."

"And that will be their mistake should they attempt to underestimate you."

I gave Anesta a knowing look. "Perhaps *you* should have been queen. I think you're much better suited for the role than I am."

She shut my cupboard and brushed a stubborn strand of hair out of her face. "Goodness, no. It's too much responsibility. I make a daily prayer, giving thanks that I'm not you."

"Hey!" My eyes widened at her blunt comment as I pretended not to be offended.

"I'm kidding," she assured me. We both knew she was not. I turned to the row of crowns before me. There was the one that I'd inherited from Lance, a smaller pearl one that might suit my jewellery better, and then there was another large diamond one, definitely more intimidating.

"You know what I mean," Anesta continued. "Though I wouldn't be opposed to being a duchess." She gave me a wink. I'd specifically asked Rhen for a lady-in-waiting of a much lower station. Someone I could trust and who wouldn't gossip about me at court. I also requested having only one lady-in-waiting. This wasn't entirely conventional, but the last thing I needed was a train of people running after me.

"Shall I arrange a marriage for you, then? Trap the poor bastard before he has a chance to run away?" I asked her.

"Maybe give me a chance to trap him first." She handed me the crown of pearls. "I'm much better at flirting than you are, anyway."

"Anesta!"

"You don't need any skill, Your Majesty. You already have more than any other girl could offer. The rest of us are reliant on our charms and wit." Where had the time gone when I was reliant on my wit?

I placed the pearl crown on my head, causing a few hairs to go astray, and after some more fussing from Anesta, I'd finally had enough. I turned and headed for the white, decoratively carved doors of my rooms, Anesta darting to catch up with me.

"Don't be offended. You're the Queen of Everness. You don't have to flirt. Men will sell their souls to marry you."

"Only it won't be for the right reasons." A few months ago, I was living in the woods, bathing in rivers and stealing from the very people who lived in my court, and here I was, multiple crowns and dresses, actually contemplating arranged marriages. The thought made me nauseous.

Before all this, I never had the particular luxury of thinking about marriage, not when my next meal was much more important.

I would admit that, at times, I thought maybe one day Ray and I would eventually marry. Mostly because there was no one else. But as Anesta said, I had the pick of them now. I could probably marry any great man I wanted. But where on earth did you find a good one? Someone worthy?

Rhen was waiting outside my chambers, ready to escort me.

"She's become a romantic," Anesta teased in response to my comment.

"Who's gone romantic?" Rhen asked, and I shook my head.

"I've not become a romantic. I simply don't want to marry a power-hungry man who will stab me in the back."

"Well, you're off to a smashing start with the Darwicks," Rhen said, though his tone didn't suggest this to be true.

"This was your idea," I reminded him.

"Yes, I said it would be to your political advantage, not that it would keep you from getting murdered." He must have seen my worried expression because he added, "Though I'm sure you'll be fine." Rhen cleared his throat. "Darwick will need an heir before he can kill you anyway."

"You two are not helping at all." I clenched my jaw, dreading the meeting even more than I had before.

We descended the staircase, before making our way down the hall that led to the throne room. After the rebellion, I'd sent most of the court to their estates while things were cleared up. And then I got rather used to the quiet of the palace, which made me picky about who was allowed to visit. The Duke of Darwick and his son, Edgar, already stood awaiting me. Good. I hoped they'd been waiting for a while.

The duke was a tall man with dark hair and dark eyes. Edgar had his father's features along with an upturned nose and deep Cupid's bow. He was dressed more finely than the last time we'd seen each other, as was to be expected.

"Your Majesty," the duke said, and the two of them bowed. I knew they did it because they had to, but it made me wonder how much they truly respected me. The lost heir who'd not been brought up in the ways of the nobles. The queen with no experience or rights to her title other than by birth, who now held their fate in her hands. I doubted their affection for me surpassed mine for them. Not beyond what my position could offer them anyway.

I halted in front of the Darwicks.

"Darwick, it's lovely to see you," I lied through my teeth.

Still in his bow, the duke took my wrist and placed a presumptuous kiss upon my hand. "Not as lovely as it is to see you, Your Majesty," he purred, in a way that caused my discomfort to grow.

I gently plucked my hand out of his grasp without trying to appear rude. "Shall we retire to the dining hall?" I felt Edgar staring at me from behind as we made our way to my private dining room, where we would not be disturbed by anyone.

I had suggested they join me for breakfast, thus keeping the conversation quiet and formal for as long as possible and giving me the opportunity to leave at any moment. It wasn't the norm, of course, and I presumed the Darwicks would think it odd. But I had to keep reminding myself of Anesta's words: it was an honour for them to dine with the Queen.

I took my seat at the head of the table and regretted for a moment that I didn't choose to wear my bigger crown; somehow, I felt as though I wasn't intimidating enough. The dining table was impeccably set, as always, with a thick white tablecloth and stitched napkins. Food was displayed from one side of the table to the other.

Plates filled with breads and cheeses, salmon, sauces, a selection of cured meats, and fruits that looked so fresh they practically glistened. Any other monarch might have found it fitting but it almost made me sick to my stomach. Sick and distraught to imagine people dining like this when, out there in the kingdom, some of my subjects were dying of hunger. How, not long ago, my own family and friends were practically starving. How I had been stealing to ensure my next meal.

The Duke of Darwick sat to my left while Edgar took a seat on my right-hand side. A servant poured us some tea.

The duke, in slight discomfort at the oddity of the meeting, looked around the room and blurted out, "If you don't mind, Your Majesty, I think the sooner we get straight down to business, the better." Lord Edgar hesitantly started filling his plate, his attention having been diverted from me to the array of food. I couldn't say I was disappointed.

"Of course." I took a sip from my cup, my throat dry. "No one would confuse you for a man fond of idle chit-chat, Darwick."

Samuel Darwick smiled. "Well, there is no need to waste time and I believe time is of the essence to you, my queen." I didn't appreciate how his words suggested I was in some sort of predicament and reliant on their cooperation, even if it was somewhat true.

I squinted. "No, I suppose there is no reason to waste time with the usual pleasantries." Of course, they didn't know that we'd met before. Darwick had no idea that I'd been to his estate, had slept in his house and made use of the horses that he'd given me. He was still under the impression that was Eloisa. And there was no reason for them to be informed of the truth.

"We have accepted your invitation to come to court because I'd like to discuss a matter of importance." Darwick tapped his fingers together, his son's eyes lingering on me as he ate.

"As you likely know, being a recently crowned queen has its challenges," he continued.

"The royal court can be a wicked place," I agreed.

"And it's our alliances that keep us protected." He clearly had a few ideas in mind.

"If you are to remain Queen of Everness, you need to secure your reign, Your Majesty. A marriage can be an immensely powerful alliance." Definitely not beating around the bush.

"Your family has a long Evernean lineage, Darwick," I admitted, "and they've always been close to the Crown, haven't they?"

He took a sip of the tea and tasted it for a moment too long. His silence gave the impression that he wanted to dominate the conversation and the room. Part of me couldn't blame him. His family was one of the oldest in Everness and he'd had his hand in noble affairs for a very long time. Now he found himself sitting across from an eighteen-year-old girl who hardly knew anything about the Crown and wanted to tell *him* what to do.

"Yes, Your Majesty. And I believe an Evernean husband would vastly strengthen your claim to the throne. As you said, our family has a long history and heritage, dating back to the founding of Everness. Our land and resources stretch far and wide and you would have the approval of your council as well as the people. All parties benefit this way." The duke wasn't lying. Every single word I knew to be true. And yet, it still felt like they were getting the better end of the bargain.

"Before I consider an agreement, I have a few questions," I responded, and the duke frowned.

"Yes, Your Majesty?" The tone of his voice gave the impression that it irked him to use my title.

"I have to consider this matter very seriously, as the future of the kingdom hangs in the balance. So, I suppose my question is, why would I want to marry *you*, Lord Edgar?"

He seemed momentarily surprised at my question. Edgar opened his mouth to speak, but before he could reply, I continued, "You would, of course, get to be king of Everness, but you are not the only wealthy family in this kingdom. And more importantly, we hardly even know each other."

I was in way over my head and perhaps risking the only alliance currently offered to me. But Anesta was right, being a scared queen who gives in to any offer because of fear wasn't going to get me anywhere either. Even with my hands shaking, I had to remind myself that I was the one with power.

I am the prize. I am the prize. I am the prize.

I stood up from the table and folded my hands together so that the shaking would be less visible. Then I took a slow, deep breath to steady myself as I walked around the table to where Edgar was sitting. I used to be the most wanted thief in Everness. I was not going to be patronised by a spoiled boy and his overbearing father. I held out a — now steady — hand towards Edgar.

"Care to join me for a walk? Perhaps we could change the latter."

His cautious expression turned into an unsuspecting grin, renewing my previous feelings of discomfort. Something about him unnerved me. I just couldn't put my finger on it.

"It would be my pleasure." It was the first time he'd spoken, and I wasn't sure I liked the way he stretched out the word "pleasure". He took my hand, rising from his seat, his plate full of food forgotten.

His hand was cold and clammy in mine, and I shifted our position so that I was holding the crook of his elbow. Together, we made to leave the dining hall.

The Duke of Darwick tried to hide his offence in having been excluded. When Rhen made a motion to follow us, I held up my hand. I needed a private audience with Edgar for various reasons and something told me he wasn't going to get in many words as long as his father was around.

I pulled away from him, pretending to fix my dress as we continued down the marble hallway and into the throne room. A servant was sweeping the floors, which seemed like a useless and impossible task with a room so large. The servant girl looked up, her eyes flashing with recognition for a moment. She awkwardly stepped out of our path.

"You've been awfully quiet so far," I commented, trying to assess his character.

Edgar shrugged, picking at a nail. "My father likes the sound of his own voice. Eventually you learn to stop listening."

I let out a "humph", thinking for a moment that perhaps Edgar did possess some sense of humour. It didn't count for much, but it was better than being married to a boring man.

I looked about the throne room, trying to come up with something for us to talk about.

"I've always thought this room to be rather cold, don't you think?"

Edgar gazed at the ceiling that stretched high above us. "I suppose on a cloudy day like today, it can be a little dark despite all the windows."

"Perhaps I could add a few tapestries to brighten it up?" Good grief, had I truly resorted to talking about tapestries?

"I'll admit, I don't know much about tapestries." At least he was honest. That had to count for something, right?

"Do you have any particular interests, then?"

"I like to read."

Of course, he liked the very thing I preferred to avoid as much as possible.

"I wish I was more of a reader, but it seems like there's always something better to do. I'm rather fond of the outdoors. That is, when I'm not occupied with my duties." I didn't want it to sound like I spent my days gallivanting around the palace, with the current state of the kingdom.

"That's nice." Edgar already appeared bored, so I decided to change the topic.

"What are your reasons for going along with your father's proposal?"

"As you said, because I get to be king," he replied, like I was some kind of idiot.

"Is that all?" I gave him the opportunity to redeem himself.

Edgar's eyes roamed over me before he smirked and finally said, "No."

A quick shiver ran down my spine and I looked towards the nearest window, not wanting to meet his eyes. It was probably too late to jump out now.

"Still, not anybody can just wake up one day and decide to rule the kingdom." I attempted to keep my voice emotionless.

"You did."

I looked at him in surprise. "Excuse me?"

"You showed up out of nowhere and became Queen of Everness."

We'd come to a standstill and Edgar looked around the throne room as if contemplating what his future here could look like. Well, not if I could help it.

"That wasn't my choice. My brother abdicated and I was next in line to rule."

"Speaking of which." He gave me a raised eyebrow. "Where is His Highness, again?"

I didn't answer.

"You have given me no reason whatsoever to accept your hand," I finally told him, letting my irritation slip into my voice.

He shrugged. "I don't have to win your approval. You need me."

"I beg your pardon?"

"Without me, you will eventually lose against the aristocrats and the unrest in the east. You have too many enemies from within. You need someone like me to protect your claim, satisfy the public and provide you with an heir."

Before I would have snorted at him, but now I was plain disgusted. Disgusted at his manners, his lack of propriety and blatant disrespect. And coming from me, the girl who'd once spat in a prince's face, that was saying a lot. I stepped back to make my way to the dining room again. "I suggest you take your leave."

Before I make you.

The meeting was over and done with, as far as I was concerned. "I'm starting to think your father isn't the only one who likes the sound of his own voice," I muttered, more to myself than to him.

As I headed for the door, I met the wide eyes of the servant girl who'd now stopped sweeping.

"You're no more a monarch than I am, thief," he sneered.

I halted, slowly turning around to face him again. "What?"

"You think I don't know who you really are?" he said in a low voice.

"You cannot try and blackmail your queen with a rumour. I can have your head for this."

"Soon the whole of Everness will know your little secret."

My heart raced. I opened my mouth to speak but nothing came out. Pure ice-cold fear filled every inch of my body. If anyone ever found out I was the Masked Bandit, they would have my head. I wouldn't even live to see the trial.

How the Darwicks knew was beyond me. It didn't matter. I was sinking into much deeper trouble than I thought. The only thing the aristocracy hated more than a young and weak queen was the bandit who had troubled them for years.

"I have no idea what you're talking about."

Deny. Deny. Deny.

"I don't make idle threats," he said, and my mind raced, trying to come up with something to say.

The servant girl moved suddenly, coming towards us.

"Neither do I. It's your word against mine." I didn't want him to see that I was scared. Couldn't let him know he currently possessed the upper hand.

"Unless you marry someone more powerful, you're out of choices, I'm afraid. And since nobody is lining up, I dare say you will be mine."

The servant girl was behind him now. She tossed the broom to the side and pulled out a kitchen knife. I watched in shock as she pushed Edgar out of the way and came straight for me.

I moved quickly, my eyes focused on the long silver blade. Taking a step back, I almost tripped on the hem of my dress. Stupid dresses that didn't have any places to keep weapons in them.

"You should never have taken the crown," she spat out, hair slightly rough, her freckled face filled with disgust.

"You don't belong on the throne." She came at me, and I barely missed her jab to my stomach. Who'd sent her? Who did she answer to? I couldn't process the thought of an assassin in my palace.

"Rhen, guards!" I shouted, watching for her next move.

Edgar stammered, mouth opening and closing stupidly. Instead of trying to help me, he stepped away.

"You're not a real queen."

"Enough," I told the servant girl. I doubted I would be able to talk sense into her. There was too much hatred in her eyes. If only I had something on me to protect myself.

"You shouldn't have come here." She attempted to stab me again and I jumped out of the way. In desperation, I took the crown from my head and used it to try to knock the dagger from her hand. But the young girl's grip was strong and her motivation more than ample. I dodged her left and right, while realising a pearly crown was not the most practical weapon. The doors burst open as Rhen and a few palace guards entered. It was only in this moment that Edgar decided to step in and help by grabbing her from behind. She kicked and thrashed, blade flashing, almost cutting him before the guards grabbed hold of her and held her hands behind her back. She continued to scream profanities as two of the guards dragged her out. As I had once been dragged out of the very same throne room. I shuddered, breathing deeply. Blood pumped wildly through my veins.

"You're bleeding." I flinched when Rhen touched my skin. The girl had managed to nick my arm, but I was shaking too much to take notice.

"Come on." He led me by my other arm. "We'll get a physician to look at that."

"No." I pulled away. "I'll do it myself. Have someone see the Darwicks out."

We both knew the best thing was to have a physician attend to the wound rather than add another ghastly scar to my skin. But Rhen also knew better than to argue with me. We hurried back to my rooms. He kept looking left and right, his body shielding me. I walked into my chambers with a few men standing guard outside.

"I need to go and deal with what just happened downstairs," Rhen said. It had been a long time since I'd seen him this shaken, though he was trying his best to not show it.

"The Darwicks?" I looked in the mirror at the small trail of blood running down my arm.

"The girl. Someone just tried to assassinate you." Right.

"What are you going to do with her?" I turned to face him.

"She committed an act of treason," he said, as if I didn't know.

"She's just a child, Rhen. She doesn't know any better." And yet, Rhen was right. She had just tried to kill me. Beyond the hate, I saw something in her eyes that I used to recognise in my own. Desperation. She had done nothing that I wouldn't have likely done, not so long ago.

Rhen met my eyes.

"I will interrogate her. Maybe she isn't the only one inside the palace."

I nodded and he left the room, allowing me to catch my breath. My heart was pounding, and for the first time in a long time, I realised that I was afraid … truly afraid.

I tossed the crown onto the bed before dragging my fingers through my hair. I wanted to be sick. My arm was still bleeding, and the pain of the cut started to settle in. How had things gone so wrong so quickly?

Without thinking, I grabbed a nearby vase and threw it at the opposite wall, watching the glass break and cover the ground beneath in little pieces. The vase was probably antique and valuable. I didn't care.

Between my servants trying to kill me and the Darwicks trying to blackmail me, I might have been better off that day of the rebellion if I'd just stayed on the damn horse and run away. Clinging to the bedpost, I sank down onto the bed, holding back tears.

Chapter 4

Cai

I pushed the food around my dinner plate. The dining table was filled with large trays of roasted meats, bowls of steaming vegetables and jugs of fine wine. Each item had been cooked to perfection and plated with precision, and I almost felt bad for not feeling very hungry. I caught my mother's glance from across the table.

"You've been very quiet this evening, Cai."

The room grew quiet apart from an awkward knife clattering onto a plate. All eyes fell on me.

"He might be sitting at this table but he's certainly not thinking about it," Thatcher murmured, loud enough for everyone to hear.

It wasn't unusual for Thatcher and Gwen to join us during our private family dinners. They were practically part of the family. But tonight, I might have preferred to eat without company. My mother hid a smile as if she could tell exactly what occupied my mind. It was one of the few smiles she'd given since Father died.

She'd always known me well enough that I could never hide anything from her.

Which only made my mischievous moments as a teenager all the more challenging. But she never yelled or screamed, and fearing her disappointment became much worse than fearing her anger. She could tell I'd changed since going to war, but we'd grown closer in the time since. Before going to Everness and then being crowned, I would go on long walks with her, and we'd talk about nothing and everything. I used to look forward to those walks and the peace they managed to bring me.

"You're right. My thoughts have been occupied with the new library we're building in the city."

Gwen coughed, seemingly innocently, at my words, and I sent a look in her direction.

"I think it's a wonderful venture. Especially with the large new children's section. We never did make enough of a priority of literature and the arts," my mother replied.

Her illness was so sudden and unpredictable, and even though she'd recovered, she seemed more fragile than the woman she was before. But I feared losing her husband had more to do with it than anything else.

It was like all the strength had gone out of her, and where she used to spend hours on end in the garden, among the flora she adored, she now grew tired easily.

She was right about the library, however. They did have more important things to worry about back in those days. Including wars and treaties and invaders and alliances. There never truly was time for privileges like reading. But I needed to keep my mind occupied, and the city needed a new library.

Being a typical boy, I'd never appreciated my education enough during my younger years. But I could not look past the value it added to my life now. Too many of our people were illiterate because of the circumstances they grew up in. I wanted to find ways to help them grow and expand our economy. I didn't want everyone to be held back by a label their entire life.

I understood better than anyone what it meant to have a title that kept you from certain freedoms, and I was speaking from a position of privilege, not that of a farmer who had to work from dawn to dusk to keep food on the table for his family. I could admit that my stay at Fairfrith had affected the way I viewed my subjects. And I believed it was a good thing. I'd been shielded my entire life, and I knew a library wasn't magically going to fix everyone's problems, but it was a start. I forced myself to take a bite of the dinner I'd been served.

"There has been recent news from Levernia," my mother said, drawing my attention. My head swivelled in her direction quicker than I would have liked. "Apparently there's been an attack at the palace."

"What attack?" I asked.

"Someone tried to kill the Queen."

I'd stopped chewing my food as a sudden wave of nausea hit me.

"What happened?" Gwen asked before I had the chance.

"Oh, you know by the time news gets here, it's all half-rumour, really. I believe it was one of her servants. As far as I know she is unharmed, but her reign remains under threat." My mother looked straight at me, gauging my reaction.

Someone tried to kill Elara.

"What about her engagement? Surely that would strengthen her claim?" Thatcher piped up.

"While engagements are promising, it's only good if you actually go through with it." My mother's expression suggested I'd been the one to break off the engagement with Eloisa. I didn't tell my family about everything that had happened during my stay in Everness, and I thought, after a while, they knew better than to ask. "The new queen is not married yet."

"What about the relationship between Norrandale and Everness?" Thatcher looked at me and I shrugged.

"I doubt Elara plans to invade any time soon," I assured him.

"And you're definitely not marrying Princess Eloisa?"

"Any documents that were signed were falsified and Princess Eloisa is missing, maybe even in hiding for all we know. Everness has shown no interest in renewing the agreement. Now may we please change the subject?"

Every memory was a vivid image in my mind. Of the time I thought Elara was her sister. Of the night in Woodsbrook Manor when Lance drunkenly used her to try to find the jewel hidden in my family necklace. A necklace I never got back from Elara. The thought made me think of her neck, of the kisses I had pressed to her soft skin. I clenched my jaw.

"Why, is it making you uncomfortable?" Gwen pried.

"No, I simply think that politics is not an appropriate conversation for the dinner table."

She grinned at me. "Liar. You're thinking that you got engaged to the wrong sister."

"I don't believe I see a ring on your finger, Gwen," I blurted, and her expression immediately changed. I cringed inwardly. I hadn't meant to insult her, but I was desperate to talk about something else, anything else.

Thatcher laughed softly. "Some poor bastard would have to be tackled and forced down the aisle."

"Thatcher," my mother gently scolded, like the second mother she was to him.

"Don't worry, Gwen darling. I'm sure you'll marry a perfect gentleman when and if you choose to do so." She tried to console her.

"There are no good men left in Norrandale, Your Highness," Gwen replied. "None with titles, anyway, and Mama would have a fit if I married below station."

I understood perfectly well where she was coming from and even felt somewhat guilty for making the joke in the first place. Gwen would have to marry someone like a duke or a prince, and even worse, if she didn't do it soon, she stood the risk of an arranged marriage at the hands of her parents. It never bothered me that I would not have the luxury of choosing my own bride. I'd been brought up with the knowledge that my marriage would be for political gain, which was why I didn't hesitate when it came to my engagement with Eloisa. It was in the interests of our people. But I was young and foolish enough to forget one very important point. That while the title of the woman I married mattered for our kingdom's sake, so did her character if she were to be a good queen to my people. Norrandale had been privileged with great queens, my mother and grandmother being two of them. I would be doing my people an injustice if I did not marry someone who measured up to them.

"You're right," Thatcher said, in response to Gwen's comment. "The only eligible man left in this kingdom is this man right here." He placed a hand on my shoulder. "I can attest to this."

This made Gwen chuckle. "No offence, Cai, but I'd really rather not be queen."

"No offence taken, Gwen." I smiled at her, trying to make amends for my earlier blow.

"And I'd really rather not have this one for a brother-in-law." I gestured with my head to Thatcher, who met my gaze.

"You wound me so."

I forced a laugh, grateful the conversation had turned away from Elara. My mind churned with the news from Levernia. I hadn't expected Elara's sudden ascension to the throne to be met without opposition, but an attempted assassination was something else entirely. If her people were trying to kill her, then my mother was right: her reign and her life were under threat.

The dining-room doors opened suddenly, and Jack stepped inside. He bowed before saying, "My apologies for interrupting dinner—" he turned towards me — "but you're going to want to see this, Your Majesty."

I followed Jack in silence, his demeanour rigid and hurried. Whatever was going on, it wasn't good. We reached the cellars of the palace and my concern grew.

It was dark — a musty smell pervaded the air. I couldn't remember the last time I'd been down here. A prison guard bowed his head as we passed.

"What exactly is going on?" There had to be a damn good reason he was leading me into the palace's dungeon. Most of the cells were empty. A single rat scurried across the floor.

"We found something, Your Majesty," he responded. "I thought it important that you be notified immediately." Jack grabbed one of the torches that lined the walls so that he could light our way.

"Well, what did you find?" I questioned with a hint of frustration at his evasiveness. Jack's pace was so quick, I almost had trouble keeping up.

He stopped abruptly in front of one of the cells and I turned to look inside.

"Oh?" I said in genuine surprise. Three men were tied up there. "Are they … ?"

"We believe them to be spies, yes. We found them on the outskirts of the city. They were staying in one of the taverns, asking strange questions about the royal guard and the palace. A fight happened to break out and someone spotted the Argonian mark and reported it. The barman says they'd been acting suspicious the whole time they'd been there."

The three men were dressed similarly to Norrandish citizens but one of them had a ripped sleeve and a symbol of the kingdom of Argon clearly tattooed on his upper arm. I immediately recognised the mark. Had seen it on thousands of young soldiers as we fought on the battlefields of Argon. If it were up to me, I'd never set foot in that kingdom across the sea ever again. The horrors of that war still haunted me.

"Do you think they were trying to scout our military forces in the city?" I asked Jack. We had no laws against Argonian citizens coming to Norrandale, but once you became a soldier in Argon's army, you were never allowed to leave. The only way out was by getting killed. Which meant these men certainly couldn't be here for a friendly visit.

"Well, they definitely weren't trying to buy bread or go for a beer."

The idea that Argonian spies had not only come onto Norrandish shores but were inside our city was concerning to say the least. Were they the only ones? Were they rebels? Why did Aries send them here?

"Have they said anything?"

Jack shook his head. "They refuse to speak." I glanced down at Jack's knuckles and noticed a bruise, but the soldiers didn't look worse for wear, which meant they hadn't been beaten for information.

"Keep them here for now." I was unsure of what to do. King Aries could have multiple intentions with sending spies into my kingdom. After the war, Norrandale and Argon had signed a peace treaty and there had been no talk of conflict between our kingdoms since. The thought that Aries could be planning to violate that agreement left a bitter taste in my mouth. It was the last thing I needed.

"Do we have any proof against them that would hold up in a trial?" Jack shook his head. "Not exactly."

"They stay here for the night. See if they're willing to share something." My fists clenched at my sides while I stared at the three men. They weren't built like ordinary citizens. Their physique could only be attributed to years of training and fighting. I'd spent months in battle against such men. It elicited one triggering memory after another, and while I knew they hadn't specifically done anything to me, I was filled with unwanted rage. Rage for what they put me and my soldiers through. Rage for everything King Aries stood for. Rage for the things that would haunt me for the rest of my life.

"Yes, Your Majesty?" Jack seemed uncertain.

"If we don't have any proof they're Aries' spies, then they might just as well be Argonian rebels or refugees of some kind."

"Then they would have said so," he argued.

I nodded. "*You and I* know that, but we'd be breaking the peace treaty if we torture Argonian men or keep them imprisoned without any proof and Aries knows that."

"There's nothing in the treaty that says we can't bargain with Argonians," Alastor said, walking into the prison. He was second in charge after Jack and had accompanied us to Everness as one of my guards and the keeper of our weapons. Despite the fact that we did not share similar titles or upbringings, I considered both Jack and

Alastor friends. Alastor tilted his head left to right, stretching the muscles in his neck. He was out of breath. I hadn't spoken to him a lot recently. Not that Alastor ever talked much, but with all my new duties, I hadn't been able to spend as much time with my guards as I used to. Jack was just about the only one I saw on a daily basis.

"Where have you been?" Jack asked.

"In the training ring," Alastor replied, tying his dark hair out of his face.

"It's dark outside."

"Exactly." He grinned. Something which did not often occur. Alastor was the sort of man you could trust with your life, but never expect to understand him or his methods.

"We can't make them talk." He turned towards the prisoners and crossed his arms. "But we can offer them immunity and a safe life here in Norrandale. As long as they never go back to Argon."

"Just so the Argonians can slowly invade us by pretending to be citizens of the kingdom? That's a terrible plan." Jack frowned.

"I didn't say it was a plan. It was a suggestion." Alastor put his hands up in defence before leaning back against the prison wall.

"What if they were to die of 'natural causes'?"

The three men didn't so much as flinch or look up at the thought of their possible demise. These men were more than willing to die for their king. It had been drilled into them from the moment they became Aries' soldiers. Argon before everything else. It made them ruthless and relentless on the battlefield and the reason not many kingdoms risked standing up to Aries, despite him being a young king.

"We can't just kill men because they're loyal to the kingdom they were born in," Alastor countered.

"Then what do you call war?" Jack cried.

"We are not at war with Argon. We cannot risk the peace treaty," I cut in. "Until we are certain what Aries' plans are, there is too much at stake. For all we know, they could have gone rogue."

"So, what do you suggest, Your Majesty?"

"Keep them here for questioning. Maybe they will eventually be willing to talk. One of you keep watch for the night."

"I believe I've got this." Alastor rubbed his hands together and stalked towards the soldiers.

The wind pressed against my back. I stumbled forwards in the tall, wet grass. My armour constricted my body. It was difficult to breathe. I stumbled on. There was a terrible smell in the air. The scent of death.

I heaved, forcing myself to continue walking. My sword dragged behind me. The sharp edge scraped along the ground with each step. With every moment, it became more difficult to breathe. It felt as if my lungs were collapsing. As if my heart had already been ripped out of my chest. I was already dead.

My head spun, the lack of food and water taking its toll. The battlefield was a ballroom of soldiers in a dance with death. Bodies collapsed on the ground beside me.

Another step.

Something grabbed my ankle and my thumping heart skipped a beat. I looked down. It was the hand of one of my soldiers. "Harris." I bent down. His eyes were wide with fear. A large gash covered his chest. He was bleeding to death and there was nothing I could do. He was barely seventeen.

I grabbed his hand.

"Your Highness, I'm afraid." His voice was hoarse.

"Do not be afraid," I said, as calmly as possible. It was an effort to keep my voice from cracking. "You have served your kingdom well."

"I want to go home," he said with sadness, his breathing becoming more laboured with every second.

"You will go home," I lied. There was no need for me to burden him with heavy truths in his last moments. He would go home … in a casket. "You'll go home," I promised. "And you'll receive a reward for your valour and bravery." I hated this. Hated every moment of this. Hated that he wasn't the first one. That he wouldn't be the last.

"A reward?" A hint of a smile. I nodded, still clutching him. "My family would be so proud."

"Yes, they will. They will be so proud of you, Harris." He had a mother, a sister who depended on him for an income. A mother and sister who were waiting for him to come back to them.

"It hurts," he wheezed. "It hurts, Your Highness."

"I know." I clenched my teeth. "It will stop hurting soon." Blood dripped from his mouth, and I held on to him until he released his final, dying breath. I closed Harris's eyes and sent up a silent prayer for him.

I forced myself to stand up and scan the battlefield again. There he was. The youngest Argonian prince and Aries' younger brother. He took pleasure in capturing my soldiers and torturing them for information. He took pleasure in the deaths of men like Harris. And it would end today. I was filled with more anger than I knew I could possess. Blind rage, searing white aggression.

My vision grew tunnelled, my sole focus on him. One goal in mind. With each step, his armoured body got closer. I watched him drive his sword through one of my soldiers, his back towards me. The man let out a cry of death. I was almost there. He pulled his sword out and shoved the soldier to the ground. I would not allow him to kill any of my men again.

I didn't hesitate. Not when he gasped in surprise. Not when he fell to the ground, with blood seeping onto the grass. I didn't hesitate to twist *the sword. Didn't hesitate when he screamed. A part of me had died in battle, had died along with every one of my fallen soldiers. I could not bring them back. I could not bring them to their mothers, or wives or sisters or friends. But I could avenge them. Their lives and their deaths would mean something.*

The prince stopped moving. I stood there for a moment, motionless. Part of me expected that I would feel something once he was gone. Satisfaction, relief maybe? But nothing. I was completely numb.

I woke up screaming.

Droplets of sweat ran down my chest. There was a knock on the door before Jack peered in.

"Everything all right, Your Majesty? I heard a scream." I should have felt embarrassed, but it wasn't the first time Jack heard me screaming myself awake and I would venture to bargain that it wouldn't be the last.

"Jack, what are you doing outside my rooms?" My voice came out hoarse.

"I was just making the rounds, Your Majesty."

"Don't you ever sleep?" I pushed away the sheets that were clinging to my body.

"I couldn't, Your Majesty. So, I thought I might as well take the night shift."

I swallowed hard. My throat was dry. "All right then."

"So, all is well, Your Majesty? I can leave you be?"

All was not well. But my nightmares were mine alone. As far as everyone was concerned, everything had to be well, always. It was my duty. My royal duty. It was not that I couldn't trust Jack. It was that I couldn't trust myself. That once the gates were opened and the dams broken, I wasn't certain I would be able to close them again.

"Get a servant to light the candles, please, Jack." I might as well get started with work. Despite it being the early hours of the morning, I was not going back to sleep. I would not be favoured with rest again before the sun rose.

Chapter 5

Elara

"Shall I get you anything else?"

I shook my head as Anesta poured the last bucket of warm water into the tub. She picked up the clothes strewn across the floor, where I had left them. It didn't sit well with me. She shouldn't have to pick up the things I'd scattered like some spoiled child.

"No, thank you. You can leave me be."

She seemed hesitant to leave me alone. I felt a twinge in my stomach. Serving the queen was one of the most highly esteemed duties a person in this kingdom could have. By tradition, a queen had many ladies-in-waiting and servants, but I preferred that Anesta handle most of the tasks herself with the help of a maid.

It was ridiculous really. A few months ago, I was pickpocketing strangers and climbing trees.

Now, I couldn't even draw a bath by myself. Not that I was ungrateful for having a warm bed to sleep in and a full belly every night. But having all this, while so many outside the palace walls suffered, seemed wrong. I was starting to become overwhelmed with guilt.

I sighed, tilting my neck back to allow my head to rest against the edge of the tub.

My arm stung from the warm water, but the cut was small and would heal quickly.

With all this power, I had yet to make any significant changes. In fact, after the past few weeks, including Lord Edgar and the maid, it was safe to say that I was only digging a bigger grave for myself. I felt doomed no matter what I did.

Perhaps I should pack a few things, slip into the stable at nightfall, and ride away as quietly as possible.

My cabin in the forest was still there and I had enough money to travel to the border and cross into Norrandale, but then what? Where would I live and what would I do? And what would happen to Everness? If I didn't do something about the state of the kingdom, then who would? Lance … perhaps not.

I groaned, sinking so that the water engulfed me completely. It was comforting to have the warm water cover me. With my eyes closed, the world became dark and silent and peaceful all at once. My anxious heartbeat slowed down.

No wonder Lance didn't particularly care to be king. I couldn't imagine anyone ever wanting to take this position willingly. My lungs ached to breathe but I wasn't ready to go back yet. I just needed a little more peace.

Rhen was right. I needed to do something drastic, and I needed to do it sooner rather than later. I emerged with a gasp, the water spilling over the edge of the tub onto the tiled floor. I had never expected this new life to be easy but becoming Queen of Everness required a lot more sacrifice than I'd been prepared for. How did people fight over these titles for ages? How did men kill each other for this position and this power? I'd been sitting on the throne for weeks and I'd yet to understand it.

The water droplets ran down my face and I brushed them away from my eyes. I knew what I had to do, but I really, really wished there were another way.

Lance sprang awake as the prison guards splashed a bucket of cold water onto his face.

"Good morning." I leaned back against the hard metal bars of the prison cell. Lance coughed and recoiled in the chair he'd been snoring in. His black hair plastered his forehead, his long lashes fluttering rapidly.

"How can it be a good morning when you're screaming and my head is pounding like a bloody drum?" he muttered. I realised that Lance hadn't been sleeping — he had passed out drunk. I should have expected as much.

"You look terrible." It'd been weeks since I'd last seen Lance. Weeks since he told me the truth about who I was. Weeks since everything changed. Lance's hair had grown, forming slight curls to accompany the newly grown facial hair. It didn't suit him. The sight of him brought back so many unwanted memories, and I wanted to hate him for all of it. But my feelings aside, I knew I needed him. Just for now. And then I could go back to hating him as much as it pleased me. But in that moment, he was all I had.

He heaved a little and tossed his hair back, properly meeting my eyes for the first time. "Well, you did throw me into a prison cell, sister. How did you expect me to look?"

I moved away from the bars and approached him. "Are you saying that you didn't deserve it?"

He grinned almost devilishly at my words and my blood began to heat in small fury. Maybe coming here was a mistake. Was there nothing that could unnerve him? He was the one who was locked up. He was the one who was at my mercy. He lost and yet … of the two of us, he was the one smiling.

"Leave us alone," I ordered the two guards, my eyes never wavering from Lance.

"Your Majesty?"

"Was I unclear?" My tone was dismissive enough that they left without another word. The prison smelled unpleasant, and it reminded me of the night I spent down here myself, not knowing if I was to be executed at any moment. It was almost as terrible as the night at Woodsbrook Manor. I tried not to shudder at the thought.

There would for ever be a small scar on my thigh because of Lance. Because of his greed and stupidity. Because he was willing to risk me for a stupid necklace that wasn't worth more than any of the other jewellery in the palace. If Lance had no problem throwing his sister in a cell, even if it was to keep up appearances, then I had no problem doing the same to him.

"You never really wanted to be king?" I crossed my arms, staring him down as if I could intimidate him.

"You know I'm not fit for the role. There is no use in beating about the bush. And—" he gestured to the cell — "I didn't have much of a choice with your little band of thieves."

"Don't play games with me, brother. You and I both know you always have ulterior motives."

"Oh, am I brother now?" He raised a dark eyebrow. "When exactly did you decide that you want to invest in our family? Was it before or after you were crowned?"

"We share the same blood, and I can call you my brother — it does not mean I have to care for or respect you."

"True." He pursed his lips for a moment. "If you did respect me, you wouldn't have locked me in a cell without the decency to come and visit."

"Don't you dare talk to me about decency," I cried. "You used me for your personal gain. You are the last person in this kingdom who deserves any respect. Uncle Arthur is dead because you were too much of a coward to put an end to the rebellion, and now I'm left to clean up your messes."

"Perhaps." Lance tilted his head, inspected me. "So why did you come to see me? Other than to remind me what a terrible creature I am."

"Terrible is too good a word." I sighed, looking away for a moment. I could still walk away while nothing had been said. The bandit in me wanted to take the easy way out. "But I'm here because I need your help."

The smugness in Lance's expression could not be mistaken. "You must be very desperate to come to me for help."

I took a deep breath before answering.

"Then you should understand the severity of the situation," I said through clenched teeth.

Lance lifted an index finger. "I have only one question."

I looked into his eyes, wondering what was going on in his head, wondering what advantage he would try to gain from this. "Yes?"

"Why the hell would I help you?" It was not what I wanted to hear. It took enough trying to convince myself to come down here in the first place. I wasn't going to grovel or beg.

"You said that you would do anything for your family. Well, look around." I gestured with my arms. "I'm all that's left here. I've taken the responsibility that you didn't want, because if I don't, Everness could have another civil war." I stepped in front of him now and hesitated, hating what I was about to say but knowing it might be the only thing to convince him. "You were right about us."

"Us?" He taunted me with the very word I hated to say. There would never be an *us* as far as I was concerned but, in this moment, I needed him more than I wanted to admit. After that he could rot in prison for the rest of eternity for all I cared.

"You and I. We do what we must to survive." I reminded him of the words he spoke during our stay at Woodsbrook Manor. "No matter what it takes."

"Well." He nodded in thought. "I can't argue with myself."

Lance looked like his old self again when I met him later in one of the studies. He was clean and neatly dressed, his hair cut, and his scruff gone.

"Took you long enough." I put down the book I had pretended to be reading. I got bored sitting still for so long but was too nervous and agitated to actually do anything.

"Well, all this doesn't just happen by itself, you know." Lance smirked, gesturing to himself. "Good things take time."

"I would advise you not to waste mine."

"Hey—" he raised his hands — "I'm here now."

"You should be thanking me for letting you out of prison." I stood up from the chair I'd occupied.

Lance didn't reply. Only crossed his arms, awaiting an explanation from me.

Perhaps this whole affair would have been easier if I didn't have to look him in the eye for the entire duration of the conversation.

"There was an attack."

"I heard. That doesn't mean you need me, though. You have guards for that."

I probably should have asked just how Lance knew what was going on outside the prison, but I figured the less I knew about his scheming and twisted ways, the better.

I pressed my lips into a line and went to stand by the window, where I could see the city of Levernia in the distance. The Evernean Forest bordered the palace grounds and the city, while beyond lay rolling green hills with the promise of freedom. I looked out longingly as one of the palace hunters emerged from the stretch of woods. Dead pheasants were hanging over his shoulder. Had it really not been that long ago that Ray and I would help hunt for the camp? My heart ached.

"Because I'm pretty sure half the council wants me dead. Rhen found out that the servant girl who attacked me wasn't working alone. And it turns out the Duke of Darwick, and his son, know about my past and intend to use it as blackmail to force me into marrying Edgar."

"Sounds like you've had an eventful couple of weeks."

I clenched my teeth to prevent myself from spitting out something vulgar and sarcastic. I still needed his help, after all.

"Rhen says I need to marry in order to secure my throne and have an heir, of course," I added, with a lack of enthusiasm.

"Rhen isn't wrong." Lance's voice came from behind me, but I refused to look at him as he came to a standstill next to me, gazing out the window. He didn't bring up the fact that he once had me believe he was going to have Rhen executed. That he had me believe, in his cruelty, he was going to murder my friend, when he only imprisoned Rhen to keep him from feeding information to the rebellion. I would never begin to understand my brother, but he seemed to know better than to bring up the subject, though Rhen would most likely have a fit if he knew I'd let Lance out.

"But if I don't marry Edgar, he's going to tell everyone about who I really am. Even if he's bluffing, I can't afford to risk it at this point. If the noble families find out I was the masked bandit who robbed them, I would be done for."

"There is no way in hell that you are marrying Edgar." I was surprised by the stern tone of his voice compared to the nonchalance he usually exhibited. "I will not have that dim-witted bastard wearing my family's crown."

I remembered how furious Uncle Arthur was when he found out about Lance's engagement. He was rightfully worried that a royal heir would only make matters more complicated for his rebellion. I didn't understand it back then. And, needless to say, once Lance was imprisoned, the engagement fell through. Lance didn't seem too upset about it. I was pretty sure he had never even met the girl and would've only gone through with it to spite Uncle.

"Well, then, what do you propose? I can't see how marrying another duke is going to solve the problem. Especially since the Darwicks are one of the most powerful families in the kingdom."

"Then, my dear sister, you marry someone more powerful than a duke."

I frowned, finally looking at him. I didn't want to admit it, but I could see the similarities in our facial features. Most of the time, I avoided looking at the paintings of my mother and father. The parents I never knew. The two people who gave me my dark hair and high cheekbones. I didn't like the fact that the more I looked at Lance, the more I started to see how we were related.

My brother. The thought was still foreign and somewhat unwelcome. "What do you mean?"

"I mean, you don't marry a duke. You marry a king."

"I'm not sure if you've noticed but they aren't exactly just growing on trees around here."

"You could always marry Cai." The mention of his name brought an image to my mind, of Cai, during our stay together at Fairfrith. It was on the night of the solstice feast that Cai asked me about the necklace. The very one Lance had tortured him for. I wasn't sure why I held on to it at the time. Part of me knew it was worth money and part of me stupidly hoped that it did, in fact, possess some sort of magic. A delusion I'd long since let go of. I'd had the necklace for months, and although it may have been a fine piece of jewellery, it certainly possessed no supernatural powers.

I was about to say something when the door swung open and a servant entered, carrying a tray with a teapot and teacups. "The tea you requested, Your Majesty?" she said with confusion, and I realised it must have been because of my shocked facial expression at Lance's words.

"Yes, thank you. You can just put it over there." I gestured to one of the tables. She obeyed and left the room in a hurry, closing the door again.

I sighed and placed a hand to my temple while Lance went over to the tea tray.

"Care to explain?" I asked.

Both Rhen and Lance had now said the same thing to me. But I was looking for every possible reason to avoid it. Cai and I had not parted in the best of ways and the silence between us only made it worse. He was the king of Norrandale now. Why would he want to marry someone who used to be a bandit? I faced the window again, staring at the outer world.

"Norrandale is a powerful kingdom, despite its smaller army. It would prove advantageous to Everness. After all, there is a reason the marriage with Eloisa was arranged in the first place. He isn't a stranger, and by the looks of it at Woodsbrook, you two had taken quite a liking to each other."

I swivelled to face Lance, feeling the frustration rising inside me. "Cai had taken a liking to me because you'd blackmailed me into manipulating him to do so."

"Ah," he said and handed me a cup of tea. "So, you don't like him, then?"

I stared open-mouthed at him, not sure what to do or say, and surprised by his kind gesture. I didn't know Lance was even capable of a kind gesture. I didn't even really want the tea, but I took the cup from him anyway.

"I didn't say that."

"So, you *do* like him?"

"I didn't say that either."

"Fine." Lance shrugged and plopped down on one of the chairs. "Don't tell me about your royal infatuation. I don't care. You've asked my opinion and I've answered you honestly."

"He can't be the only option." I took a seat on the chair opposite him, taking a moment to adjust my layers and layers of skirts.

He wore a sly grin. "Why do you think I didn't want to be king? If it was easy to rule a kingdom, everyone would do it."

"Yes, thank you. Remind me to think up some gruesome punishment for you regarding that."

"You left me to rot in prison, dear sister. Haven't I been punished enough?"

I clenched my teeth.

"Now I get to enjoy the parties and the drinking and the women and the food, all without taking any responsibility. So, if the people get restless and want to decapitate the monarch, I am completely safe and sound."

"If I couldn't trust that you don't want me dead, you'd still be in that prison cell." I rolled my eyes at him. He wasn't exactly the ally of my choosing, but I needed anything I could get at this point.

"Of course I don't want you dead. That means no more drinking or women. My face is too pretty to be decapitated."

I wasn't going to dignify that with a response.

"So, what, I invite Cai over for tea and politely ask if he wants to marry me?"

"Of course not," Lance scoffed. "Don't be ridiculous. Cai is never going to come here now. You must go to Norrandale."

"And who will rule in my place while I'm gone?" I took a sip of the tea. There wasn't any sugar in it, and I wasn't sure if Lance somehow knew that I didn't have sugar in my tea or if he'd just forgotten to put any in. I was going for the latter of the two.

"I wouldn't mind keeping an eye on things for a few days."

I had to fight to keep from spitting the tea back into the cup.

"You're not serious? You want me to leave you in charge. After you've just, once again, reminded me why you should not rule?" The fool wasn't making any sense.

"Ruling as regent for a short period and as king for the rest of my life aren't exactly the same thing. Call it a family favour."

"Don't push me, Lance. Even if I did go over there and …" I hesitated, "propose … who's to say Cai's even going to say yes?" I couldn't imagine looking like a bigger idiot than if he rejected me.

"He can't exactly say no. He'd already agreed to marry you."

"What?" I said, a little too loud, and my teacup clattered in the saucer.

"Cai signed a marriage contract back at Woodsbrook. He agreed to marry the eldest daughter of King Magnus. His signature is on the paper. He can't take it back now."

"But surely you gave him a falsified document to sign?" I gently put the teacup down on the table.

"No," he responded nonchalantly.

"But you knew that was me and not Eloisa. Why the hell would you let him sign it?"

"For a day such as this when it could be necessary to help us." Us? There was that word again. I was starting to regret every life decision I'd made up until this point.

"Lance, you have to stop blackmailing people."

He took a small flask out of his coat pocket and poured the liquor into his tea. "And you need to learn that sometimes to be a monarch you have to make difficult choices."

"Well, what if I don't want to make difficult choices?" I threw my hands up in the air.

"Then abdicate. Run away. But you'll never be able to blame the problems of this kingdom on anyone else. Not when you had a chance to fix it."

I hated the fact that he was right. Hated that for most of my life I'd complained about the way this kingdom was ruled and now I actually had a chance to make a difference.

"What about Eloisa?" She was next in line for the throne after me. And if I hadn't been born a few minutes earlier, it would have been her sitting here today.

"Well, no one's found her yet, right?" He took another sip of his tea as if he was pondering his next words carefully. "And to be completely honest, I think you're much better suited for this role than our sister."

I huffed out a laugh. "How on earth can I, a thief, be a better queen than a princess?"

"Eloisa is … special."

"That's a nice way of saying someone is troubled." Whether or not I was ready to hear more of the truth, it needed to come out.

"Eloisa is many things, but a ruler isn't one of them."

"Where is she?" I didn't expect him to know. No one knew. It was like she'd disappeared off the face of the earth. But I asked him anyway.

"I don't know." His slightly worried expression made me believe him. The subject clearly bothered him, but he didn't look eager to share more on it.

"Well, are you going to send someone to find her?" He was the one responsible for her when she'd gone missing. He knew the best place to start.

"I have. More than once. No one has returned with any news of her." I considered for a moment that somewhere along the road something could have gone terribly wrong and Eloisa might no longer be alive.

"I'll see what I can do about it." I attempted to regain focus on the important matter at hand. "A lot of loyalists won't be happy if I marry a Norrandish king."

"You can't make everyone happy, Elara."

I suppressed my discontent at his use of my real name. "Still. If the people are happy, they're not trying to assassinate me."

He put his cup down and leaned forwards, his elbows resting on his thighs.

"Well, if you cannot be loved, then you must become feared."

"Wise words from a former king," I muttered.

"Norrandale has had a long line of prestigious queens, and it would not be easy to measure up. If you want to be accepted, then you must be respected. By our people as well as theirs." It felt like asking an awful lot of someone with no experience.

"As well as Cai," I added.

"You don't think Cai respects you?"

"I have no idea what Cai thinks," I replied in earnest. "I was so angry when I found out he knew the truth about me that I told him to leave and I haven't heard anything since."

"Cai might have been a bit hurt." Lance stood up, pulling his tunic straight. "But I do doubt he hates you."

"You seem very confident in my ability to pull this off." I cast a side-eye in his direction.

"I've always been confident in your abilities. Even if I didn't show it."

"You know most older brothers would just settle for giving me lessons in sword fighting or something." I scrambled for the right words.

The corner of his mouth twitched as he attempted to hide a grin. "But I'm not most brothers, am I?"

I didn't reply.

"You don't have to do this. But it could be your best chance at a successful reign. And you can do a lot worse than Cai."

I certainly could. But Cai could also probably do a lot better than me.

"I thought you two didn't like each other? Why would you want me to marry someone you were willing to torture?"

"He is a little ... princely for my taste," he admitted. "But what happened at Woodsbrook had nothing to do with Cai and everything to do with the necklace."

I caught him looking at my neck, which was free of jewellery. "Princely?"

Lance rolled his eyes. "All heroic and dashing, always saving everyone and following the rules. I don't know how he doesn't bore himself to death."

I bit my tongue to refrain from defending Cai.

"Yes," Lance continued. "The charismatic prince and the rogue bandit. What a lovely couple you'll make."

I took the last sip of my tea and placed the cup on the tray. "Well, as much as I enjoy your company, you'll have to excuse me. I have a kingdom to save."

"Oh no, you're already starting to sound like him."

Chapter 6

Cai

How did I get myself into this?

I escorted Lady Meredette outside while making a mental note to extract some sort of revenge on Thatcher for placing me in this position.

Meredette was the complete opposite of Elara.

It probably wasn't fair of me to compare them. I walked alongside her through the palace gardens. Meredette had eyes of coal and a long, sharp nose above full red lips. She was tall too, her height almost reaching my own. I watched her mouth curve up into a smile.

Our conversation thus far had been rather strained. Thatcher hadn't told me about the visit until the last moment. He knew I would find some sort of excuse if I'd found out about it in advance. I'd merely been informed that I had a meeting with one of the nobles regarding an urgent matter. It was only as Lady Meredette's carriage rounded the gravel path in front of the palace entrance that Thatcher appeared alongside me with a wicked grin. I was certain he now stood somewhere by a window, enjoying my discomfort with that same grin.

"You certainly have gardens that can be boasted about, Your Majesty," she offered, trying to make conversation, but it felt formal, forced. The truth was we probably didn't have anything in common other than being born into rich families. I missed the way Lara always spoke her mind. She didn't care for things like propriety or worry about offending me. Most of the time, she was brutally honest. But she was real.

"Well, if there is to be boasting, it definitely won't be me doing it."

She looked at me from under long lashes. "No? How so?"

"I can take credit for spending a lot of time outdoors, but I definitely can't take any credit for the state of the gardens. My mother manages them," I explained.

I had placed my arms behind my back in the gentlemanly fashion I was used to. But this did not keep Meredette from hooking her arm into mine as we continued our stroll, my arm now bent in an uncomfortable manner. And yet, changing my posture would give offence. We weren't alone, of course, my guards trailing closely behind, just far enough for them to pretend they couldn't hear our conversation.

"Do you like to be outside?" I attempted to continue the overly polite exchange. I didn't have the time or capacity for courting. Not that I could stay mad at Thatcher for this either. He was only trying to help as he saw fit. He was trying to be a good friend.

"Good heavens, no. In the winter, it's much too cold to go outside. And the Norrandish summers have too many insects."

I couldn't argue. The summers here could not only become uncomfortably hot but were accompanied by the annoyance of flying insects, especially around bodies of water, of which Norrandale had plenty.

"I prefer to be inside painting if I'm not on social calls."

"You have an interest in art?"

"Very much so," Lady Meredette replied with sincerity.

"Well, you know the palace has a lovely art gallery should you ever wish to visit it."

"A garden, an art gallery — what do you lack, Your Majesty?" Her smile was flirtatious.

"Oh, I lack plenty, to be certain."

She chuckled. I hadn't meant to flirt back. I was just trying to be … nice.

"I heard rumours that you were planning to host a ball soon." Which could only be attributed to Thatcher. Damn him. Her eyes gleamed with hopefulness. Was she entertaining the idea that she would receive an invite from the King himself?

"And do you always believe everything you hear?" I replied, trying to dodge the question.

Her face fell.

"You're not hosting a ball, then?"

I half smiled, attempting recovery. "I wasn't planning on it but perhaps a ball could be fun."

Her grin quickly returned and there was no doubt she would leave our meeting and tell every person she came across that she had personally been informed by me about a ball I would be hosting.

I looked at Meredette again, but she was occupied with some pink flowers that I couldn't remember the name of. I half listened as Meredette made some comment about the flowers while I looked to the horizon where the kingdom of Everness lay. I hated her hopefulness when I had no intention of courting her. I had no intention of courting anyone for a while. Especially if there were Argonian spies in my kingdom.

"I'll admit I was surprised at Your Majesty's invitation." Meredette drew my attention back to the conversation.

"Oh?" was the only word that escaped my lips.

"Well, with all the changes at court, I didn't think you'd have time for … social affairs." She chose her words carefully as if testing the waters. Of course, she would make assumptions of her own even if no clear intentions had been stated. Who wouldn't?

"Well, I like to stay busy," I replied without thinking and then realised the words hadn't come out exactly the way I wanted to. This only seemed to encourage Meredette.

"I'm very glad we finally got a chance to meet properly. Lady Gwen mentions you so often and she always has the nicest things to say."

"She is like a younger sister." Whom I was going to have a very stern conversation with regarding her interference in my affairs, or rather the lack of affairs.

"She's been a very kind friend to me."

I wasn't sure how to reply, so I gave her a polite smile.

"And what else does His Majesty like to do in his free time?" It was becoming practically torturous now. And even though most men would probably have killed for the chance to be on a walk with a beautiful girl like Meredette, I could only think of the million other things that required my attention.

"I've been out horse riding a lot recently." It always seemed like a good excuse to get out of the palace.

"I'm quite fond of horses," she said softly.

"We are fortunate, our stables have magnificent breeds."

"I have no doubt, Your Majesty."

The conversation seemed to have run out, and with nothing left to say, we continued our stroll in awkward silence. I noticed Alastor near one of the palace doors. "If you'll accept my apologies, my lady, I'm afraid I must cut our conversation short."

Raised as a lady should be, Meredette kept face, though I could tell she wasn't too impressed.

"I have a very important matter at hand that needs to be discussed," I said, gesturing towards Alastor.

"Of course." She bowed. "Don't let me keep you away from your duties." I nodded when she said, "Don't forget the promise you made of a ball."

"I won't." I forced a smile before hurrying off.

"Everything all right?" Alastor asked upon seeing my expression.

"Just keep walking," I muttered under my breath, not looking back as I walked past him.

"That bad?" he questioned carefully, as he followed me inside.

"No." I sighed, slowing our pace. "I just …" I shook my head, not wanting to continue the subject. Despite the tapestries and curtains, our voices still echoed off the stone walls.

"What news is there regarding our prisoners?" I looked around and made sure there was no one nearby to eavesdrop.

"Nothing," Alastor replied. "If Aries sent them, whatever he promised or offered made them willing to risk their lives. We all know how loyal those damn Argonians can be."

"Well, something's got to give," I replied. "We can't keep them there for ever. It's too much of a risk."

He nodded before stalking off.

The palace was bustling, every servant and courtier appearing to be on their own mission. Most of the time, I preferred to have the palace lively and full of guests, but today everything felt like a distraction from my duty. I saw Meredette climb into her carriage as I passed one of the open windows. Soon gossip would begin to circulate about whether or not I was courting, as well as the prospect of a future queen. I knew I couldn't put it off for ever but ... I sighed again.

When I got back to my chambers, I locked the door behind me. I couldn't remember the last time that I had locked my bedroom door. But I needed to be alone. Even if it was for a few seconds. It was a hot day, though we were well into the autumn season, and I pulled off my jacket with frustrated impatience. I opened one of the windows and sat on the bed. Lying back, I tried to enjoy the breeze that entered through the open window. There was the undeniable scent of wild thyme in the air. It grew vigorously in the meadows close to the palace, in clusters of purple during the summer months. I didn't know flowers, but I'd know wild thyme anywhere because its sweet scent reminded me of Lara.

I didn't have any appointments scheduled until much later in the day and I was perfectly happy to hide away. I needed time to think. Needed to make sense of everything that had happened in the past few days.

The matter regarding the Argonian spies weighed on me like a chest plate that was too heavy and constricting.

Across the ocean, Argon was a kingdom that'd been after our land for centuries.

Our forefathers had battled each other on and off until the time came for me to step onto the battlefield myself. King Aries had barely inherited the throne at that time. Though I'd met him on a few previous occasions, it was his younger brother whom I faced on the bloodied field. I knew Aries couldn't easily forgive me for the act of killing his only sibling, but had I been a fool to hope the peace treaty would be a standing agreement?

I wasn't alone in my room for long before there was a knock at the door. I sighed heavily. Maybe if I pretended to be sleeping, whoever was there would go away.

"Your Majesty?" It was Jack. Jack didn't make a habit of asking for me if it was not important.

"Yes, Jack, what is it?" I called out.

"I think Your Majesty should come downstairs."

"Why, did the Argonian spies finally decide to speak?" I sat up quickly.

"No, Your Majesty. I mean, I think you should come down to the throne room."

The throne room? What kind of matter required my presence in the throne room at this time of day? No events had been scheduled as far as I could remember.

"What's the matter?"

Jack hesitated on the other side of the door. "You have a visitor."

I really didn't feel up to socialising. Nor could I think of any possible guest who would immediately require my attention.

"Tell them I will see them at dinner when I have finished my other duties for the day." I waved a hand in dismissal even though Jack couldn't see me, and rolled onto my stomach, pressing my face into the sheets. Sleep. Sleep would be so wonderful.

"I really think you should come down now, Your Majesty."

With a huff I stood up and marched to the door. "Who is it, Jack?" I unlocked the door and yanked it open. "Who could possibly be so important that they need to see me right this instant?"

Jack looked at me with his mouth slightly open. He shifted from one foot to the other nervously.

"Queen Elara, Your Majesty."

Chapter 7

Elara

"This is so exciting!" Anesta practically leaned halfway outside the carriage window. "Isn't this exciting?" Her eyes were wide with wonder and part of me let myself think about what Norrandale must have looked like. But I didn't dare look out the window. I couldn't afford to get distracted. I had to prepare myself mentally for what lay ahead, and even though I was exhausted from several days of travelling, I didn't allow myself to sleep as we got closer to the palace.

I had to ask a king for his hand in marriage, and not just any king, but Cai of all people. How was I going to see it through without my nerves getting the best of me?

"This is not a holiday, Anesta," I reminded her. "We have a very important matter at hand and I'm going to require your help every step of the way." Technically, that wasn't true. Although I would have been more than willing to let her do the proposing for me, should it have been appropriate. But I needed her to help me look my best, and more importantly, I needed her as a friend.

"Right." She nodded but I could see she wasn't listening. This was her first time outside the kingdom of Everness and I couldn't blame her for being excited. I'd never set foot outside Everness myself, but I had plenty of reasons to be sick to my stomach.

"What do you think he's going to say?"

"Who?"

"His Majesty, of course," she said, as if it were obvious.

I didn't want to think about how Cai would react or why he hadn't reached out since the rebellion. Though there was obviously something between us at Fairfrith, our circumstances had changed so drastically, there was no guarantee that he would still feel the same.

"Do you think he'll take your hand with a smile or perhaps pull you into his arms and spin you around in the air?"

This was exactly one of the many reasons I didn't take pleasure in reading the same way Anesta did. It filled your head with foolish notions and unrealistic expectations.

"Well." I pulled at my bodice, attempting to make it sit more comfortably, but it was useless. "Hopefully he will see that this is a smart choice for both of us and will agree without hesitation."

"I cannot believe I actually get to witness this. It's so romantic." She clasped her hands together.

"I wouldn't go as far as saying it's romantic."

Anesta suddenly met my eyes, and I watched her expression grow into some form of understanding.

"This is a political agreement. Nothing more and nothing less," I said, knowing that was the only way I would allow myself to think of the situation. Allowing any kind of personal feelings to get involved would only complicate the matter so much more.

"You're right, I'm sorry," she apologised. "I have spoken out of my place."

"There is nothing to be sorry for," I reassured her. Anesta looked so hopeful, I would hate to be the one to ruin her mood. But we also needed to stay focused. This alliance was important for all of us.

"Could you tell me about him?" she asked with a hint of caution, folding her hands in her lap. The carriage continued to bump along the rocky road.

"About whom?"

"About His Majesty. What's King Cai like?"

I sighed and crossed my arms in thought. "He's ... he's kind."

Anesta smiled softly.

"He's a good soldier. He cares deeply for his kingdom. He loves the outdoors."

"He sounds lovely," she replied.

"I expected him to be stuck-up and spoiled." I chuckled at the memory of my first encounter with Cai. Back before I knew he was the crown prince of Norrandale. "But he can be very sweet and caring."

"You should see the way your eyes light up when you talk about him."

"Don't be ridiculous," I scoffed. "We're here for a political alliance, remember?"

"Right."

"We're almost there, Your Majesty," Rhen called from outside the carriage, where he was leading the party on horseback. I relaxed a little, thinking about Rhen's presence. I had no doubts that he would give his life to keep us safe. If it hadn't been for him, that girl with the knife might have ... I shuddered, not wanting to think about it. At least with him and Anesta, I didn't feel quite so alone. Before I was queen, being alone was a normality. And yet, I'd become dependent on these two people. Elara, the Masked Bandit, needing someone … what an ironic thought. Part of me wondered if I should have left Rhen to keep an eye on things in Everness. There was no telling what would happen while I was away. I pushed the thought from my mind. Sitting here with worry wasn't going to change anything anyway.

Focus. Focus. Focus.

When we entered the palace gates, I finally dared to look outside the carriage window. I wished I hadn't. I gulped at the majesty of the large building, boasting tall towers and massive gardens. It made the palace in Levernia look small.

"It's incredible. Have you ever seen a palace to equal it?" Anesta was in awe as well. I didn't quite allow my mouth to hang open as hers did.

We made our way up a long gravel road and then around a large fountain, splashing with crystal-clear water.

When we finally stopped, Rhen dismounted, looked around and walked to the carriage door, where he stood ready to help. I reached for him before stepping out.

"Your hands are shaking," he said under his breath.

"Shut up." I didn't need him to point out the obvious now. Of course I was terrified. Even if I didn't know what exactly I was so terrified of. Rejection maybe? No. This was only Cai. The prince whom I'd spent days on end with. My friend. The man with the blond hair and enchanting green eyes.

You haven't spoken in months, my mind reminded me. We were no longer the same people — we were a king and a queen.

Rhen announced us to the palace guards, highlighting the importance of our visit.

I toyed with the ring around my finger, which bore the royal crest. Not wanting to appear overbearing, I didn't wear a crown today. The guards were clad in blue and gold uniforms as they approached us. I straightened my back and tried to keep my expression neutral. The palace guards looked uncertain while Rhen spoke to them, but eventually, one hurried off inside. I eyed the large doors, the clean stone steps and perfectly cut hedges.

Finally, two of the guards led us towards the throne room. The halls were long and wide with more guards stationed around each corner. They stood so still — one could almost mistake them for statues. I attempted not to let my eyes wander too intently over the décor and architecture. It was a distraction, and I needed to mentally rehearse the words I was going to say.

However, once those two doors were opened with a heavy, hollow thud, my thoughts were temporarily forgotten. I had once reckoned the throne room of the palace of Levernia was majestic and intimidating enough to make you feel as though you were shrinking. But that was nothing compared to the vast stature of this great hall. Massive windows lined the walls, allowing heaps of sunlight to sweep into the room as it reflected off the white surface of the marble floor.

I was stuck taking in the canopy of the arched ceilings above when I heard my name and words sounding vaguely like "Queen of Everness" being announced. Bringing my attention back to the people in the room, I made sure my mouth was clamped shut. A few courtiers stood close to the large fireplace and all eyes landed on me as the throne room fell slowly silent. My heartbeat rang in my ears. I was sure everyone in the room could hear it.

It wasn't difficult to spot Cai's mother. She looked so much like him, and I wondered what features he had shared with his father.

At the mention of my title, she turned away from the conversation she was in.

"Do my ears deceive me or has the Queen of Everness graced us with her presence?" The queen mother's face formed a smile as she approached me. Though graceful, her steps were slow, and she appeared somewhat fragile. The illness must have affected her quite seriously.

I bowed my head in acknowledgement.

"Please call me Elara. It's a pleasure to meet you."

"Well, I admit, Elara, I've certainly heard plenty about you." Her smile remained soft, and I wasn't sure what she meant by the comment. My cheeks flushed. What kind of news about my reign had reached across the border of Everness? And even worse, what had Cai told them about me?

Don't flatter yourself. He probably doesn't even mention your name.

"And here I had come, hoping my reputation didn't proceed me," I admitted honestly, trying to hold up my brave facade.

"Good things only, my dear."

"You must be surprised by my abrupt visit. Especially with no prior notice. I must apologise for this. But you see, I come to Norrandale with a most serious matter, which I'm afraid I could not delay."

It was an effort not to fidget with my hands.

Stand still, head up high and keep calm.

"I see." Cai's mother took in my travelling party before glancing at the throne-room doors. "I'm sure my son has been sent for. Perhaps we can arrange some refreshments for your company. Everyone must be tired and hungry after your journey."

"That would be very kind of you."

The rest of the room had returned to their hushed conversations but kept eyes on the two of us.

85

"Did you have a good journey? Especially across the border?"

I can still remember the feeling inside my chest when Rhen had told us we were crossing into Norrandale. So many times had I planned that very moment, my escape to freedom from Everness. And there I was, riding into the kingdom with a carriage and a royal guard, not as a bandit but as a queen. I could almost laugh at the irony.

"Yes, we did, thank you. The nights are definitely getting colder for travelling, though. I think I'm already starting to miss summer."

"That's good to hear. I'm glad you didn't come across any bandits on your way here."

I let out an awkward laugh. Oh, if only she knew.

"Thankfully that problem seems to have eradicated itself."

"I am sorry to hear about the attack in Levernia, though." She gently placed her hand on my arm that carried the small scar.

"I suppose it comes with the territory." I tried to shrug it off casually.

"Still, it must have been such a horrid experience. No young woman should have to go through such a thing." Her sympathy provided me with a sense of comfort, and I was starting to see why Cai cared for his mother so much.

"It was definitely not my finest hour as a queen," I confided. "But I can only hope such a thing will not happen again."

With every passing moment, I anticipated Cai walking into the room, and I could feel my nerves growing.

"Yes, let's hope," the queen mother agreed. "Everyone's had more than enough tragedy in the past few months."

"Speaking of which, I'm very sorry for the loss of your husband and the former king." My eyes trailed over her black mourning dress. A lovely design but undoubtedly melancholic.

"Thank you, dear." There was a sadness behind her eyes, which was entirely understandable. "I think it's been harder on Cai than anyone else."

"Oh?" Cai didn't often talk about his father, so I had no idea how close they were.

"There was much he still wanted to learn from his father before stepping into the role. He's putting a lot of pressure on himself to live up to the man." That I could believe.

"But I'm certain he will be very happy about your surprise visit." She turned the conversation back to my presence.

"Oh, I don't know." I tried to smile through my embarrassment, wondering how much Cai had told his family about who I was and what the two of us had gone through. My hope was as little as possible.

Before Cai's mother had a chance to respond, Jack walked through the throne-room doors.

"His Majesty the King." My stomach did a thousand twists and flips, and I momentarily wished I was anywhere but there.

I held my breath as Cai walked into the room. Apart from the slightly messy hair and his on-edge expression, he still looked the same.

The King of Norrandale's eyes landed on me.

Chapter 8

Cai

One of the last times I'd seen Lara, we were both covered in blood and dirt, exhausted from fighting in a rebel uprising.

And then she'd told me to leave.

Now she stood in front of me, no longer looking like the wild girl who used to climb trees. She looked like a woman who'd lived at court all her life. In the months since we had last seen each other, her appearance had changed. The darkness under her eyes was gone, the colour having returned to her cheeks. She looked stronger. Healthier. It was good to see her face again.

"Lara" was the only word that managed to come out of my mouth.

She gave a small curtsy. "Hello, Cai."

Her voice was soft and elegant, and, in a moment, she felt like a stranger.

"How are you?" I cleared my throat, attempting to be polite instead of carrying a shocked expression.

"I am very well, thank you." She folded her hands in front of her skirt, gazing at me through long lashes.

At first, I'd frozen when Jack told me she was here. Not just in Norrandale but in the palace. My mind raced with questions. What was she doing here? Did she see Lady Meredette leave? Did it matter? Would the court be knee-deep in gossip tomorrow about my two female visitors in one afternoon?

I'd followed Jack to the throne room, wondering what Elara thought of Norrandale. She'd never left Everness, but she'd talked about coming to Norrandale before the rebellion happened. As I'd approached the door, I could already smell the sweet scent of her, and my heart raced at the memories it elicited. I could picture her hair, her neck, her mouth, her eyes.

"I apologise for my sudden visit. I would much appreciate if we could discuss a rather important matter."

I watched the courtiers in the room as they pretended not to be staring and listening to our conversation.

"Of course." I cleared my throat again. "Would you join me in the study?"

She turned to my mother, who'd been standing next to her. "It was lovely to meet you."

"You as well, dear."

Elara gave her a smile. She followed me through the doors of the throne room, the chatter of the courtiers quiet, allowing our steps to echo across the floor.

"It's good to see you again, Jack." Elara greeted him with a warm smile.

"You as well, Your Majesty."

I led her to the nearest study and opened the door, only to find Thatcher calmly reading near one of the windows. He smiled upon seeing me and put down the book.

"Ah, I was looking for you. I was wondering how your—"

He trailed off as Elara walked in behind me and I watched his expression turn curious.

"Thatcher, I would like you to meet Elara, the Queen of Everness." I gestured to her, and Thatcher quickly got out of his seat and gave a deep bow.

"Pleasure to make your acquaintance, Your Majesty."

"Lara, I suppose you remember me telling you about my oldest friend, Lord Thatcher?"

"I've heard a lot about you." She gave him a weary smile.

"All bad, I hope." He gave her a cheeky wink, at which she seemed surprised, and I remembered Elara didn't have the pleasure of knowing Thatch's boyishly charming character.

"To what do we owe the pleasure of your visit, Your Majesty?"

Something I would very much like to know, too.

Elara looked in Thatcher's direction and then back at me. "May we speak?" And then she added, "Privately?"

I opened my mouth to ask Thatcher politely for some privacy, but he was already halfway to the door.

"If you'll excuse me, Your Majesties, I'd best be on my way. I need to go and find my sister." Doubtful, but I appreciated his effort.

"Give my regards to Gwen," I tried to joke, if only to stop the astounding beating of my heart. Elara was here.

Why was she here, and why did she carry such a worried look on her face?

The doors closed behind Thatcher, leaving the two of us alone in the study, with our guards waiting outside. We'd been alone so many times before. But this was different. Our last encounter wasn't how I'd wanted to leave things between us, and I was sure both of us could sense the clear tension.

"Shall I call for some refreshments?"

Elara shook her head, taking a seat on one of the settees. "No, thank you."

I sat on a chair opposite her, putting some distance between us.

"I'm sorry about your father," she said, folding her hands in her lap. I'd never seen her act this proper, not even when she was pretending to be Eloisa. "You must miss him very much."

"Some mornings I wake up and it takes me a moment to realise he's not there, that I am now king."

"Your mother seems well." They had appeared to be in a discussion when I entered the throne room. I wondered what they had been talking about.

"She has mostly recovered from her illness, but I think my father's death is taking its own toll." Most of the time, I believed my mother pretended to be doing better than she actually was.

"It's going to take time." Elara offered me a sympathetic smile. I appreciated her condolences, but I doubted she'd come all this way to enquire about my mother's health.

"You've travelled very far." It was the only thing I could think to say without directly asking her what she was doing in Norrandale, which I feared might come across as a little rude. Did this have something to do with the attempt on her life? Was she in some kind of trouble?

"I haven't heard from you in a while." There was a hint of resentment in her tone.

"I didn't think you'd want to hear from me," I replied honestly. I'd hated walking out of that palace without a proper goodbye. I didn't want to leave her to face the unknown obstacles of the new Everness. But she had been so adamant in telling me to leave. I felt I had to respect her wishes.

"I understand you had your mother's illness and then your father's death, but I didn't expect this complete silence from you," Elara admitted, a trace of hurt in her expression.

"Well, I hardly thought it appropriate, all things considered." She was the one who'd ended it, and nothing had prevented her from writing to me either.

"All things considered?" she frowned. "What is that supposed to mean? Because I'm queen?"

"Of course not," I retorted. "Because you're engaged. I think that more than enough reason to believe that you didn't want to hear from me unless it regarded a political matter."

"Engaged?" she cried out. "Engaged to whom?"

"I don't know. Some Evernean lord." Based on her expression, I was beginning to feel rather ridiculous. Had it truly just been a rumour, then?

"With all due respect, I think I would know if I was about to walk down the aisle with someone. I'm not sure where you came upon this news, but I can assure you that I am certainly not engaged."

I didn't know why a sense of relief flooded my chest at her words. I didn't want it to.

"All this time, I thought it was because of my family or my title," she said, more to herself than to me. Her eyes turned to the floor, and her hands unclenched in her lap.

"I should have told you the truth."

"I shouldn't have told you to leave like that." She pressed her lips together. With her stubbornness, it must have taken a lot for her to admit she was wrong. My body was screaming at me to be closer to her. But things were different between us now. She had me longing for things I couldn't have. She always did.

"You didn't have to come all the way to Norrandale just to tell me that." It wasn't my best attempt at a joke, but I needed something to lighten the mood between us.

"That's not exactly why I came." She sighed and the worry in her face returned.

I finally decided to be brave and moved so that I was sitting next to her on the settee.

"Why are you here, Lara?" I asked more gently, tempted to reach for her hand, but I held back out of fear of making her uncomfortable. She turned to look at me.

"Things in Everness have become dire."

I frowned. They were hardly in good shape before.

"If I'm being honest, I fear a civil war. The people have had a difficult time adjusting and I am surrounded by enemies. As queens usually are."

I noticed a faint, small scar on her arm, and I realised it must have been from the attack. She was almost killed in her own palace.

No longer able to stop myself, I reached my fingertips towards the line on her upper arm. I half expected her to flinch. Instead, she froze at the touch of my fingers on her soft skin.

"Is this from—?"

"Yes," she answered quickly and swallowed hard. I dropped my hand, fearing the intimacy of the moment.

"I suppose …" She hesitated. With her hands clasped, she took a deep breath, and I saw the determination grow in her. "I suppose I've come to ask you to reinstate the alliance between our two kingdoms."

"I beg your pardon?" I blurted out too quickly, not sure if I understood her correctly. "I mean—" I cleared my throat. "Sorry, what did you say?" My thumping heart wouldn't return to normal. In her eyes, dark shadows appeared. Her face grew serious.

Elara sucked her teeth in disapproval at my making her spell it out. "I have come to ask for your hand."

"In marriage?" I let out a partial sound of disbelief.

"Well, yes." She looked at me as though I were an idiot. "What else could I mean?"

"Your solution to a civil war is marrying the king of an enemy kingdom?" I was in too much disbelief to consider my words before they left my mouth.

"I have threats all around me. My people are trying to blackmail me, my servants are trying to kill me, and I need someone powerful at my side if I am to protect my reign. I don't exactly see eligible kings lining up, so unless you know of someone else?"

"Good grief, Elara, you certainly know how to make a proposal." I sat back, considering her words. "Please marry me because there simply isn't anyone else?"

She seemed taken aback. "I didn't mean it like that, and you know it. You should understand making political decisions regardless of your emotions better than anyone."

"Then what did you mean it like?"

"You were going to marry Eloisa anyway. How is this any different?"

Because she's not you.

"It's different because the political situation in Everness has changed. I would need to discuss this with my council before any serious decisions are made," I explained. "I understand your predicament, but things are complicated." My father had just died, and I had Argonian spies in the palace prison. The timing could not be worse.

"So that's it? Nice to see you after months of silence but please leave until further notice?"

"That's not what I said," I stated, realising I might be coming across as a bit harsh.

"Then what would you have me do?" she exclaimed. "Who else am I supposed to go to? Do you honestly expect me to simply disregard everything that happened between us in Everness?"

I'd told her to give me a chance until the rebellion was over. I'd told her to escape to Norrandale and that I would find her and then … then what? I didn't think about the future. Living in the woods at Fairfrith felt like another world most days. It was easy to set aside my duty and the harsh reality of our circumstances. And now …

"But you're not here because of what happened between us in Everness." She wasn't here to make some declaration of love, to say that she'd missed me or wanted to be with me. She was here because she needed the strength of my new title.

"I came to you because I thought I could trust you." She was begging.

"You can trust me."

"Can I?" It was a punch in the gut. I clenched my jaw.

"I suggest you stay here as a guest for the time being and we can discuss the matter." This was after all, the usual procedure for these kinds of matters.

"Very well." Elara stood up and brushed invisible flecks of dust from the skirts of her dress. "I'll leave you to your duties, then."

"Elara, wait." I stood up as well. This was clearly not the way either of us had hoped this conversation would go.

"Cai," she said, like she was drawing a line under the conversation, before she walked out the door.

* * *

"I'm such an arse." I sat with my hands in my hair.

"That could have gone better," Thatcher responded, after I'd told him about what happened. "Although when I said she would come crawling back once you started courting other women, I did not imagine she would show up the same day." He smiled at his joke.

"I wasn't prepared to see her in the first place, much less for her to ask to marry me." I was still in a state of shock over what had just happened. Had Elara really just showed up here and proposed? And had I really just said no?

"You said you'd discuss it with your council." Thatcher tried to reassure me.

I continued to stare holes into the carpet of the study.

"I couldn't have just said yes, could I? I mean, this would make me king of Everness and unite the kingdoms in a whole new way. It would have a massive impact on Everness and Norrandale. A new agreement would have to be drawn up. This is a serious matter."

"Of course it is," Thatcher agreed. "It's not a simple yes or no. Elara will see that."

"I don't want her to hate me."

"She doesn't hate you." He smiled. "You can stop moping like a lovesick puppy."

"I am not a lovesick puppy," I mumbled.

"Forgive me, what kind of lovesick animal would you prefer to be?" If one of the books had been any closer, I would have thrown it at him.

"I am curious, though." Thatcher relaxed back into his chair and tilted his head. "Politics aside, if you weren't the king of Norrandale and she wasn't the queen of Everness, what would your answer have been?"

"What do you mean?"

"If you were just a farmer and she was just a peasant girl? Would you have said yes?"

"If that were the case, I probably would have asked her to marry me, not the other way around," I blurted without thinking.

"That's evading the question," Thatcher pressed.

"I used to know a girl in Everness. She was wild and fearless." I sighed. "She called me out and pressed my buttons. There was a fire inside of her and I used to believe I could marry a girl like that."

"And now?"

I turned to look at the door she'd walked through. "Now, I'm not so sure that she's that girl anymore."

Chapter 9

Elara

I rushed through the palace hallways, trying to put as much distance between me and the study as possible. Rhen gave one look in my direction and read enough from my expression to follow a safe distance behind, along with Anesta.

He said no.

How could he say no?

I couldn't decide if I was furious with him or myself or perhaps downright embarrassed at the feeling of rejection coursing through me. I had come all this way to make a complete and utter fool of myself and at the hands of the king of Norrandale, no less.

Cai had said no.

Or at least, he hadn't said yes.

Most of my time on our journey here had been spent practising what to say leading up to the proposal. I was so focused on how to go about it that I hadn't prepared myself properly for what to do if he didn't say yes. Of course I knew it was always a possibility. But this was Cai. I knew him. Or at least, I thought I did.

A proper queen would see all of this as a challenge instead of defeat. But I knew, in the back of my mind, that I was no proper queen. I was just a masked bandit with a title. Perhaps I would always be a masked bandit, playing pretend with her crown.

I hadn't told Cai what Lance had said regarding the marriage agreement.

Whether Cai liked it or not, he was technically engaged to me according to a paper that he'd willingly signed. I hadn't even considered bringing the documentation with me because part of me believed I truly would have no need for it. And if I did, waving it in Cai's face to pressure him to marry me would make me no better than my brother. Was it so terrible that I didn't want to force Cai into this alliance? I'd never expected us to be lovers for the rest of our lives, but having the past we did, I thought us, at the very least, capable of doing this as friends. There were worse fates, after all.

Most of all, I hated myself for the fact that I had genuinely hoped he would say yes.

"I cannot believe that man."

Anesta remained quiet as she took the pins out of my hair. After my failed proposal in the study, I spent the remainder of the afternoon hiding in the guest chambers. I didn't have it in me to face anyone else. Poor Anesta had no choice but to listen to my venting.

"He was the one who told me to wait for him, to give him a chance. And now he wants me to believe he doesn't care for me whatsoever? That he's just numbed himself to all emotion regarding my existence?"

"He really said he wouldn't marry you?" Anesta said, with disbelief.

"Not exactly," I huffed. "He said he needed to think about it. That he would have to discuss it with his council. Does the king have no power in this damn kingdom to marry whomever he wants? This would make him the king of Everness." I was agitated. Because it was easier to be furious than to be sad or allow any other negative and self-deprecating emotion to slip through the cracks. I didn't want to consider Cai's reasoning either. How much of it was political and how much was personal?

"I suppose that's kind of a polite way of saying he doesn't want to marry you," Anesta took out another pin.

"Anesta!" I groaned. "You're supposed to be making me feel better, not worse."

"I'm sorry." She began brushing out my hair. "You're right. The man doesn't deserve you. You can do so much better, Your Majesty." Her tone wasn't entirely sincere, but she was trying her best to cheer me up.

"I don't know about that. There aren't exactly many eligible kings running around."

"What about King Aries?" she asked, while combing the locks of my dark hair.

"King Aries?" I really did have to start paying better attention when Rhen discussed politics with me.

"Yes, the king of Argon."

Memories of his name and the kingdom being mentioned resurfaced. "Oh, right."

I crossed my arms. "I don't know anything about him. He'd be a complete stranger. And even though there is technically peace between Argon and Norrandale, I heard the war was pretty devastating. Something about going to a kingdom that's as good as Norrandale's enemy feels wrong."

"What are you going to do then, Your Majesty?"

"I don't know." I had my elbows perched atop the dressing table and hid my head in my hands. "This feels so humiliating."

"Don't think of it as humiliation." Anesta tried to sound optimistic.

"Then what should I think of it as?" I peered through my fingers and met her gaze in the mirror.

She pursed her lips for a moment. "Think of it as an opportunity."

"An opportunity?"

"Yes," she said. "So that the two of you will have the time to get to know each other better. He said you could stay here as a guest, didn't he?" She finished my hair and put the brush down.

"Somehow my world seemed a lot easier when I knew a whole lot less," I muttered to myself, standing up. I paced across the room before falling back onto the bed, my feet dangling off the edge. "We need a proper plan. I am not going to beg Cai."

"No, we do not beg, Your Majesty," Anesta agreed.

"And I am not crawling back home empty-handed with my tail between my legs."

"Of course not. You're Queen of Everness and we do not accept defeat," she encouraged, taking a seat next to me.

"We just need to make Cai aware that this is the best decision for him and his kingdom." I looked up at the ceiling, momentarily biting the inside of my cheek. "Surely it cannot be that difficult."

"Surely not, Your Majesty."

There was a light knock on the door, and for a moment my heart leaped. It could be Cai, coming to apologise for the mistake he'd made. But even I knew I would not be so lucky.

"Come in." The doors opened, and a smile quickly stretched across my face as I jumped up from the bed. "Cordelia!"

She let out a laugh and wrapped her arms around me. "I missed you so much!"

I pulled back to look at her. "I missed you too! You look so well."

Her expression and sense of self were warmer and calmer than I had seen them before, and though I hated to admit it, I could see that living here had done much good for Cordelia.

"Oh, where are my manners?" She curtsied and dramatically said, "Queen Elara."

I let out a chuckle. "Don't tease."

Anesta stepped forwards and I introduced them. "Cordelia, this is Anesta, my current lady-in-waiting. Anesta, this is Cordelia, my previous lady-in-waiting, I guess you could say."

"I've heard so much about you," Anesta told Cordelia.

"She's a handful, isn't she?" Cordelia gestured with her head to me and Anesta laughed. "I can't believe you're really here." Cordelia looked back at me.

"Well, it's not exactly under the best of circumstances."

"What do you mean?"

"Things haven't settled in Everness. There is a lot of opposition to my reign, and I need a strong alliance now more than ever."

Her eyes widened.

"But, unfortunately, Cai isn't exactly eager to unite the two kingdoms."

"He hasn't been the same since his father and the coronation. Jack worries about him a lot."

"That doesn't solve my problem, though." I sighed.

Cordelia placed a hand on my arm. "I have full faith in you and that everything will work out as it should."

I wished I could believe it too.

"Speaking of which, how are things with you and Jack?"

"Never better." She swayed, with her hands behind her back. "I care for him very much and everything is so wonderful here, but I do miss my home some days, as can be expected."

"Rhen and I miss you too."

"I'm so glad he's here with you. I feel better having him by your side."

"He is very good at his duty," I acknowledged. "But don't tell him that or it might go to his head."

She chuckled. "Now that my relationship with Jack is no longer secret, I'll have to keep them away from each other before Rhen gets all brotherly."

"You know, I would pay good money to see Rhen and Jack take each other on in the ring."

"Tease all you want but I'm not nursing those two big babies if they decide to beat each other up."

"Jack is a good guy, though. I'm sure everything will be well."

We spent the remainder of the evening in each other's company, catching up and telling stories about the time we had been apart. I was pleased at how easily Cordelia and Anesta seemed to get along, and for the first time in a long time, I wasn't overcome with my own feelings of solitude.

Norrandale grew dark slowly, as if the night crept up on you. Though the darkness certainly didn't bring silence. There was a liveliness in the air, something I'd never associated with the palace in Levernia. I could hear the hall bustling with courtiers long past the dinner hour. Cordelia said goodnight and Anesta made sure a servant lit the fire in my room, and that I was comfortable, before she left. The bed was large, with soft sheets, not unlike my own back home.

But once I'd blown out the candle next to my bed, and was left alone with my thoughts, my mind became plagued with worry. I thought about the Darwicks and how many of the council members they might have turned against me by now. I thought about Lance and hoped he managed to avoid causing too much trouble. I thought about Cai … even though I really didn't want to.

It seemed the more I tried not to think about him, the more my mind created images of him. Memories resurfacing of our time spent in the Evernean Forest, of whispers in the dark, in my cabin and the time he treated the wound on my leg. Memories of his hands and the way he looked at me sometimes, like he was looking into my soul.

He'd said no.

And I wasn't going to force Cai down the aisle. I had a little too much pride left in me yet. But with everything going on around us, something was bound to give.

Chapter 10

Cai

I woke up nauseous and with a fierce headache after I'd spent a mostly sleepless night rolling around in my bed. There was a council meeting this morning, which I cancelled because I truly didn't have the mental or physical capacity. Not to mention the mountain of work that awaited me on my desk. I had so many things that were supposed to be occupying my mind, and yet I could only think of Lara.

A training session in the ring seemed like a good idea. The weather was cool, and the fresh air felt nice. The palace grounds were bustling with servants and courtiers, while soldiers filled the training yard. Thankfully everyone appeared to be minding their own business, though I had no doubt that I was still being observed in several peripheral visions.

"Permission to speak freely, Your Majesty?" Jack asked with a light tone. He flexed his wrist and prepared to strike with the blade in his hand.

"Yes, Jack?" I said, knowing that I most likely wasn't going to like the words coming out of his mouth.

"Your mind is not currently on our practice. Is everything all right, Your Majesty?"

Jack struck my sword with his, almost knocking it out of my hand.

"You're right, it's not," I confessed and dropped my hand. He stopped too, huffing out a breath. We'd been outside for over an hour, if I had to guess. Yet, it still didn't feel as if I'd been able to release any of the tension inside my body.

"Is this about Queen Elara, Your Majesty?" he asked gently.

I sat down and took a sip from my flask of water. My shirt clung to the sweat on my skin, increasing my irritation. "You have a marvellous talent for pointing out the obvious, Jack."

He sighed, and hesitated before deciding to speak up again. "I don't mean to be intruding on your personal affairs, Your Majesty. But what happened?"

"She asked me to marry her," I blurted out.

His expression filled with surprise, and I wondered for a moment how I had looked when Elara asked me. Probably much more shocked.

"And?" He drawled out the word.

"And I didn't say yes."

"Hmm." He took a seat next to me. "May I ask why, Your Majesty?" Jack had seen the best and the worst of Elara and knew her almost as well as I did.

"I don't know," I confessed. Maybe part of the not knowing was the reason I was so angry with myself. I could practically run myself through a wall with frustration. I'd been a mess the day before. I hadn't said a single thing right. Had I spent so much time trying to push Elara from my mind, these past months, that I didn't take time to survey all the damage done between us? All the actions and secrets and lies we had webbed ourselves in that one could almost believe it was for the better. I'd kept too many things from her. We were different people now. We were as good as strangers.

"She's different though, no?" Jack observed. "I mean—" he let out half a chuckle — "she's still Elara but being on the throne has certainly changed her."

"In some ways, yes." But the fire behind her eyes had not yet burned out. Determination and steadfastness lingered there.

She was a force of nature before, unpredictable in her ways. There was no telling what exactly was going on inside her wild mind. We'd become foreign to each other in our time apart, and I was unsure what to feel, what to think, what to do.

"Too much has changed in too little time. There is a lot to take under consideration here and it couldn't hurt for me and Elara to spend some time together until the agreement would be revised. See exactly what kind of king and queen we turned out to be."

"I would imagine Her Majesty didn't respond to your answer very well."

"In a way," I told him.

Jack seemed to hesitate again.

"Yes?" I encouraged him, being able to tell after all these years that he had plenty on his mind.

"Forgive me, Your Majesty, it's just, before, when you were set to marry Eloisa, you seemed to have no quarrel about the fact that you two were strangers. You were happy to marry for duty. So why not now, when the matrimony would benefit Norrandale and Everness?"

I let out a breath, attempting to release the tension in my jaw. I'd come out here to practise duelling with Jack for the purpose of avoiding the subject of politics and Elara. But simply ignoring it wouldn't make it go away.

"If I'd married Eloisa and things were different with my parents, she would have been princess in Norrandale for a long time. She would have had the ability to get to know the kingdom and the people, to be taught our ways. Elara would be thrown in the deep end, and with the Argonian spies ..." I sighed. "I just have a bad feeling. I have to meet with the council. If Aries is planning on breaking the peace alliance, we need to reconsider what an alliance with Everness could mean. Besides, it's not as if I'm being cruel. Elara isn't in love with me or anything of the sort ..." I trailed off.

"Don't tell me, you've changed your mind and wish to marry for love now."

I gave him a look. Jack and I didn't really have secrets. I trusted the man with everything. But there was something about my relationship with Elara that I wanted to keep to myself. I didn't have to share everything that was on my mind with everyone all the time.

"Afraid she'll break your heart, Your Majesty?" he teased.

"Shall we get back to it?" I stood up and gripped my sword.

"I must say, Your Majesty, I often forget your pride since you hide it so well." He laughed to himself but stood up nonetheless.

"I think you forget yourself." The words sounded like a king's warning, but Jack and I both respected each other too much to forsake honesty for the sake of propriety.

"Very well." Jack came into position with a smirk. "On your guard, Your Majesty."

I took comfort in Jack being head of my guard and part of the reason was his excellent swordsmanship. Which was why I knew he let me win the round. It was probably meant well, but it only made me feel worse.

"Is that how a king fights these days?"

We turned to see Lara approaching. She was in her riding attire, and I wondered if she'd gone horse riding in the morning. At the sight of her, appearing so calm and collected, my stomach tightened in a knot. Her expression suggested that our conversation yesterday had never happened.

"Not at all," Jack countered. "Today was a good day. He's usually much worse." I sent half a glare his way as Lara grinned, walking into the sand ring.

"What do you say, Cai, want to give it another go?" Her head tilted to the side innocently.

"Mmm" was the only sound I managed to let out. "I'm not sure. If you can remember, last time didn't end so well for you." I used my shirt to wipe the sweat off my face and caught Lara's eyes on my torso. "Your Majesty," I added, trying not to smile at the memory of our duel in Camp Fairfrith. Right before Ray broke it up anyway. He wasn't there on the day of the rebellion, and though I had no idea of his whereabouts, I wondered if he was back in Levernia. If perhaps he stayed at the palace with Lara. I felt an unwanted prick of jealousy at the thought.

Her eyebrows rose at my choice of words. "Well, if you're so confident, then it shouldn't be a problem for you."

"Are you sure?" I teased. "We wouldn't want to bruise your ego too many times."

Lara's eyes flared in challenge and she held out her hand to Jack, waiting for him to hand over his sword. I had meetings. I had duties, and yet we both knew I would not be able to drag myself away from a challenge such as this. I wouldn't be able to drag myself away from her.

"This is ill-advised, Your Majesty," Jack murmured under his breath, with a smile, but I chose to ignore him. He stepped out of the ring.

"You know what I think?" Lara purred. "I think you're afraid of losing against me."

Giving in, I held up my sword and she stood frozen in temporary surprise, as if she didn't quite expect me to actually agree.

"Well, come on, then." I cheekily beckoned her closer with my free hand.

With a devious smile across her lips, Lara clutched Jack's sword and held it up. "Prepare to lose, King of Norrandale."

"My dignity or my heart," I boldly teased, not being able to help myself. We both knew that should Lara really have wanted to cut out my heart, I probably would have let her.

"Both." She winked and came at me.

Her speedy attack caught me off guard for a moment before I regained focus.

Lara aimed high and I countered her strikes one after the other. After a few minutes, I expected her to get tired or perhaps even frustrated, but she seemed to be at ease. I struck left, and as she blocked the blow, I realised Lara wasn't trying to beat me yet. Instead, she was toying with me. Playing with me like a cat played with its prey before it ripped it to shreds.

"You've been practising," I commented.

"Mmmhhh," she replied with nonchalance.

I decided to go on the offensive moving more swiftly. She narrowly dodged one of my hits and it threw her slightly off balance. Sparks practically flew as the metal of our swords clashed above our heads. Her arm was stretched above her, and I could tell it was taking most of her strength to keep it up so high.

Our eyes met. "What are you looking at?" she asked.

"Just waiting for you to surrender." I tilted my head down so that our faces were slightly closer.

"That's very bold of you to assume, considering you're currently losing." Her eyebrows slowly rose and her lips pressed into a line of satisfaction.

"Oh, am I?"

"Look down, Your Majesty." And sure enough, while one of her hands held the sword above her head, the other pressed the tip of a dagger to my jacket.

"It doesn't count if you cheat."

"You didn't say anything about not using daggers." We hadn't moved from our position yet, and I heard Jack mumble something about duties before walking off.

"You didn't say we *could* use daggers."

"If it were a real fight, I would be allowed to use a dagger."

"If that's the case …" I grabbed her wrist, holding the dagger, before she could react. I used her surprise to knock the sword out of her hand and twist her wrist so that her back was turned to my chest. Though there was resistance from her side, my physical strength easily overpowered hers. She looked down to where the sword was lying on the ground, and I thought I heard her mutter something like "bastard".

Sword still clutched in my right hand, I brought it around to her front, keeping it a safe distance away from her neck.

"What were you saying about losing?" My mouth was next to her ear, and I imagined she shuddered.

"Well, this is obviously all still part of my plan to win, letting you think you have the upper hand and all."

I couldn't help but chuckle. "I'd really love to see you get yourself out of this." She was so incredibly close and just the scent of her had me forgetting why I hadn't accepted the proposal yesterday.

"That won't be a problem." She moved her shoulders but we both knew there was no way she could escape my grip.

"Surrender now and we can forget this ever happened. I'll promise not to bring it up again."

She huffed out a laugh. "How very chivalrous of you."

"Well, I am nothing if not chivalrous."

I tilted my head in an attempt to stretch out the discomfort in my neck.

"Your Majesty?"

"Mmmhhh?" I looked up towards one of my council members, Lord Burrow, and realised that I hadn't been listening to a word he was saying. Most days, I didn't mind the meetings too much. Half of the council members weren't currently at court, but I felt it necessary to address the issues at hand as soon as possible.

A large table sat in the centre of the room and the drapes and windows were open, allowing a bit of the autumn air to filter in. The walls were lined with portraits of all the previous kings of Norrandale, their eyes overlooking my reign. Our family was proud of its long history of great kings. It was a lot to live up to. I looked at the faces of my forefathers as if their painted expressions held all the answers for me.

"I asked what you propose we do with the Argonian spies?"

Whatever was going on in my head, I needed to gain control of myself. Elara's proposal wasn't the only matter requiring my considera-tion and my council would soon lose respect for me, if only because of my lack of attention.

"We have not been successful in extracting any information from

112

them," Lord Burrow reminded me. He was many years my senior, a strong-willed man who'd been on the council since the beginning of my father's reign.

"It leaves us with two options. We can keep them imprisoned here or we can send them back to Argon," I answered.

"Is there any possibility that this could be their plan? That they wanted to be captured in order to gather information about the palace and the monarchy, just to take it back to King Aries once they're released?"

"That is entirely possible." I nodded and there were murmurs of agreement from the others. "So what do you propose? That we should keep the prisoners in Norrandale until further notice?" I needed to get out of this stuffy council room. I was drained, both mentally and physically, and I wouldn't have been surprised if I started yawning.

"If I may interject," one of my other council members said.

No one has ever managed to stop you from interjecting, I thought. Lord Stapleton was a rounded man with a weakness for gambling and cake, but he'd been very loyal to the Crown his whole life, thus earning him a spot on the council despite his vices. Most of the men in the room had been around during my father's rule, and despite my personal feelings towards each of them, I knew I could trust my father's judgement.

"Is it not also possible that the longer they remain here, the more information they are able to get?" Lord Stapleton asked, and I wondered if it was a speck of icing in the corner of his mouth.

"They are in prison," Burrow retorted.

"Though we'd like to believe our guards to be loyal, we must also assume that anyone can be bought off," Lord Stapleton suggested.

"What do you propose, Your Majesty?" All eyes turned to me.

"We know that the Argonian spies would more likely kill themselves before abandoning their king. And it's like you say, Lord Stapleton, our men could be feeding them information. But we must also consider that if Aries does not get his spies back, he is likely to send more. Perhaps we may benefit from sending them back to Argon."

"That can be arranged, Your Majesty," Lord Stapleton commented.

"Yes, we must consider every possibility," Lord Burrow agreed.

I stood up from the table. "Send them on the first ship back to Argon, and I want an increase in security at all the coastal borders. I would prefer not another one of them set foot in my kingdom."

"There is another matter, Your Majesty." Lord Burrow ignored my clear intention to escape the council room.

I refrained from letting out a sigh and slowly fell back into my seat. "Yes, Lord Burrow?"

"Well." He folded his hands atop the table. "It has come to the council's attention that you've recently had the company of the young Lady Meredette."

I could already sense where this was going.

"Now we understand Your Majesty has only recently come to the throne and that the kingdom has many fine young ladies. But does this mean there could be the possibility of a new Norrandish queen somewhere in the near future?"

It was a very delicate way of asking me whether or not I was intentionally courting. Of course, many of the council members had their own daughters and nieces they'd be more than happy to send to court.

"Lady Meredette is a close friend of Lady Gwen, who you all know is as good as my sister," I responded in a monotone. "We merely enjoyed an afternoon stroll together. At present, my only intention is Norrandale's safety and prosperity."

"As long as Your Majesty remembers the safety and prosperity of an heir," the Duke of Mannik chirped, as if I was likely to forget such a thing.

"A wealthy and titled young woman from Norrandale," Lord Stapleton said. "That's what the people need. Norrandale needs to be a united kingdom, now more than ever." I nodded but had stopped listening again, my thoughts with a woman who was both titled and wealthy but very far from Norrandish.

Chapter 11

Elara

I woke up to the sound of my bedroom door opening and closing.

My eyes, fighting to open, made out a blurred figure approaching the bed. I sat up, the silken sheets falling to my waist. Goosebumps formed on my arms from the cool breeze coming in through one of the open windows.

"Cai?"

He placed one of his knees on the bed and leaned towards me.

"Elara."

For a moment, I entertained the idea that this wasn't real. That there was no way Cai's shirtless form was actually in my sleeping chambers in the middle of the night. Before I could say anything else, his lips were on my own and the scent of him overwhelmed me.

The kiss was different to the ones we'd shared before. My hands found his shoulders of their own accord. Had they always felt that strong? The warmth of Cai's lips chased away the cold of the night, though this did not stop me from shivering when his mouth moved away from my lips and down my neck.

"Cai, what are you doing here?" I couldn't help myself from asking.

He pulled away far enough that our foreheads were touching, and we shared a breath. "I missed you." It wasn't enough for me. I wanted more of an explanation, wanted more words.

But Cai wouldn't give me that kind of satisfaction. He pulled the bed sheet away, exposing my legs. I didn't let go of him as his arms wrapped around my waist and pulled me up and into him. His tongue traced my bottom lip teasingly and disrupted the last of my common sense. My fingers ran through the hair at the back of his head.

"Aren't you going to say you missed me as well?"

Cai laid me back, letting my head rest against the soft pillow. I couldn't stop myself from letting out a laugh.

He smiled against my neck. "Sshh, you're going to wake up the entire west wing with your laughing."

Were there guards stationed outside my door? Did Rhen see Cai come in? I decided too quickly that I didn't care.

"I'm taking that as a yes." His breath was hot against my skin.

"Maybe I just missed the sparring." His hand slowly ran up my leg.

"Liar."

My hands traced down his back, digging into his skin as he pressed a kiss to my collarbone. I took his face into my hands and brought his mouth back to mine. Cai continued to kiss me as if it would be the last kiss we would ever share. His hands were everywhere until I had lost track of them — in my hair, my waist, my thighs.

I pulled away merely for the desperate need of taking a breath when his eyes locked with mine. Those beautiful eyes …

I gasped, sitting up in bed. The room was empty. I was alone. It was the sound of the window blowing shut that woke me from my dream. I shuddered, still able to feel Cai's hands tracing my skin. I

117

slipped out of the sheets, walked over to the window and pushed it open again.

The cool night air was a relief while I attempted to calm myself. *Just a dream*, I repeated over and over. Just a dream, though every part of it felt real. Had I really given into Cai that easily? Was him whispering my name in the dark all that it took?

It wasn't real.

Cai wasn't here and he'd said no.

I'd asked him to marry me, and he'd said no.

So, I pattered back to bed, hoping that a dreamless sleep would take me this time.

"I'm so happy we finally get to spend some time together again." Cordelia grinned as we climbed out of the carriage. The city, which bordered the palace grounds, was so much bigger and busier than I could have imagined. I definitely wasn't in Levernia anymore.

"Me too." I tried not to gawk. She linked arms with me and led me through the vibrant streets while Rhen followed behind at an appropriate distance. Gone were the days that I walked through the cities alone. Gone were the days I scaled rooftops and sneaked through markets. The air was crisp and fresh, and somewhere in the distance, someone was playing a fiddle. The streets swarmed with people as we walked past colourful window displays of hats, dresses, glassware and art.

I couldn't face Cai that morning. Just the thought of the dream made me blush, and I knew I would struggle to look him in the eye. But our council meeting couldn't be pushed back for ever. I'd heard some of the council members weren't currently at court and had been asked by Cai to return to the palace. But I needed something more substantial than a potential meeting. It felt as though I had a ticking clock, and the time was slowly running out.

I attempted to focus while Cordelia talked about which vendors and merchants she liked and which bakeries made her favourite pastries and cakes. We walked the cobbled streets while I took in the signs and window displays. There was something lively about the atmosphere. Cordelia led me inside a merchant's shop filled with trinkets and gifts.

How could it be that less than a year ago I would have risked my life to steal some of these things and now I could afford as many of them as I wanted? I couldn't decide if it made me feel relieved or filled with guilt.

"Do you think I should get this for Jack?" she asked, holding up a small flask. I turned my attention to her from where I had been staring out the window at the people passing by in the street.

I contemplated the flask for a moment. It was silver with a decorated leather strap attached. The craftsmanship was impressive. A lovely gift indeed. I knew the two of them cared for each other, but it made my heart warm to see her this happy.

"I think he would really appreciate that, Cordelia."

Her smile grew. "Great." I waited while she purchased the flask and finally convinced her to take me to one of these bakeries that she kept raving about. I would, embarrassingly, admit that it was the best cake I'd ever had in my life and that I practically inhaled it. How had I managed so long without chocolate?

"You seem to be thriving here," I commented when we made our way back to the carriage, Rhen's arms full of small boxes filled with sweets and pastries.

"It sure is different from my life in Everness," Cordelia agreed. "But that doesn't mean I don't miss it sometimes." She gave a backward glance towards her brother. Rhen only gave her a small smile.

"Do you think you and Jack will ever get married?"

"He talks about it all the time."

"But?" I nudged her to tell me more.

"But I think he's afraid his station isn't good enough. He's always on about saving money and so forth." She shrugged.

"He's captain of the king's guard."

"He doesn't have a title or assets. Starting a life of our own won't be easy." And while Jack was young now, what would happen when he grew too old to serve in the king's army? Endless thoughts and questions raced through my mind, and though I knew it was none of my business, I wondered if I should speak to Cai about it. If he knew what Jack's intentions with Cordelia were, he might find a way to help his friend.

"It will all work out," I tried to reassure her. "You'll see."

I found myself walking into an empty dining room by the time lunch rolled around. Well, empty apart from one person lounging at the head of the table with a book in his hand.

"Hello, Lord Thatcher," I greeted him sheepishly. I'd mostly tried to avoid his gaze during our first encounter but now I had a chance to fully inspect Cai's friend. They shared a similar hair colour, but Thatcher had a wildness and ambition in his eyes that I couldn't quite name.

"There is no need for such formalities, Your Majesty. Please just call me Thatcher," he said, putting the book down and turning his attention to me.

"In that case, you can call me Elara." It was strange introducing myself by my first name. But there was a sense of truthful relief to it. I could practically hear Rhen lecturing me that it was improper, but I didn't really care. I was getting tired of being called "Your Majesty" all the time. It only managed to remind me of the massive responsibility I had to carry on my shoulders. "Are you having lunch by yourself?" I gestured to the empty room and half-dressed table.

Thatcher shrugged. "I was going to have lunch with Cai, but he's decided to take lunch in his study instead."

My stomach rumbled, the cake from earlier long forgotten.

"Would you care to join me, Your Majesty?" Thatcher asked, not calling me by my first name as I'd requested.

"Oh, I don't know." My hands involuntarily fidgeted behind my back.

"It would be an honour." He seemed to catch onto my hesitation and called for a servant to set the table. Everything smelled so wonderful.

"Perhaps His Majesty might join us later," he suggested hopefully, as a servant helped me into my seat.

"I've been meaning to see him all day, but I believe he had other plans this morning, so I explored the city with Lady Cordelia instead."

"And what do you think of Norrandale thus far?"

"It's beautiful. Everything feels so lively and full of colour. The people look really happy."

Thatcher shrugged, taking a bite from the food on his plate. "Looks can be deceiving sometimes."

"Oh, don't I know that." I almost laughed. A servant placed a plate full of food in front of me and I thanked him. In my peripheral vision, I saw Thatcher observing me. Probably because I was paying more attention to the servants than I should have. *Let him stare.* I knew what it was like to be even lower than palace servants. I knew how people treated you when you weren't born with money and a title. They were no less human than I, and I wasn't going to let propriety stop me from showing common decency.

"Are you suggesting some kind of trouble growing in the kingdom?" I asked.

"Every kingdom has its troubles as you well know, Your Majesty." There was no arguing with that. "Though Cai isn't quick to confide in anyone about the things he's dealing with."

"When I first got to know him, I honestly didn't think he had a single problem in his life. He's good at hiding his feelings." It felt somewhat strange to talk to Thatcher, a man I hardly knew, about Cai. But, to my understanding, this was his oldest friend. Thatcher was like Cai's brother. If there were anyone to discuss Cai with, it would be him.

"What was my friend like in Everness?"

"More ..." I thought about it for a moment. "More carefree, I suppose." I bit my lip. "He didn't consider the future with every decision. He was more likely to follow his heart."

"Sounds like him." Thatcher nodded. "These days he's working most of the time. I worry about him."

I forced myself to eat more slowly and cleared my throat. "What about you?"

Thatcher had put his book away entirely by now. "What about me, Your Majesty?"

"Well, I know you're Cai's friend and I know you used to get into a lot of trouble when you were younger."

A smile formed at my words.

"But other than that, I don't know anything about you."

He sucked in a breath and relaxed back into the chair. "I'm to inherit all of my father's money and business. Though he does have excellent men running most of it, which leaves me more free time for ..." He hesitated. "Certain pleasures."

"Cai seems awfully fond of you." I tried to steer the conversation.

"He's like a brother. I've known him my whole life."

"I have a friend like that," I said, thinking about Ray. Wondering where he was and hoping that by some miracle he was still alive.

"I didn't know queens had friends," Thatcher replied coyly.

"Maybe you're right." I sighed, taking another bite. "Maybe we only have allies and enemies."

"Perhaps." He took hold of the nearest cup and started filling it from a porcelain jug. "But it would be awfully boring otherwise."

"I could use a little boredom." I chuckled. "In fact, I wouldn't even mind a lot of boredom."

"Well, you certainly won't be bored if you marry Cai." Seeing my expression, he added, "Forgive me, Your Majesty. Cai confided in me about the matter."

"I see." I couldn't blame Cai for telling Thatcher but felt embarrassed, nonetheless.

"Don't worry, Your Majesty." He winked. "I won't tell a soul." He said it with enough sincerity that it made me feel a little bit better.

"Thank you. I appreciate it."

"It's none of my business anyway," he continued. "Though I had to keep myself from giving that man a smack on the back of his head."

"Why?" I frowned.

"I understand Cai needs to view everything from a political angle now. But some men would kill to marry a queen."

"I suppose." I shrugged. "Though not all men are fit to be king." I thought back to Edgar wanting to blackmail me.

"Now that—" Thatcher raised his cup — "I couldn't agree with more."

"What are you reading?" I nodded towards the book on the table.

"Some old poetry collection. I didn't want heavy reading material for lunch."

"So, you decided on poetry?" I asked in slight surprise. I always thought poetry was to be examined, dissected even, read between the lines.

"You don't prefer literature as a pastime, Your Majesty?"

"Not even if someone paid me."

He laughed at my response. I dabbed my face with my napkin and pushed the chair back.

"Thank you for lunch. I'm going to see if I can find Cai."

"It was my deepest pleasure. Thank you for keeping me company." Thatcher picked up his book again.

I walked from the dining room to Cai's study. It wasn't the same one we'd spoken in when I'd proposed, and it took a while of searching and eventually awkwardly asking one of the servants. Why did this palace have to be so damn big? After much protesting, I'd finally been able to convince Rhen not to follow me around everywhere, that I was safe here. But it was difficult to find my way through all the halls and rooms.

I pushed open the door without knocking. Thankfully Cai didn't have company.

I wouldn't want to look like a complete fool … again. He looked up as I entered the room, his expression carrying uncertainty. Flashes of my dream came to mind and my eyes involuntarily travelled to his hands. I could still feel his breath against my skin.

Cai set down the papers that had been in his hands. "Lara. Please come in." The study housed a large dark oak desk and many books lining the walls. I wondered if this had been King Eric's study before it was Cai's. Or had he chosen a different room, something that was his own? Regardless, there wasn't much thought put into the decoration. It was simple and neat, suited to Cai.

"We need to talk." I tried to keep my posture as straight and confident as possible. It felt like that was the only thing I'd been doing since arriving in Norrandale — trying to appear more confident than I actually was.

"Yes, of course." He looked down at the papers on his desk and hesitated. "It's only that now is not exactly a good time and—"

"Are you avoiding me, Cai?" I cut straight to the point.

"No, why would I be avoiding you?" he asked.

"I wanted to have breakfast with you this morning." I stepped further into the study.

"I'm sorry, I was in a meeting," Cai responded with sincerity.

"So I heard, and then I thought perhaps we might have lunch together."

The study remained awkwardly quiet.

"But I see you're busy." He probably had many things on his plate, but was it too much to ask for a moment of his time? I turned to leave.

"Lara, wait!"

"Listen, Cai, I understand you have your priorities, but I have mine too, and whether I like it or not, you're involved with that. I'm asking you to treat me like an equal and not a problem to be solved."

"That was not my intention," he responded swiftly.

"I believe you." I sighed. He sat back in his chair. "But pushing me away is not going to make me leave. It's not going to make any of this change."

"I'm not trying to push you away. This is so much bigger than you and I. There are procedures and documents and protocol and—"

"I don't care about the damn documentation, Cai. I just wanted an answer from you."

"I … it's not …" He stumbled over his words.

"Figure out what you want, Cai. I know why I'm here," I said, walking out of the study.

Chapter 12

Cai

I watched her hair spiral in slight waves down her back as my horse started to fall behind hers. Elara's riding attire was elegant, with the Evernean royal crest stitched onto the back of her jacket. Her legs dangled next to the horse's sides in such a manner that it gave away her lack of formal training, growing up. She might have been taught to ride like a bandit, but she certainly hadn't been taught to ride like a queen, sitting astride like that.

The thought made me smile. I wasn't sure if asking her to accompany me for a ride through the forest would make up for any tension between us, but she seemed content enough, even though she hadn't said a word since we left the stables.

"You know, if you paint a picture, it will last longer." She looked back with a smile, and I felt my cheeks flush. This only seemed to widen her grin, her eyes playful.

"I'm simply admiring the horse's flanks. They've been doing well exercising her over the last few months." The attempt at redemption was futile and almost a little bit sad, but it was too late to stop myself.

I managed a smile, however, when I heard Elara say "Horse's flanks, my arse" to herself. "Where are you taking me, by the way?"

"There's a hill beyond this stretch of woods. The view is quite something."

"You do realise we'll get into an insurmountable amount of trouble upon returning to the palace."

It probably wasn't the best idea to sneak out of the palace without any of our guards to accompany us for our safety. But there was something in the forbidden that reminded me of the time I spent with Elara in Fairfrith. It was the first time since then that I was completely alone with her. And maybe we both needed it.

"I'm the king of Norrandale, I can only get into so much trouble."

"I see your new title has made you arrogant." She chuckled.

"Perhaps I was always arrogant and you simply didn't notice."

My words made her laugh softly, as though trying to contain it.

"Pray tell, what is so amusing?"

"You would make an awful spy, you know."

"I would?" I questioned, curious to know exactly why.

"I hate to be the one to tell you, but you're a terrible liar."

"Well, I can't be good at everything, now can I?"

"I thought kings were supposed to be good at everything."

I played along. "A common myth, I assure you."

"Ah, I see. Forgive my ignorance, Your Majesty." She drew out my title.

"You've changed, though," I commented, and she turned her head to face me.

Those wild, beautiful eyes, which had flames dancing in them. Just looking at her ignited sparks inside my chest.

"What do you mean?"

"You used not to fear getting into trouble. I see your responsibility must have caught up with you."

"Oh please, I was only fearing for your sake." Elara urged her horse into a gallop and they raced away.

I chased after her, the wind swirling past us, my horse huffing underneath me as he pushed forwards. She ducked under a low hanging branch, which almost hit me. The trees moved past us in a blur of green. The sound of our horses galloping echoed through the woods. Elara remained ahead all the way through the trees and up the hill.

"Careful that you don't fall," I called out.

Her laugh was carried away by the wind until she finally reached the top of the hill. She stopped to catch her breath. "You were right." Elara loosened the reins, allowing her horse to eat the grass. "It really is something."

Ahead were hills and valleys of lush green surrounding a long winding river that gathered water from the mountain slopes. My eyes travelled to Elara's face, and I watched her take in the view.

"Now are you going to tell me why you really brought me out here alone?"

"I told you, I wanted to show you—"

"Cai." She raised an eyebrow.

"And …" I added. "Because I wanted to apologise for yesterday. I have a lot on my mind."

"I'm not asking you to drop everything for me," she said gently. "But don't you think it would ease your mental burdens if you talked to me about what's bothering you?"

I shook my head. "I'm not making my problems your problems, Elara."

She sighed. "I know I'm here on political business. But you're my friend, if nothing else. A lot has changed, I know. Maybe it wouldn't be the worst thing in the world for us to spend time getting to know each other again."

I glanced her way, to meet her eyes, but she was looking at the horizon.

"Sometimes, I wish there was a way to take a break from being a monarch." Not many people would understand. But she would. "I'm not blind to the privileges I was born with but …"

"I know," Elara replied. "I haven't even experienced this kind of life for long, but a break would be nice."

"I'll make you a deal," I offered.

"Oh?"

"One day, when we're old and retired, we'll travel somewhere."

She laughed. "I thought you only retire from this role when you're dead."

"Will you just play along?"

"Fine, so where would we go?"

I thought about it for a moment while trying to keep my eyes away from her mouth. Had it always been so alluring? "Some island somewhere warm and far away."

"I could work on my swimming in the sea."

"I thought you could swim?" I frowned.

"I can. I'm just not a very strong swimmer, I'm afraid." Elara shrugged.

"I could fish," I added, imagining it. "And we could eat whatever I caught."

"How very rugged for a king." She chuckled.

"Well, I wasn't always king, remember?"

Elara closed her eyes and breathed in as if she could see it in front of her, the warm white sand, the crystal-clear water. I couldn't pull my eyes away from her.

"It sounds lovely."

It was wishful thinking and we both knew it. But it was nice to think about the possibility of someday.

Chapter 13

Elara

My grip tightened on the hilt as I took a swing at Rhen.

He stepped back and my sparring sword struck nothing but air. "Too predictable. You need to exploit my weaknesses."

I stretched my neck by tilting my head side to side. "Well, that would be a lot easier if I knew where your weaknesses are."

"You're too focused on where you're aiming and not observing where my lack of defence is." He was right. "Let's go again," Rhen said patiently.

We'd been at this for most of the afternoon. I needed somewhere to channel my frustrations.

It felt good to be in a pair of breeches and out of a dress again. Not that I minded the dresses as much anymore. It was a lot better now that they were specially made to fit me and I could request the seamstress make them as comfortable as possible.

I gathered my strength and struck towards Rhen. He parried.

"A little better. Again."

"You don't have to talk to me as if I were a child who's never done this before. I do have some swordsmanship skills." I attacked again and again. He managed to block each blow, and I looked to see if I could find him off balance when he countered my attack. I noticed a slight wobble in his sword when he made a swing from the lower left.

"I'll stop talking to you like a child when you stop fighting like one."

"Hey!" I grunted and pressed forwards, my hands moving as if to attack from the right.

"What about your time with the King yesterday?"

"What about it?"

I saw him commit to defend and then swivelled, my sword aiming low and left.

"Has he accepted your proposal yet?"

"It's not that simple," I begrudgingly quoted Cai.

Rhen was momentarily taken by surprise by my move but managed to defend just in time. He was completely off balance now.

"You don't have that much time, you know."

"I'm trying!" I argued, no longer giving Rhen the opportunity to strike me as he tried to defend against each swift blow.

"Well, maybe you should try harder."

That did it. I gripped the hilt of the sword tighter than ever before, and with all the strength I could muster, I hit the sword out of his hand. We both watched as it fell to the sand.

"Interesting," he said, more to himself than to me.

"What is?" Sweat started to gather on my back. All these weeks of eating expensive foods and not exercising properly had left me out of shape.

"You fight better when you're angry."

"What do you mean?"

"There was a short period of time when I was responsible for helping train the palace guards in Levernia. I would tell them not to let their emotions get the better of them when fighting. I've told you the same thing, many a time."

"I'm aware," I said, teeth almost clenching.

"However, I've also noticed that when you get riled up, you seem to be better, more focused, oddly enough. Like you channel everything to a single place. You use your emotions to your advantage."

"Ha." I barked out a laugh. "Never heard that one before."

"I'm serious, though." He shrugged. "I think it's your passionate spirit that drives you."

"How about less talking and more sparring?" I said, though I couldn't pretend I'd not heard his words.

"I wish I could oblige, Your Majesty, but you appointed me for a reason. I'm sure you know how vital our discussions are to your reign."

I wished I could argue with him, but it didn't mean I looked forward to Rhen's regular commentary regarding politics.

"If you insist." My tone was sarcastic, but he knew I understood the seriousness of the matter. I dropped my sword.

"Have you recently been in contact with Lance about how matters are faring in Levernia?" Rhen asked.

"I've sent a messenger. I should think a response will arrive in a few days."

"I certainly hope so."

"You're the one who worked with him first."

"I worked with him so we could get anyone on the throne that wasn't him."

I raised an eyebrow and he shrugged.

"You know what I mean."

"And how's that working out for you?"

"I exchanged one child for another." He sighed.

"Very funny." I rolled up my sleeves, the heat of exercising continuing to catch up with me. *A cool bath would be delightful.*

"If I can get Cai to marry me—"

"If?" he asked, and I sent a glare his way.

"When." I corrected myself. "When Cai marries me, I'll secure my place on the throne. Lance can do whatever he wants with his time and fortune, and Cai and I only have to see each other on occasion."

"Do you think Cai would agree to that?" Rhen asked as we stepped out of the sand ring.

"Are you suggesting Cai wouldn't agree to that?"

"Cai is not above marrying for duty, no. But his council would want him to be certain that this alliance benefits him too. If he's not marrying for love, anyway."

He mumbled the last part, and I pretended I didn't hear him. I was thankful that Cai had made some time for us to spend together but I could still sense a distance between us. Distance I could probably only blame myself for. Was it possible that Cai was still hurt about how things ended in Levernia? Or did he simply no longer possess the feelings he once had? Even if Cai had said my past had nothing to do with his silence, what if his hesitance towards the alliance had something to do with who I was underneath my crown?

"Regardless, I trust Lance's reply will be positive." I turned the conversation back to the original subject. Rhen didn't respond, as if he wasn't quite sure of this. The air around us was quiet for a moment apart from our footsteps and the birds happily chirping.

"It's probably not my place to ask," Rhen started hesitantly. "But do you want to talk about what happened with the Darwicks?"

I shuddered. "The part where Edgar tried to threaten me, or my servant tried to kill me?"

"Both."

"I don't know. I'm used to people not liking me, but the stakes are somehow higher now and I can't just run away to safety."

"I'm sorry I didn't step into the room sooner. I was trying to give you the privacy you asked for and ..."

"You don't need to apologise, Rhen. You were only doing your duty. I'm starting to learn that privacy is a luxury I can no longer afford." Which seemed ironic considering how many luxuries I could, in fact, afford.

"I'd better go and get ready. I'm having dinner with Cai's family."

"You have much to do, Your Majesty." Rhen smiled, taking in the state of me.

We walked towards the single door leading back inside the palace. I looked up, spotting movement. There was a window high up, overlooking the grounds and the training yard. Despite the glass's reflection, I made out a tall figure with blond hair. Thatcher. He smiled and waved. I returned a slightly awkward smile and waved back.

"You know, sometimes I think you're a little too honest, Rhen."

"Whatever you say, Your Majesty."

I was lucky that Anesta knew what she was doing.

Not too long ago, my hair was a mess and I was covered in sweat, but Anesta managed to make me look like the picturesque queens I always saw in the portraits in the palace. I hadn't realised how long Rhen and I had been sparring. Needless to say, it would have been very rude of me to arrive late to a dinner held in honour of my visit.

My stomach churned, and I wasn't sure if it was due to hunger or nerves. I held on to the heavy skirts of my dress while trying to hurry through the hallways without looking like a fool. Though lavender wasn't my favourite colour to wear, Anesta always found a way to make it work. The soft material cascaded down my legs in waves of light purple, while the sleeves hung about my arms, revealing my shoulders. My footsteps were soft on the carpeted floor beneath me. Candlelight illuminated the wallpaper-covered wall panels and decorated side tables.

I wasn't even entirely sure how to get to the dining room from this part of the palace. And I would have hated to ask for assistance again. If Rhen had been at my side, he probably could have shown me the way. But I had too much pride to walk all the way back and ask for his help. Especially after I'd insisted he didn't escort me everywhere.

My eyes caught the large portraits hanging on the walls. Some of the faces looked familiar. Which meant the dining room had to be left.

I veered down the next hallway and stopped short for a moment. In the middle of the hallway stood a woman well into her later years, looking up at one of the paintings. Cai's grandmother. There was no doubt about it. I gulped.

My disrupting presence was impossible to miss and my blood chilled slightly as her head turned to take me in.

"Queen Grandmother." I bowed my head. It didn't matter that she hadn't ruled a kingdom for a very long time. Everything about this woman's stature and attitude labelled her a queen. A real queen. Everything I could never be.

"Ah, the young queen, Elara. Come closer," she ordered, and I didn't hesitate to obey. I could see Cai's green eyes in her, but her hair had long since turned grey. Her dress and jewels, however, were still of the most elegant and expensive kind.

"You're a very pretty thing." Her eyes took in every part of me.

"Thank you." I attempted a smile even though everything about her made me nervous.

"Pretty things can be dangerous, you know."

My smile dropped, and I remained quiet only because I had no idea how to reply.

She turned to walk away, and when I didn't immediately follow, she stopped to look over her shoulder. "Well, aren't you coming?"

"Of course." I quickly fell into step beside her.

"Usually, in nature, we find that the more beautiful something is, the more poisonous it can be."

I still had no idea how to respond.

"I see you're wearing my necklace."

I couldn't help but look at her with surprise.

Her necklace? I hadn't planned on bringing the infamous necklace to Norrandale, but Anesta must have packed it with my other beautiful pieces of jewellery. I decided to wear it tonight as a reminder for Cai. A reminder of the things we used to fight for. Of the past and friendship we used to share, in the hope that it would aid me in gaining this alliance.

"But Cai had given the necklace …" I began.

She watched realisation settle on my face. Cai had talked about giving the necklace back to the original owner when we were in Fairfrith. And I had refused to return it to him. I was afraid of what it could be capable of. And I selfishly wanted to keep it if I ever needed to exchange it for money someday.

It had belonged to Cai's grandmother all this time, and I was parading it around in front of everyone tonight. Could the embarrassment be worse?

"Here." I stopped walking, quickly reaching for the clasp. "I'm so sorry. I didn't know."

But Cai's grandmother held up her hand as she faced me.

"You can keep it. I gave it to Cai a long time ago and told him it was for his future wife."

There was a time when it was meant for Eloisa. If I had known the sentimental value of the necklace, I never would have held on to it.

"But I'm not ... we're not ..." I struggled to find the right words.

"It's just a piece of jewellery, my dear. But it represents a history of the strongest and most adored queens the kingdom has seen."

I swallowed hard.

"Make sure you are worthy of wearing it." She turned and walked towards the dining room, leaving me speechless in the hallway.

Chapter 14

Cai

"This is going to be wonderful." Thatcher rubbed his hands together as if he had some kind of diabolical plan in mind, and I chuckled.

"Why would you say that?"

"Your previous suitor against your current suitor. Don't tell me you don't love a cat fight?"

"I'm also competing in the archery competition, and in case you forgot, so are you and Gwen." I tested the string of my bow, not bringing up the fact that Meredette was not my suitor. It was a cloudy day but there was no wind. A large target had been set up in the distance. The thick rope was rolled into a disc, with a white dot, the size of a saucer, painted in the middle.

"Yes." Thatcher rolled his eyes at me. "And we all know Gwen is going to win anyway. Unless your Elara has a hidden talent up her sleeve."

"I'm afraid not when it comes to a bow and arrow, unfortunately." I pretended I didn't hear him say *my* Elara. Like the sound of it didn't stir something primitive in me.

"If she's not good, then why is she participating?" We looked to where Elara stood next to Rhen, observing the tip of one of her arrows.

"I could be wrong, but I do believe she's trying to prove a point."

"And that point would be?" Thatcher cocked an eyebrow.

"That is the question."

"Do you know if Lady Meredette is any good?" he ventured.

"I didn't even know she could shoot with a bow and arrow at all." I shrugged. "We didn't exactly cover that topic at our last meeting."

"Then what did you talk about?"

"Gardening, mostly."

Thatcher muffled a laugh at my response. "I have a feeling this is going to be very interesting indeed."

"When was the last time you had any practice?" I held up the bow in my hands.

"Don't fret, my friend." He placed his hand upon my shoulder. "Who needs practice when you were born with raw talent?"

I laughed. "Very well, may the best man win."

"Indeed, may he do so."

My eyes shifted to Elara, who appeared to be in serious conversation with Anesta. Her expression was coated with worry. So she had been practising the sword but not the bow and arrow.

"Are you ready to proceed, Your Majesty, or do you fear a little competition?"

Meredette boldly spoke up, making all our eyes turn towards her. She wore a deep red gown, her lips once more painted the colour of rubies to match.

"On the contrary, I was simply trying to be a gentleman and let the ladies go first."

Thatcher cleared his throat next to me, hiding a smile behind his fisted right hand.

"Very well." Meredette shrugged nonchalantly and stepped forwards, her weapon in hand and ready to be drawn. The target wasn't set at an impossible distance, but still, one would require definite skill to hit the white circle.

The air became deathly quiet, all eyes on Meredette as she pulled the bowstring taut. By the sheer confidence and focus on her face, one could tell it wasn't her first time. She let go and the target sounded as the arrow impaled it. Not quite dead centre but not far off either.

Thatcher let out a low whistle and Gwen stiffened next to me, her face blank. "Looks like you have some competition," her brother said, almost in satisfaction. She sent a look of disapproval his way.

"Who would like to go next?" the assigned judge dared to ask, but when no one volunteered, I had no choice but to step up.

"I guess I'll go, then."

My arrow managed to hit the target almost dead centre and there was a small round of applause.

"Well done, Your Majesty," Meredette said. "I had no idea you were such a skilled archer."

"Nor I you," I admitted. Over her shoulder, I saw Elara watching us carefully.

Gwen took her turn and hit the target in the middle of the white circle. She turned and made a vulgar gesture towards Thatcher, who'd been trying to distract her throughout the whole process.

Next was Elara. Even from a distance, I could see her hands shake. This was not going to go well. She bit her lip in displeasure as the arrow hit near the outer edge of the target.

Thatcher was the last to go and he managed to hit the target a little further off than Meredette had. We continued for another few rounds, gathering points with each.

Unsurprisingly, Gwen came first and I second, with Meredette a very close third.

"This was certainly very entertaining." Meredette handed her bow to a servant before we started making our way back to the palace's veranda. "We must do it again sometime, Your Majesty."

"I'm at your disposal," I replied, without thinking. "You name a time and place."

"I quite like the idea of that," she said, with a hint of flirtation, before I caught Elara staring. Was she jealous?

"In that case, would it be too much to ask you to host a ball? I'm sure the whole court would be very pleased," Elara asked sweetly, but her tone wasn't entirely sincere.

"I suppose it's possible," I agreed, not quite knowing her motive. Was she trying to win my affection or simply peeved that my attentions had been elsewhere?

"Yes, please host a ball." Gwen jumped into the conversation. "It's been forever since we've had a proper ball at the palace."

"I think a ball is a great idea." Thatcher slapped Gwen on the back, causing her to elbow him. "And since poor Cai is so terrible at planning them, I think he should leave the planning to us. Don't you ladies agree?" he asked, looking at Elara and Meredette. He didn't wait for a reply to continue. "We should all convene for lunch in, say, an hour or so?"

"I could do with something to eat," I agreed.

"Me too. All that winning has built up quite an appetite," Gwen joked.

"Then it's settled. I shall see you at lunch." He gave an exaggerated bow before strutting off, leaving me shaking my head at him.

I turned to speak to Elara, but she was gone.

"Something the matter, Your Majesty?" Meredette asked.

"I just remembered something I need to take care of, if you ladies will excuse me."

I presumed she'd taken the long way around through the gardens. And I walked along the hedges and around the potted ferns until I reached the path where the majority of the flower beds were planted.

It was there that I spotted Elara. At first, she didn't notice my presence and I watched in amusement while she scolded herself. After a moment, she let out a heavy sigh and took a seat on the waist-high wall that formed part of the path. She leaned her bow against it and brushed her fingers through her hair.

"Enter the archery competition because *that* will be a good idea," she mumbled to herself.

"I didn't think it was that bad."

Elara's cheeks coloured as she noticed my presence.

"How long have you been standing there?" she asked as I walked over.

"Long enough." I chuckled while she attempted not to blush further and failed miserably.

"Well, I hope you enjoyed having me join in on the archery." She straightened her dress, trying to regain some composure. "As it is unlikely to occur again."

"Do you want to go for a walk?"

She looked up at me with pleasant surprise.

"Very well."

We walked slowly and in somewhat of an awkward silence. I could see her forming sentences in her head and tensing herself to say something before thinking better of it. I was equally unsure of how to begin the conversation.

"As you can clearly see, I have not improved at archery." Elara finally broke through the quiet.

"You weren't that bad," I replied too quickly, not sounding quite sincere, though I was only trying to make her feel better.

"Not that bad?" she exclaimed. "You're such a terrible liar."

"And here I thought you were letting me win for my ego's sake."

Her lip twitched as she attempted to hide a smile.

"I appreciate you trying to lift my spirits, but we'll just have to accept that I'm a lost cause when it comes to a bow and arrow." She crossed her arms. We'd stopped walking.

"Such a shame." I shook my head in a teasing manner.

She moved to lean back against one of the walls overgrown with ivy. It had been like that for as long as I could remember, but my grandmother always insisted we keep it that way.

I'd opened my mouth to speak when Elara suddenly fell backwards, through the wall, head disappearing in the ivy. I hurried over to help her up.

"There's a door there." She stood up, dusting off her skirts. I took out a twig that had got caught in her hair. Her eyes followed my hand and then she looked back to meet my gaze. She stared for a moment before looking away somewhat self-consciously.

"Yes, it would appear so," I stated rather obviously, with a smile on my face, taking too long to look away from her eyes and mouth.

"It's a private garden," Elara mused.

I recognised it as one of the places where I used to play and hide as a child. I hadn't been there in so many years, and I'd practically forgotten where the door was. I was so focused on Elara, I didn't even realise we were in that part of the garden.

"Why do you think it's sectioned off from the rest of the gardens?"

"It was done during my grandfather's reign." It was clear that no one had been here in a very long time and nature had taken its toll. "He made many changes to the palace and this part of the garden was cut off."

"You can tell it was pretty at some point, though."

The garden was like a small courtyard, containing broken water features, and the remains of what had once been flower beds with trees creating a canopy above. There were weeds everywhere, the grass almost reaching my knees. But yes, at some stage, before I was born, it must have been beautiful. It was a shame, really, that everything was now in such disarray and that the garden was no longer in use. Perhaps I needed to speak with my mother about getting someone to clean it up.

"It's the kind of place one can go to be alone with one's thoughts."

"I don't know if that's such a good thing," Elara admitted earnestly. She stepped further into the garden, picking at one of the weed flowers.

"Maybe, maybe not," I agreed. I was so far gone into my head these days, it seemed like the last thing I needed was more time to overthink. "Either way, it would be nice to get it reclaimed from the weeds and overgrowth. Then at least the garden could be put back into use."

"With discretion, of course." She looked around as if she could already imagine the water flowing from the water features again and the rose bushes that would no doubt be planted.

"What do you mean?"

"Didn't you say you had a secret hiding place like this as a child?"

I'd forgotten I'd told her about this place. It seemed like it was a lifetime ago. Much less did I think she would remember.

"You're right. It used to be my secret hiding place, but I haven't been here in ages."

Elara looked around again, her eyes gleaming with mischief. "If I had a place like this to hide as a child, I don't think I would ever come out." That I could believe.

"I'll see what I can do about getting it cleaned up."

"I bet it's going to look really beautiful."

"I had a thought." I changed the subject before my nerves got the better of me.

She looked over her shoulder at me. "Yes?"

"Maybe we could go for a picnic sometime? Only if you want to, of course."

"You're not otherwise occupied with your duties?" She referred to the schedule that had been keeping me from spending time with her.

"They can wait," I assured her.

"I'd like that very much."

"Excellent, I'll have a servant arrange it."

"I'll arrange it," Elara suggested, surprising me.

"Are you sure? You don't have to."

"I want to," she affirmed.

"Very well, then. I look forward to it." I couldn't help the smile on my face.

Chapter 15

Elara

Having left the bow and arrows somewhere in the gardens, I made my way through the palace halls. How could I have been so stupid as to agree to an archery competition, knowing full well that I was going to achieve nothing apart from embarrassing myself? Not to mention the knot that seeing Cai and Lady Meredette created in the pit of my stomach. Convincing him to agree to this alliance already carried great difficulty without the additional obstacle of beautiful potential suitors.

I stepped into my chambers and asked Anesta to draw me a hot bath. Slowly, the room filled with steam and the scent of roses and lavender, which she'd added to the hot water.

The archery may not have been a success, but at least Cai had made an attempt to spend some time with me.

I undressed and sank into the bath. Whatever the soaps were made of in Norrandale, they smelled heavenly. Anesta undid my hair while I washed.

"Should I ask about the archery competition?" she enquired, and I shook my head.

"I have single-handedly managed to continue to humiliate myself in front of the King of Norrandale and his courtiers. Of all things, why did it have to be archery?"

"I'm sure King Cai doesn't care about such simple things."

"Speaking of which, I must ask your assistance," I mumbled through the water while washing my face.

"Of course, Your Majesty."

"Cai has suggested a picnic for us."

"Oh, how lovely." She yanked at a knot in my hair from excitement and I cringed.

"I need to find out what Cai's favourite desserts are so that I can make sure we have them."

"You don't know the King's favourite dessert?" Anesta grinned, still fighting the knot. Her eyebrows lifted as she discovered a small ivy twig in the process.

"We were in the midst of a rebellion the last time we saw each other, so no, there wasn't really time or opportunity to discuss pastries and cakes."

"I'll find out what food His Majesty likes," she reassured me, smiling in satisfaction as the offending knot untangled painfully.

"Thank you." I scrubbed my arms. "Anesta?"

"Yes, Your Majesty?"

"Are royal picnics similar to other picnics?"

"What do you mean?"

"Well." I hesitated. "I've never really been on a picnic. Not a proper one, anyway. I have no idea what these people do on such occasions."

"I don't think it really differs or that there are any special rules regarding picnics."

"Really?" I said, unconvinced. "With the kind of fuss they make,

I would think they would forbid a king and queen from sitting on the ground."

"Oh no, you'll probably have chairs and a table and a tent to keep you out of the sun and servants to dish up the food."

I gave a grunt of dissatisfaction. "That's not the kind of picnic I had in mind."

A loud knock sounded from the outer door before Anesta could reply. I frowned, wondering who it could be.

"I'll get it." She stood up and walked out of the bath chamber into the bedroom. I heard Anesta open the door and greet someone.

I tied up my hair and wrapped myself in a warm robe before freezing at the sound of his voice. No, it couldn't be.

"Ray?" I asked in disbelief, hurrying out of the bathing chamber.

"Lara."

I blinked twice, making sure what I was seeing was, in fact, real.

"It's really you," I cried out, and before I could stop myself, to Anesta's horror, I ran towards him in my robe.

Ray caught me in his arms, and I let out a laugh of pleasure. "What are you doing here?"

He put me down but held on to my shoulders.

"And where the hell have you been?" I rammed a fist into his chest. "You practically scared me to death."

"I know, I'm sorry." His face was tanned from spending time in the sun. He'd grown a beard and his hair was longer. But he was still Ray, all the same. My oldest friend. My partner in crime.

"After our last conversation, I rode through the night into Norrandale to alert the King. I thought maybe if he knew his son's life was in danger, he would help."

"You came to Norrandale?"

He nodded. "By the time I got here, I found out the queen was practically on her deathbed, and he'd sent for His Highness."

I sighed. "But why didn't you come back? I thought—" I shuddered at the memory — "I thought you were dead."

"I almost was," he said. "I took ill on the road and had to take up lodgings in a boarding house while I recovered. Luckily, the lady in charge used to be a healer and could take care of me. When I finally returned to Everness, I heard about you …" He trailed off, not sure what words to use without making the conversation awkward and confrontational.

"If I'd known the truth sooner, things might have gone down differently. Fewer people would have been hurt." My shoulders sagged.

"I heard you were temporarily in Norrandale, and I couldn't wait for your return."

I placed my hand on his arm. "I'm glad you didn't. It's really good to see you."

He shook his head as if in realisation before bowing. "Where are my manners, Your Maj—"

"No, please don't." I pulled him upright by the shoulders. "I'm not entirely used to the idea of being queen yet."

Ray smiled almost in disbelief. "Well, you are such a hooligan, it's a miracle they haven't removed you from the throne yet."

He had intended it as a joke, but it only served to remind me exactly what kind of a mess I was in.

"You're not far off," I replied. "Why do you think I'm here?"

Ray's expression grew solemn.

"I'm here to make an alliance with Cai and Norrandale," I answered myself.

"You're not serious?"

I slowly nodded.

"Have you gone mad, Lara? You cannot marry someone you don't love and spend the rest of your life in misery just because you're a queen now."

I wasn't sure what reaction I'd expected from him, but it certainly wasn't this kind of outburst.

"Things have changed, Ray. I have changed. If I don't do this, I risk losing the kingdom's safety."

"But …" He searched for the right words. "What about your happiness?"

"It doesn't matter." I sat on the bed in dismay. Anesta had quietly busied herself in the corner of the room, trying to be as invisible as possible. "Happiness is for people who don't have crowns."

"I'm sorry you've had to go through this alone." He came and sat next to me.

I let out a long sigh. "Ray, I'm going to ask something of you, and you have every right to say no."

He raised an eyebrow. "All right?"

"I would love for you to stay here with me for a while, but then I need you to go and find Princess Eloisa for me. At first, I thought Lance was keeping her hidden, but apparently she's disappeared, and you're the only person I trust for the job." I glanced up at him hopefully.

"Why? Do you think she could be in trouble?"

"Maybe. And Lance also mentioned she has—"

"What, you've been speaking to Lance?"

"Well." I looked away from his eyes.

"Well?"

"I released him from prison," I admitted.

"You did what? Lara, have you forgotten what he's done to you, to Uncle Arthur, to his people?" Ray ignored my title.

"Of course I haven't," I retorted. "Lance will always have his own best interests in mind, but right now, I need his help." I reached for his arm. "Just like I need yours. Will you please help me find Princess Eloisa?"

He sighed and bit his lip. "Why do you always make it so difficult to say no to you?"

My lips curled up into a smile. "It means a lot to me that you're doing this."

"Then it would be an honour, my queen." I felt relief wash over me at finally having my friend back.

Cai suggested we all have dinner together that evening, even though we'd shared lunch earlier. Though Lady Meredette did finally go home which I had no complaints about. Cai didn't appear very excited at Ray's return, but I was grateful that he allowed him to stay at the palace in Norrandale.

"Do I really have to go?" Ray asked when I knocked on his door to share the dinner invitation. "Can't I just have it in my room or something?"

"The King of Norrandale has requested our presence at his private dinner. It would be very ill-mannered not to go."

Rhen looked at me like he almost no longer recognised me.

"I don't want to spend the entire evening in the company of people who think they're better than me."

"It's not like that." I was quick to come to Cai's defence. "I'll be right next to you the whole time and you can tell me all the stories of your travels here and back to Everness."

Ray didn't look entirely convinced. I knew this would not be easy for him. Just like me, he'd grown up with very specific beliefs about people in Cai's position. Something which was not likely to change in one evening over the course of dinner.

"Please." With matters being as tense as they were, I didn't want to risk offending Cai or any of the court members. "Just this once and I promise I won't ask again."

"You're asking an awful lot of favours today." The corner of his mouth turned up in half a grin.

"I know, but I promise I'll repay you for it. Lots of gold and you can even have your own estate if you want, anything." Going after Eloisa, with no clear tracks or any clues as to where she might be, would be a very difficult task. But this matter could no longer be left unresolved, and if anyone could do it, it was Ray.

"I don't want your money, Lara," he replied softly.

"I know you don't, but I'll pay you anyway. I don't take any of it for granted, I promise."

When he didn't respond, I playfully put my hands on my hips. "Now, as your queen, I'm ordering you to be dressed and ready for dinner in an hour."

When I arrived at the dining room and discovered Ray wasn't there, I worried he might have bailed on me. Much was my relief when he walked into the room less than a minute later.

I'd never seen Ray in something other than his brown breeches and old linen shirts, but it was clear a servant had helped him pick out something appropriate for the occasion. His black boots were new and recently polished, and the navy jacket fitted him perfectly.

"You clean up nice," I said in a low voice when he came to stand next to me.

"Why are these shirts so damn uncomfortable?" Ray pulled at the collar.

"I'm afraid it's something to get used to."

His eyes took in my dress with the wide skirts and small beads on the bodice and the edges of my sleeves.

"I don't think I'll ever get used to seeing you like this."

"I'm so glad you could join us." Our heads turned at the sound of Cai's voice. "It's good to have you back." I knew Cai had never been very fond of him, but I appreciated him making an effort to make Ray feel welcome.

"Your Majesty." Ray cleared his throat and gave an awkward bow.

"Please, there's no need for such formalities. We're all amongst friends here." He gestured to Gwen, Thatcher and Anesta.

Everyone took their seats at the dinner table, and I was about to reach for the chair next to Ray's when I heard Cai say my name.

He'd pulled out the chair to his left, waiting expectantly for me to take my seat. Even if things did run a little differently in Norrandale, I knew that kings did not pull out chairs for their dinner guests. It was a way of showing me much respect, and I couldn't help but feel a flutter in my stomach.

"Thank you." I gave him a warm smile as he stood at the head of the table.

"To friends." He lifted his glass, and we all toasted with our wine.

The first course was served, and Ray looked at the cutlery with uncertainty. I gently placed my finger on the knife furthest away from the plate. He gave me a grateful smile from across the table.

"So how are you finding Norrandale?" Gwen asked Ray. She sipped on her wine with interest.

"I'll confess I haven't seen much of it apart from the main travelling roads, but the palace really is something."

He looked at all the food as if he were unsure where to start. Ray's discomfort made me realise how accustomed I'd grown to this lifestyle.

"Cai's recently had a new library built in the city for all the public to use. It's the biggest library Norrandale's ever had."

I was grateful that Gwen found it so easy to make conversation with strangers. If it were up to me, the whole lot of us would probably be sitting in dreadful silence.

"Though I don't suppose you read much." Thatcher spoke up before Ray had a chance to say anything.

I looked up from my plate in slight surprise. Was that supposed to be some kind of insult?

I saw Ray's jaw clench at the comment. "No, I'm more of an outdoor person."

"Cai's the same," Gwen continued, unbothered by her brother. "If he didn't have to work in his study, I'm sure we would never find him inside."

"That's not true," Cai countered, with a grin. "I don't mind sleeping inside."

"You know what I mean." She waved him off.

"Cordelia and I were in town the other day, but unfortunately, we never got around to the library. Then again, I'm not much of a reader either." I made my best attempt at contributing to the small talk.

"Yes, if anyone were planning to punish you, it would take nothing more than forcing you to go through a thick book."

I met Cai's eyes and shook my head at his little joke.

"What about you, Lady Anesta?" Gwen turned her interrogation to the next victim. "Are you fond of reading?"

"I don't mind it." Anesta shrugged, though I wondered how she ever got around to reading when she had to run after me all day.

"Are you planning on staying here for a while?" Cai asked Ray, who looked like he'd rather be anywhere else in the world.

"Not long, no." He met my gaze. "My queen has sent me on an important mission."

"That sounds exciting," Gwen replied. "What kind of mission?"

Cai looked to me, and his eyes seemed to ask the same question.

"I've asked Ray to look for my sister." My voice came out softer than I would have liked.

Servants entered the dining room and removed our plates, which were quickly replaced with a new dish.

"You mean the rumours are true that the princess is missing?" Gwen's eyes were wide with intrigue.

"Unfortunately, yes." I reached for my glass and took a long sip of wine.

"That seems like a very personal mission. You must be very well acquainted with Her Majesty."

I couldn't tell who was more peeved by Thatcher's comment, Cai or Ray. No one responded.

"Please remind me, again, how you and Her Majesty know each other."

It was enough for Ray to suddenly push out his chair and stand up. "I'm actually quite exhausted from the journey here, if you would be so kind as to excuse me." He looked towards Cai. "Thank you for the invitation, Your Majesty."

Cai gave him a curt nod in response, and I watched Ray walk out of the dining room.

"You can't ask people you don't know personal questions like that." Gwen clapped her brother on the shoulder.

"I didn't realise my question was so personal," Thatcher defended himself.

"Ray and I have known each other since childhood," I said, hoping to break the tension and that no further questions would be asked on the subject. Once everyone had finished their dessert, I excused myself from the table and made my way to Ray's room.

He didn't answer the door when I knocked, but I heard a distant voice say, "Come in." When I stepped into the room, Ray was in the midst of packing a small bag. His weapons lay spread out on the bed.

"What are you doing?"

"Leaving. If we want Eloisa to be found, I'd better get on with it."

I placed my hand on his arm, forcing him to look at me.

"I'm really sorry about dinner. Thatcher didn't mean to be rude. He's just a little—"

"It doesn't matter, Lara." Ray pulled himself free and shrugged off the borrowed navy jacket. "I'm glad you've found somewhere you are comfortable, but I don't belong among these people."

His words stung like a cut. That he thought I was here having the time of my life like I couldn't care less about the things that mattered.

"At least stay the night. You can't go out in the middle of the night, and you need the rest."

Ray licked his lips and rubbed his tired eyes. "Fine," he responded coldly.

This wasn't the way I wanted us to part.

I took a step back towards the door. "Please come and say goodbye before you leave tomorrow."

He nodded, looking out his bedroom window.

"Goodnight, Ray."

The next morning, Ray came to see me before breakfast. It wasn't a long or dreary goodbye. After last night, it felt as though some kind of rift had been created between the two of us but there was nothing I could do to change it now. We both understood the importance of Ray's mission. I could only hope he would find Eloisa.

It was a mission to arrange a private picnic unlike the one Anesta had explained we were likely to get. However, I managed to get my way in the end, with a simple basket and a large blanket suited for the outdoors. I'd also sent Anesta to the kitchens early in the morning with a note, requesting some particular desserts.

Cai's expression was bright and eager when he greeted me, almost like he'd been looking forward to the event. I leaned back against the trunk of the tree we were sitting under and paged through the book of poetry Thatcher had suggested. Though I wasn't overly fond of reading, it seemed like a good pastime.

Cai made himself comfortable lying on the blanket with his hands behind his head, listening to each word I read. I took the moments he closed his eyes to study his face secretly while I pretended to search for a new poem. He hadn't changed much in our time apart and yet there was something different in his expression. A look I couldn't quite place.

"'The birdsong added to the pleasantry then, for the lovers were finally together again.'" I closed the book with a small sigh, having had my fill of literature for the day.

"I'll admit, I quite liked that last poem." Cai glanced at me from under his lashes. We were alone again. I understood his new title kept him busy with endless duties, but I had a kingdom on the brink of civil war and I still didn't have a matrimonial agreement.

The late morning had been quiet and sunny, a warmth settling over the palace grounds.

"It wasn't too bad."

"You didn't like it?" He frowned, playing with a blade of grass between his fingers.

"It's not that I didn't like it. I simply thought it lacking."

"Lacking?"

"Yes." I raised my chin. "While it was sweet, I thought it could have been a little more romantic."

Cai laughed. He actually laughed. "When, dearest Elara, did you turn into a romantic?"

"Who said I wasn't romantic?"

Well, his expression certainly does.

"I could be romantic."

"Oh, you could now?"

I shifted my position and Cai decided to sit up. Leaning forwards, I reached for the picnic basket. "I asked the servants to make us some things to eat."

"How kind of you." His tone was still teasing.

"I even asked them to make your favourite." I pulled out a small blueberry tart and held it towards him. Anesta, who performed her duties exceptionally well, had managed to find out that blueberry was, in fact, Cai's favourite flavour of dessert. It was an effort to keep my hands from shaking. Why was I so nervous?

"How did you know these were my favourite?" He didn't hesitate to take it.

I shrugged. "I have my ways."

"Am I hallucinating or are you, Elara, Queen of Everness, trying to flirt with me?"

"A gentleman would just say thank you."

"Thank you for the blueberry tarts, Elara." Why did my name sound like that only when he said it?

Cai surprised me by giving me a kiss on the cheek, and then he proceeded to dig into the picnic basket as if it was nothing. I couldn't help but stare at him. It wasn't fair. How could he be so calm when it felt as though at any moment my heart was going to jump right out of my chest?

This was dangerous territory. I wanted the alliance to be nothing more than political, believing any kind of feelings between me and Cai would only make the matter so much more complicated. What if I allowed myself to be vulnerable and only ended up getting hurt? What if Cai realised he could never grow to love me again? Would I spend the rest of my days pining after someone who didn't want me?

I quickly cleared my throat, trying not to appear unnerved. "Do you have many other things to do today?"

"There are still heaps of papers and things that I have to get through on my desk, and then, of course, I need to follow up on the planning of the ball."

"I thought you were letting Lord Thatcher plan the ball?"

Cai held up one of the blueberry tarts for me to bite into. Tempted as I might have been, my nerves got the better of me and I reached out to take it instead. Cai's expression remained unchanged.

"If I allow Thatcher to plan a ball on his own, not only will it be too expensive, but the drunken revelry likely to take place would not be appropriate."

I suppressed a smile. "You and Thatcher are so different. I wonder how you ever became such good friends." The blueberry tart was deliciously sweet, and I wondered how I had never tasted anything like it before.

"I think circumstance was the main driving force. We grew up together." He tilted his head to the side. "We used to be much more alike."

"I remember you told me stories of your younger days together and some of the mischief you got up to."

"I'm afraid there wasn't much else for a spoiled young prince and his friend to do."

"You, spoiled?" I raised an eyebrow, holding back a laugh.

Instead of replying, Cai reached towards me and brushed remnants of blueberry tart away from the corner of my mouth. The air around us turned quiet and I watched with avidity as he brought his thumb to his lips. Cai's green eyes seemed to smile, studying me.

"Perhaps I was a little spoiled."

I swallowed harder than intended, suddenly flushed at the intimacy of his action. After pulling out my handkerchief, I dabbed at the corners of my mouth, hoping I look more composed than I felt.

"What about you?" Cai changed the subject.

"What about me?"

"What other matters require your attention today?"

"Nothing," I confessed. "My only plans were this." I gestured to where we were sitting.

"Good." Cai pushed himself back against the wide tree trunk so that we were sitting next to each other, shoulders touching. "Do you have anything else for us to read in that picnic basket?"

"What about all your paperwork?"

"It will still be there tomorrow."

Chapter 16

Cai

I found Rhen standing guard outside Elara's room.

"Good evening, Your Majesty." He bowed his head.

"Good evening, Rhen." I could see the question in Rhen's face, his uncertainty at my presence there. I couldn't sleep, and I'd been wandering through the palace and somehow found myself at Elara's bedroom. I didn't know what I was doing there. It wasn't like I was going inside. On the other side of the door, Elara was probably sound asleep.

"Couldn't sleep, Your Majesty?" Rhen broke the silence.

"It would appear so." I opened the nearest hallway window and looked out, my arms resting on the edge. The night air was cold, the gardens quiet and asleep along with the rest of the world.

"She doesn't sleep much either."

"What do you mean?" I turned to look at Rhen. His expression was blank, or maybe there was a hint of a smile.

"I can hear her pacing her room at night." I could believe that. Elara often paced in Fairfrith as well.

"When do you retire for the evening, Rhen?" It was very late and he was still standing guard.

"I'm about to change shifts, Your Majesty."

"Oh." I turned to look out the window again. The moon hung low, as if watching us through the glass. "Well, goodnight, then."

"Goodnight, Your Majesty." The new guard on duty had yet to arrive but Rhen bowed and left me alone in the hallway outside her door.

I'd always thought him to be a good man. He'd saved my life, after all. It was clear that Rhen and Elara had grown much closer since her coronation. I could tell he cared about her wellbeing.

I stood alone in the quiet hallway for a while before I started heading back to my rooms. When I was about halfway down the hall, a scream erupted through the quiet of the night. Elara was screaming. My mind barely had time to register the thought before I burst through her chamber doors, half expecting to find someone in the bedroom, attempting to kill her. But Elara was alone in her bed, thrashing around with her eyes closed. She was having a nightmare.

I hadn't realised how fast my heart was beating until I let out half a breath of relief. I stalked over to her bed, taking a seat next to her on the mattress.

"Elara?" I tried to keep my voice as calm and soft as possible. She didn't wake.

Her hair was damp, her forehead sheened with sweat, and I didn't even want to imagine the kind of dream she must have been having.

"Elara," I said again, placing a hand on her shoulder. This time, her eyes flashed wide open and she sat upright with a start, immediately reaching around as if looking for a weapon of some kind.

"Cai," she breathed out. "What are you—?"

"You were screaming."

"Oh." She looked down at her nightclothes in embarrassment, her fingers digging into the sheets.

"I'm sorry, I didn't mean to just burst into your rooms, but I thought something had happened to you. Are you all right?"

"Yes." Elara brushed the hair away from her face. "It was just a dream." She said it dismissively, but based on her state, I knew some sort of hell must have visited her in her sleep.

"I still get nightmares too." We'd had this conversation before, on our first night travelling together through Everness. I supposed some things *didn't* change.

"What do you dream about?"

"The war with Argon."

"The same ones you had before?"

I turned my face and looked towards the corner of the room, the light and darkness having a never-ending battle, as the flames from the candle rose and fell.

I nodded. "They're always the same and they don't get better with time."

She took a deep breath, and I moved my hand towards her in comfort.

"Would you tell me about them?" she asked carefully, another question underlying it.

Would you trust me with your deepest, darkest, subconscious thoughts? With the things that you fear, that secretly haunt you?

I moved so that I could sit with my back against the headboard and Elara curled up next to me.

"Most of the time, I'm on the battlefield. My men are dying

around me, crying for me to help them. I can never get to anyone fast enough. Never save anyone. It's as though I'm stuck."

"That must be terrifying."

I nodded slightly. "It is. But it helps if there's someone there when you wake up."

"Oh." She sounded disappointed and I realised what it sounded like. As though I had a string of lovers in my bed.

I should not be making conversation in the middle of the night when I'm not fully awake.

"No, that's not ... I mean it *would* be nice ... if there was someone, or you know." She seemed to grasp what I meant, and I stopped talking.

Elara was silent for a moment before she scooted closer to press her side into me. "Will you stay until I fall asleep again?"

"Of course I'll stay." I draped my arm over her shoulders, and she tucked her head into my neck. Her hair smelled sweet. Having her this close was magnetic. The more I got, the more I wanted. I pressed a kiss to the top of her head and then another to her forehead. She pressed closer to me in response.

I sat next to her until her breathing became even, and then long after.

"I heard you and Her Majesty were out for a picnic." Thatcher placed his feet on one of the coffee tables and leaned back.

"I need the names of your spies in the palace." I looked up from where I was sitting behind my desk.

"Just always looking out for you, Your Majesty." He lazily picked up one of the books that someone seemed to have absentmindedly tossed there earlier. "So, no more strolls with Lady Meredette?"

I contemplated ignoring him, my eyes glued to my desk.

"If you remember correctly, you tricked me into that meeting."

"Just not the woman for you, was she?"

"I don't know what you're talking about," I responded, trying to focus on the papers in front of me.

"Don't evade the question."

"I'm not like you, Thatcher. I can't fall in and out of love every day. And I don't mean that offensively." I signed a page, moving on to the next one. "Lady Meredette was polite and well-versed."

"But?"

"But whomever I marry will become queen of Norrandale. She will be in charge or ruling my people alongside me. I do not consider the matter lightly."

"Are you afraid Queen Elara's not up to the task?"

I didn't want to admit it aloud, much less have Elara know.

"She hasn't been queen for very long. She's still finding her feet." My concentration was no longer on the pages in front of me. I could only think about our picnic yesterday and how much I enjoyed it. "She's unpredictable and impulsive. I just ... I don't know. What if all of this breaks her somehow?"

"Are you afraid she won't be a good queen or that Elara is going to change her mind and your matrimony will be nothing more than a piece of paper as each of you reside in your separate palaces?"

There could be no doubt that I was infatuated with Elara all those months ago. It was easy to make vows when you were free of responsibility and it seemed like the world was going to hell.

But everything had become shockingly real when my father died and suddenly I was in charge of running a kingdom. My choices had consequences now, not just for myself but for countless others.

Leané Giliomee

"I think I've been spending too much time with you." I signed another document.

His head tilted back with laughter. "For what it's worth, I like her a lot."

"I know," I mumbled. "Me too."

Chapter 17

Elara

Most evenings, dinner was a quiet occasion, the conversation mainly small talk. Tonight, current political affairs were the main topic of discussion. Thatcher and Gwen sat alongside Cai, while his mother had dinner separately.

"Argon signed a treaty swearing peace between our two kingdoms after the war." Thatcher leaned back in his dining chair with a crease between his eyebrows.

"Thatcher, you know as well as I that treaties are made and broken." Cai had his hands folded on the table. He'd barely touched his food. I realised that, in the past few days, he hadn't done a lot of eating or sleeping. Dark circles ringed his eyes, accompanied by an ever-present faraway look on his face. He looked exhausted, and quite frankly, I would have been lying if I said I wasn't a little worried.

"And why do you think Aries would consider breaking the peace treaty?" Gwen took a sip of wine.

Cai crossed his arms, looking down at his plate. "There is news that Aries has been growing his army and talking about military campaigns. We have to consider every possibility."

I, of course, had never met King Aries. But I hadn't heard anything good about him either. If the news was true, then it was no wonder Cai had been so worried and preoccupied since I'd arrived. I took a bite of my dinner, listening to the conversation.

My eyes didn't waver from Cai. Even with his worried expression, he still somehow managed to look quite handsome. Eventually my gaze seemed to draw his attention.

He looked at me almost inquisitively and I decided to continue my stare without remorse. Daring to do what I would have never previously had the courage to — which I blamed only on the expensive Norrandish wine — I lightly knocked my foot against his under the table.

Cai bit his lip, trying to hold back a smile. Thatcher was saying something to him, but I could tell from his expression that he wasn't listening.

"Do you believe King Aries intends another attempt at conquering Norrandale, Your Majesty?" Gwen drew his attention back to the conversation.

"It's too soon to tell," Cai replied. "We cannot act based on the assumption that he would do that." His gaze returned to me. "What do you think, Queen Elara?"

All the eyes shifted to me. I jerked my foot back from his leg. Why on earth would he ask me a question he knew I had never considered? There was a mischievous look on his face.

"I, uhm," I stammered. "I really don't think I know enough about King Aries to make an educated remark." It was the best thing I could have said without making a fool of myself. I could already feel the heat pulsing in my face, as if my body was preparing itself for the embarrassment it knew was coming.

"I hope King Aries hasn't grown arrogant regarding the matter," Thatcher spoke up again. "Taking on the king of Norrandale is one thing but if Norrandale and Everness are united, we are considering a whole new situation."

I hadn't even considered it. I'd been so preoccupied with what Cai's union would do in my own kingdom, I hadn't thought about the fact that Norrandale's enemies would now be my enemies too. And the last thing I needed was a longer list of enemies. Was this something I needed to discuss with Lance? How had I grown so unconfident in my own choices over the last few months, second guessing myself around every corner?

Regardless, I should probably let Lance and the council know that if we were to go through with the alliance, Norrandale already carried the potential risk of hostility with the kingdom of Argon. But if they were aware that alliance came with risk, would they baulk and oppose it?

"Maybe that's exactly why Aries is growing his army," Gwen responded. "He could fear the opposition it would pose to Argon."

I took the napkin from the table and dabbed the sides of my mouth. "My apologies, but I think I'm going to retire early this evening." I stood up from the table. Cai seemed surprised. Did I spot a hint of disappointment in his expression?

"Good night, Your Majesty." Both Thatcher and Gwen bade me farewell. I left the dining room, my footsteps echoing on the tiled floors before I reached the carpeted hallways.

Halfway back to my room, I let out a yawn, feeling tired and sleepy. Too much wine. The more I thought about it, the more my bed with its silken sheets and soft pillows called out to me.

171

There were sudden footsteps behind me, and I barely had time to look around before Cai pulled me into the nearest room, which happened to be the library.

"Cai, what are you—?" He didn't give me time to finish my sentence, kissing me with surprising intensity. All sense and dignity forgotten, I grabbed onto him as he pulled us taut against each other. My hands were in his hair, my arms wrapped around his shoulders.

He walked us into one of the bookshelves and I let out a yelp.

Cai pulled back with a worried expression.

I let out a chuckle and took out the book that had protruded from the shelf just far enough to press into my back.

"Just a book spine." I tossed the book somewhere and pulled his mouth to mine.

Cai's hands ran up my sides and I tilted my head back as he kissed my neck.

Heat and something I couldn't name coursed through my body with every breath. Cai had never kissed me like this before. Flashes of my dream about him slipped through the pathways of my memory. His mouth pressed a kiss to my collarbone before he made his way back to my lips.

"I should go back," he whispered between torturous kisses.

"Shut up," I breathed out, and I felt Cai grin against my skin.

"Your wish is my command, Your Majesty." His kisses slowed, grew soft and sweet. More than anything, I just wanted him near me. There was no denying the sense of safety I felt when we were this close. And as much as I hated to admit it, it was all-consuming. It consumed my mind and my body and the very core of all my senses.

Cai's hands were on my hips, my lower back, pulling me closer still. I held on to his neck, ran my hands over his strong shoulders.

I couldn't fathom how someone or something could be so compelling. I had forgotten where I was on my way to before, why I was on my way there, and I was pretty damn close to forgetting my own name.

My leg lifted to wrap around Cai's waist, but the skirts of my dress made it nearly impossible.

Cai's lips didn't stray from mine as his hand found its way underneath the heavy material. His fingers started their journey from my ankle to where my stocking ended just above my knee.

As if he had all the time in the world, Cai delicately took hold of the stocking and pulled it down. My entire leg was now exposed to the library as he pulled my skirts up, but I didn't care at all, not even while knowing that someone could walk into the room at any moment.

Cai's fingers dug into my thigh as I let out what must have been a gasp. My hands rested on his cheeks, which had a day or two's worth of scruff.

Part of me found it difficult to comprehend that I was in the library of Mistwood Palace, fighting to catch my breath while the King of Norrandale caressed my upper leg. And I had no complaints at all.

Cai's mouth moved to my neck again and I would have been content to stay like that for ever. He pressed long kisses from my jawline down to my faded birthmark, where he lingered, allowing his teeth to graze my skin.

Something sounding like my name came from his mouth before he kissed me again, parting my lips. My hands were in his hair again as his fingers continued to trail up and down my thigh, teasing me relentlessly.

He pulled away from my mouth for a moment so that he could shift my skirts, lifting my other leg so that both were now wrapped around his waist.

A sigh of delight escaped me as he pressed our bodies together against the books.

There was a sudden knock on the door and a moment of silence before we heard Jack's voice. "Your Majesty, I'm afraid I require your presence immediately."

"I'm going to kill him."

Cai's breath was warm against me as I tried not to think about how Jack knew exactly where we were and most likely what we were doing.

I let out an uncomfortable chuckle and he gently set me back down.

"I'm coming now, Jack!"

My chest heaved and I wondered how I was ever going to breathe normally again.

"I'm so sorry. But I have to see what it's about." Cai apologised while attempting to help me fix my stocking and skirts.

"It's fine, really." My mind slowly returned to reality, asking me what the hell I thought I was doing.

He gave me another soft kiss before leaving me alone in the library, still trying to compose myself.

A few days later I received a letter from Everness while readying myself for the day. I anxiously tore open the envelope.

Sister dearest,

I rolled my eyes and shook my head at Lance's cursive handwriting. He always did have a flair for the dramatic.

*You'll be pleased to know that I am in excellent health
and spirits.*

Which could only mean he was drunk on spirits. I'd been relieved
when the messenger arrived with Lance's letter. But I should have
known he wouldn't be able to take it seriously. After a whole para-
graph of talking about himself, he informed me that matters were
still in hand in Everness … for now, anyway. Though the council
wasn't overly fond of his regency, Lance had been a monarch a lot
longer than I had, and he always knew exactly which strings to pull
to keep people just content enough. Many rumours were going
around about the possible alliance with Norrandale and a lot of
them were quite hopeful. No pressure for me. I placed the letter
down and looked at Anesta.

"Good news?"

"Well, Lance hasn't burned down the palace yet."

"I sense a but, Your Majesty."

"But," I confirmed her theory, "that doesn't mean he still can't.
Above all, Lance only has his own interests in mind, and he'll only
help me as long as it serves him."

"On a more positive subject." She held up two dresses: one of light
blue and another of a pale cream colour. "Which dress is the Queen
of Everness going to wear for her birthday?"

"I was really hoping we could keep the whole birthday thing quiet."

Which was my polite way of begging her not to make a big deal
out of it.

She dropped her arms with slight disappointment. "Why? Birthdays
are the best day of the year. And you're queen now. The whole court
should be celebrating and feasting."

With my past, there were many reasons why birthdays weren't the best days of the year. Though Uncle Arthur had kept track every year, there were no presents or cakes or any form of celebration. Instead, he would use it as an opportunity to measure my skillset as a bandit, claiming every year that I had to be better, more skilled, quicker, smarter than the last. Sometimes Ray would give me a birthday gift. He was always a better hunter, tracker and provider for the clan than he was a thief. But every now and then there would be a little trinket or extra food, which he must have got from somewhere.

"I have too many other things to think about today. And if I'm lucky, no one else will find out that it's my birthday."

"You mean we are not going to do anything special, Your Majesty?" Anesta was clearly not pleased.

"How did you find out about my birthday anyway?"

"Lance told me before we left. He said that we might still be here by today and that I should make sure we have some cake, which, by the way, I have been looking forward to all week." She sent a disapproving look my way.

Of course Lance would know when my birthday was. I hadn't even thought about it or the fact that he was there the day I was born. He'd been celebrating on my birthday every year with Eloisa. The thought left a knot in my stomach. I hoped Ray would find her soon. Or maybe I didn't. I honestly didn't know anymore.

I sighed, knowing there was little value in arguing with Anesta. "If it makes you happy, I'll wear the cream-coloured dress."

"Happy birthday, Elara." The voice behind me halted my steps through the throne room.

I pressed my lips together, turning around.

"Thank you," I said to Cai, with as much of a smile as I could muster. "Now, if you'll excuse me, I need to find Rhen—"

"Wait." He took hold of my hand. His hand was warm and immediately created a mental picture of where his hands were while we were in the library. "I have a gift for you."

"Cai, that really isn't necessary."

"Of course it is. You're the Queen of Everness now. We should be hosting a ball in your honour."

I knew he meant well, but the thought alone made my stomach churn.

"I'd really we rather not."

"At least say you'll accept my gift." He looked so genuinely excited that I couldn't help but smile. "Close your eyes and hold out your hand."

I raised a curious eyebrow.

"Just trust me."

I obeyed and felt cool metal against my skin.

"All right, open them."

"Your dagger?" The one I'd wanted to steal on the night we'd first met.

"Well, you tried to steal it so many times that I figured you've earned it."

My heart surged. The memories were still so vivid and yet they felt like a lifetime ago.

"Cai, you love this dagger. I can't accept this." I held my hands out towards him, but he closed my fingers around the knife.

"I want you to have it, Elara."

I couldn't help but notice the beautiful sparkling jewel that looked so similar to the one on that necklace. Had it always been there?

"Thank you." I held on to the dagger like it was the most precious thing I'd ever owned. Perhaps it was.

"I have one more surprise."

"Cai, please," I pleaded.

"Come on." He laughed and pulled me after him. I really needed to see Rhen to discuss Lance's letter. But Cai's childlike excitement was enough to convince me. I let him drag me all the way to the kitchens, with servants stumbling and bowing every few seconds in surprise at seeing their king on the lower levels of the palace. It reminded me of a time not so long ago, though it felt like ages, when we ran through the forest of Everness, unaware of how much would change.

Is it possible for us ever to have that again?

"Where are we going?"

"You'll see. I figured there would be hell to pay if I made a big scene in front of everyone at court." He gestured with his head to the upper floors. We entered the kitchens, where Anesta stood at one of the large tables in the centre of the room. Brutus, whom I had not seen since the rebellion, was standing next to her. A few other servants were in the kitchen, though they pretended to ignore us respectfully.

"Surprise, Your Majesty!" Anesta held out her arms to a small cake on the table. The cake had been decorated with little colourful flowers that I recognised from Everness.

"Did you make this, Brutus?"

He nodded almost shyly.

"Thank you."

Cai handed me a large cutting knife.

"You shouldn't have."

"I know." He winked at me. "But I wanted to."

Anesta forced me to blow out the candles before cutting the cake. It was dense chocolate and perhaps the best thing I'd ever eaten in my life. In that moment, with the group of us standing around the cake, I could almost forget everything else.

"King Cai won't be able to keep his hands off you tonight," Anesta said. I met her gaze in the mirror as she gently placed a tiara atop my head.

"Do you think so?" I raised a recently trimmed eyebrow. Anesta insisted that one doesn't go to royal events with uneven eyebrows and therefore thought it appropriate to attack me with a small pair of metal tweezers. The act was mostly a combination of her telling me to sit still and me yelling "ow!" with each hair she removed from my face.

"I know so," she replied. "You'll be the most beautiful queen he's ever seen."

I proceeded to tilt my face side to side, inspecting the reflection as if not quite believing her words. I had managed to convince Cai not to have a ball on the evening of my birthday but rather a few days after. That way I could at least pretend it had nothing to do with me.

"Everyone's been urging Cai to throw a ball, but now that it's happening, I feel like I'm going to be sick." I groaned.

There was a soft knock on my chamber doors before Cordelia strolled in. Her eyes widened at the sight of me. "Your Majesty, you look beautiful."

I stood up from the dressing table and swished my skirts from side to side. "Thank you."

"I must say, I'm proud of my work." Anesta placed her hands on her hips in satisfaction, and I grinned. The silk dress cascaded down my body in waves of blue. The bodice was tight and flattering, my sleeves of a see-through material.

"Do you know if Lady Meredette will be there tonight?" I dared to ask Cordelia, who seemed to know everything about everyone at court.

She hesitated for a moment, and I noticed her jaw clench.

"What is it, Cordelia?"

"Not only will Lady Meredette be there but it turns out she is close friends with Lady Delany, who has also been invited."

Lady Delany who'd been betrothed to Cai since they were children and ended up marrying his cousin. The woman Cai's family *actually* wanted him to marry.

"Delightful," I muttered.

"Come now, Your Majesty." Anesta placed a hand on my shoulder. "Surely you're not jealous or intimidated by her?"

"Why would I be jealous?" I pretended to inspect my reflection again. "Cai only used to be in love with her."

"His Majesty was a boy back then. He didn't even know what love was." Cordelia tried to reassure me.

I squared my shoulders. "It doesn't matter anyway. I need his throne, not his heart."

Anesta smiled, and I sent a look her way.

"You keep telling yourself that, Queen Elara." Cordelia linked her arm with mine and led me out into the hallway.

The ballroom was lit with a thousand candles hanging from the chandeliers illuminating every corner of the room. The orchestra plucked at their stringed instruments while ballgowns of every colour swished across the recently polished floors.

I lifted the hems of my dress while ascending the few stairs that led into the ballroom. My eyes scanned all the faces until they landed on a tall figure with broad shoulders and an unruly head of blond locks.

Cai was as finely dressed as ever, in his black polished boots and blue tunic.

As if he felt my gaze, his head turned away from the conversation he'd been having with one of the court's council members. Those deep green eyes met mine for a moment before a smile spread across his lips. Cai turned back to the gentleman and gave what I presumed was an apology before he started making his way across the ballroom floor.

He met me when I reached the final step.

"Elara, you're—"

"Beautiful, ravishing, exquisite?" My nerves forced me into a sense of teasing.

"And shockingly humble too." Cai grinned while holding out his hand. He led me to the other side of the room, towards the refreshments, while having to stop every two seconds for someone who wanted to greet him. Still, Cai didn't once show a hint of agitation. He patiently engaged in every conversation.

"You're astoundingly popular, Your Majesty," I told him when we finally reached the table filled with refreshments.

"I'm fortunate to have grown up close to my friends and family. Though I suppose in some ways this resulted in them raising me as the king they wanted me to be," he said, with a hint of disdain.

I wanted to ask him if this was a bad thing, but a servant stepped in front of us with a wine jug and asked Cai if he would like some.

"This is George, my wine steward." Cai introduced him to me while I politely declined his offer of pouring me a glass.

"Is this from the new vineyard?" Cai asked after taking a sip.

"Yes, Your Majesty."

"It's lovely, thank you."

George bowed before moving on to the other courtiers.

"You have a wine steward? I don't have a wine steward."

"That's because Lance would drink him out of his job," Cai joked.

"Don't tease. I'm trying to get him to sober up."

"How very noble of you."

I let out a heavy sigh. "You're telling me."

Cai held the glass towards me, and I gave in, taking a small sip. It was *good* wine. Even I could tell with my spectacular lack of knowledge of the subject.

"George was employed by my father. Norrandale has a good climate for winemaking. The man takes a lot of pride in his art. Who am I to take that away from him?"

I nodded in understanding, my eyes darting across the room, over all the unfamiliar faces, until they landed on two that I recognised.

"I see Thatcher has taken quite a liking to Lady Anesta."

Cai noted the direction of my gaze as I handed him back the glass. Thatcher and Anesta were in close proximity, her cheeks wildly tinted red while she twirled her hair in a flirtatious manner.

"Although from what I've heard, Thatcher takes a liking to just about every woman he sees."

"You're not entirely wrong," Cai replied with a slight grimace.

"You need to tell your friends to lay off my ladies-in-waiting. At this rate, I won't have any left."

I took the wine glass from his hand without asking and indulged myself with another sip.

"Is that resentment I sense in your tone?"

"Of course not. I'm very happy for Cordelia and Jack."

"But?"

"But I miss her sometimes. She was my friend. And even if things did get … complicated near the end, she was good for me."

"I'll tell you what, if Thatcher should make any serious advancements towards Anesta, I'll make sure they stay at court so she can remain your lady-in-waiting."

"I appreciate it. But I wouldn't want to stand in the way of someone's happiness."

"I wouldn't be too concerned, though. Thatcher is quite fond of the drama here and isn't likely to leave anyway," he reassured me. "In fact, he might have spent more time at court than I have."

Cai reached for the wine glass but I pulled my hand back.

"I thought you didn't want anything to drink?"

"That was before I tasted George's talent."

Cai shook his head with a slight smile, before his expression changed. I looked towards where he was staring, at the entrance to the ballroom.

"It's my cousin, the Duke of Orrington." There wasn't a hint of loathing in his voice. In fact, he seemed quite eager to greet the duke. And next to him, an angel made woman. The duchess had long waves of golden hair and a bright, warming smile. She seemed to radiate elegance and grace as the couple made their way across the room.

Behind them, Lady Meredette also had a gentleman at her side. Though it seemed her only interest was in pretending he didn't exist as her eyes scanned the ballroom.

"Charlie!" Cai called out and greeted the duke.

"Please, cousin, will you never refrain from calling me Charlie when you know I prefer Charles?"

"Well, I need to keep you humble in some way." Cai chuckled, inclining his head to the duke's wife. "Delany." She bowed with that same warm smile at the sound of her name.

Cai placed his hand on the small of my back and pulled me closer. "May I introduce Queen Elara of Everness."

"Your Majesty," both of them said, and I watched the duchess slip into a deep curtsy. "It's an honour to finally meet you," she met my gaze. Even her eyes looked like they sparkled. How was it possible for someone to be so beautiful and charming? It made me want to hate her, while wishing I was her at the same time.

"I've heard much about you," I replied, and her expression faltered, though she tried to hide it. Did I sense nervousness? How could I make someone nervous when I was the one intimidated by every person in this room? Perhaps I would never get used to my title.

"All good, I hope," Charles chose to reply.

"Of course. Cai only ever speaks fondly of his family."

"I simply adore your necklace, Your Majesty." At first, I was unsure whether or not to wear the necklace that actually belonged to Cai's family but it looked so beautiful with the dress Anesta had picked out and I seemed to have Cai's grandmother's permission to wear it for the most part.

"Thank you." I looked down at the sparkling jewels. "It was a gift."

I met Cai's eyes as I said the words and he gave me a knowing grin.

"I've never seen its equal," Delany continued. "It's practically glowing."

"It must be all the candlelight." I shrugged it off, but my eyes glanced down at the jewelled necklace, nonetheless. A strange feeling settled in my stomach, which I blamed on nerves.

"Do you intend to stay at court?" Cai asked his cousin.

"Perhaps for a few days. I don't want to be away from the estate for too long. We have quite a few hunts arranged." Charles shrugged.

"You must come hunt with me on the palace grounds sometime." Cai's hand didn't move away from my back. Instead, his thumb started making idle circles. I tried not to shiver.

"I'll come as soon as I am invited, cousin." The duke had a dashing smile.

"Matters at court have been keeping me busy," Cai apologised. "But we must arrange something soon."

"If you'll excuse us."

They both bowed again before going to greet their other acquaintances.

When Cai didn't say anything for a long time, my own nerves rose. I wished I knew what was going on in that mind of his. "You know, I didn't look forward to tonight, but this is actually very pleasant."

"I know a ball seems frivolous and unnecessary with everything that's going on, but I feel like we all needed one night where we don't have to make important decisions. One night where we don't have to feel guilty for enjoying ourselves."

"You're too hard on yourself." I turned to better face him. He didn't notice my stare as he continued to look out towards the crowd.

He had to have been the most handsome man I'd ever seen. Just by looking at him it was as if I could feel his mouth on me again, the way he held me in the library. We'd not had a proper chance to be alone since, or to discuss how this affected our relationship or the alliance. Maybe it was the wine or the built-up stress from the past few weeks, but I couldn't help myself any longer. I pressed up next to him, my head leaning on his shoulder. I just wanted to feel him near me.

"Would you like to dance, Queen Elara?" His voice was soft enough that only I could hear.

But I shook my head. "No, I just want to stay right here with you."

"Afraid you'll embarrass yourself on the dance floor?"

"Oh, I think we both know I'll embarrass myself on the dance floor." I felt him smile into my hair.

I straightened when a servant approached us with a tray of wine. This time, it wasn't George himself. Feeling bad for having stolen Cai's glass, I took one off the tray and handed it to him.

"You know, I think Lady Meredette will be deadly disappointed if you don't ask her for a dance tonight." I tried to find her in the sea of people. "She's probably been the person most excited for this ball." I could no longer spot her or her escort in the crowd.

But Cai didn't reply. I jolted as glass shattered on the floor next to me.

"Cai?"

He remained expressionless, his face deathly pale.

"Cai?" I said again, with more panic, and then he dropped to the ground.

I must have screamed something, but I was kneeling next to him when the servants and the guards rushed over in a sudden frenzy.

I was pushed out of the way as his attendants tried to help him. Someone shouted that the king had been poisoned.

I sat next to Cai's bed while the physician examined him.

"It's definitely poison."

My foot tapped on the carpeted floor and I clenched a fist.

"Can you determine what kind?"

Cai's mother had been in the room when the physician arrived but was now pacing in the hall outside, talking with servants to try to track down the perpetrator. I could hardly sit still myself, but I didn't dare take my eyes off him.

"Based on its immediate effect, it narrows it down to a possible few, but as I cannot be certain, it will be difficult to give him the correct antidote." It wasn't what I wanted to hear.

"Can't you do anything in the meantime?"

The physician nodded. "I can try, Your Majesty. But unfortunately, I cannot promise any results."

He hurried out of the room — I presumed to the infirmary.

Cai looked like he was sleeping peacefully, but with every minute, his breathing became shallower and the pounding in my heart increased to the point where I could feel it thumping in my ears.

The doorknob turned and I looked up.

"How is he doing, Your Majesty?" Jack asked, and I shook my head.

He walked over, his expression of distress showing through the mask of calm he tried to keep up.

"It's my fault. If I hadn't taken his glass, he wouldn't have—" I trailed off, my eyes watering.

Jack placed a hand on my shoulder. It wasn't protocol, but it was as if we both knew I needed the comfort. "If anyone is to blame, it's me. I don't even know how the assassin got in the palace in the first place."

He looked at Cai. "I failed him."

"No, Jack, you can't think like that," I said, though I knew my words wouldn't change his mind. Wouldn't change my own mind from feeling like I'd failed Cai.

I sniffed and Jack handed me a handkerchief. "I'm afraid," I admitted. "What are we going to do?" I asked because I genuinely had no idea. Because I desperately needed an answer.

"Hope for a miracle." Jack stood back, regaining his soldier's posture. "I hate to leave but there are matters that need my attention now. That man needs to be tracked down. I have to go and do my duty and you have to do yours."

"Which is?"

He looked at me sincerely. "Taking care of Cai, Your Majesty. You're the only one who can." I knew he didn't mean the words literally, but I appreciated his faith in me. I nodded and Jack departed, leaving me and Cai alone.

With my hands still clutching his, I tried to hold myself together, refusing to believe that this was the end of the line.

"Listen to me, Cai. You're not going to die on me. Do you hear me? I won't allow you to abandon me."

I shifted my position to sit next to him on the bed, one hand holding his and the other on his cheek. He was hot with fever.

"You still have a long life ahead of you. Your kingdom needs you to be their king. Your family needs you." I sucked in a breath. "I need you."

The doors burst open and the physician rushed in with a small bottle in his hand.

"How long until it takes effect?" I asked while he administered the antidote.

"There is no telling, as I can't guarantee its success."

"All right, you can leave us."

He bowed before exiting the room.

So I sat and I waited.

I waited into the long hours of the night.

And when Cai's fever got higher, I called for a pitcher of cold water and a cloth that I could hold against his skin when I wasn't holding his hand.

His mother sat there for a few hours too and then went to check on Jack's progress identifying the assassin and then back to pacing in the hall. Still too weak to wait up the entire night, she told me she would get a few hours of rest and then return to check on Cai again.

My dress began to grow uncomfortable, and as I shifted the skirts, Cai's birthday present fell out of the pocket. I felt better carrying it by my side but had forgotten about it with the events of the night.

I picked the dagger up from the floor and delicately turned it in my hands.

"This dagger got us into so much trouble, didn't it?" I couldn't help but let a smile form at the memories. My thumb brushed over the new jewel that had been embedded in the hilt. There was no denying it looked exactly like the jewels in the necklace. It was a beautiful gift.

I placed the dagger in his hand, covering it with my own. "Do you remember the night in the tavern when you insisted on sharing the room and I was so infuriated?" I managed a small grin. "It was the night I found out you were a prince." I rubbed my thumb over his hand.

"Come back to me," I whispered into the deathly quiet room. "Please come back." A single, rogue tear ran down my cheek. Every memory of Cai flashed through my mind. Every smile he'd given me, every caress, every kind word. My heart ached at the thought of never experiencing any of it again.

I sat for hours with our hands linked like that. Every second seemed to go by slower than the last. The candles in the room burned out, one by one, and I didn't call for a servant to relight them. I sat until my head started to grow heavy, and I eventually fell asleep, half draped over the bed, next to Cai.

Dawn approached with its light and birdsong when something woke me. Not something: movement.

I held my breath as I watched and waited.

And it happened again.

Cai's hand moved in mine. I swallowed hard.

"Cai?"

The world stood still in that moment in Cai's room where I held on to him as if I was holding on to dear life itself.

His grip tightened slightly.

And then his eyes opened. His movements were slow and uncertain, and I had to keep myself from crying out in relief. His forehead still gleamed with a little sweat, but although the colour had yet to return to his cheeks, his breathing wasn't as laboured as before.

"Elara?" he croaked, and I resisted the urge to wrap my arms around him.

"You're okay," I promised, though I had no form of confirmation. "You're going to be okay."

Chapter 18

Cai

My headache was growing worse by the minute. I reached for the pitcher of water and filled a glass.

"Your Majesty, George confirmed that he'd employed the servant months ago."

Jack stood on the other side of the table in the council room. He looked tired from lack of sleep and completely overridden by anxiety. "He'd needed more hands in the cellar."

"Did he say where the kid came from?" The assassin had been only a few years younger than me.

"Some small village not too far but we have rechecked the references he'd given George and all of it was falsified." Not a very good sign.

"Any chance he had an Argonian tattoo?" one of the council members asked, and Jack shook his head. "George said he's seen him working in short sleeves or shirtless on multiple occasions. No tattoo, my lord."

"He wouldn't have had a tattoo, even if he was Argonian. Soldiers only get the tattoo when they're eighteen. Some symbol of manhood while also claiming fealty to their king."

"We have no proof that the boy was working for Aries," Lord Burrow argued.

"But we do know that Aries has most likely been sending spies into the kingdom and now someone has tried to assassinate the King. We cannot ignore the possibility of a link," someone else said.

"The point is, we have an assassin on our hands, with no idea where he's come from or where he's going. How do we plan on finding him?" Lord Burrow exclaimed.

"He couldn't have gotten that far. We know what he looks like, and we have sent scouts to the nearest villages and cities, my lords," Jack assured them.

"What about George?" Lord Burrow asked. "Will there be any repercussions because he hired the young man?"

"George had no way of knowing. The boy has been working in the cellars for months. Whatever this was, it was pre-planned. I'm not going to punish George for something that wasn't his fault," I stated, and then looked at Jack. "Let me know if the search is successful."

"Yes, Your Majesty." Jack bowed before marching out the room.

"What about the young queen, Your Majesty?" Lord Stapleton changed the subject.

"What about her, Lord Stapleton?" I wasn't sure if I was ready for this conversation.

"It's no secret Her Majesty is here to make an alliance. The council has yet to discuss what a marriage to the Queen of Everness could mean."

"On the one hand, it would be a great aid military-wise," the Duke of Ryker spoke up. "Everness is known for having a large army."

"We don't know what King Aries' plans are. If we ally with Everness, he could take it as a threat to his throne. It could give him the motivation he needs to launch an attack," Lord Burrow replied.

"We also have to consider that Everness is currently in a weak state. The new queen has yet to properly establish her reign, and with all the opposition she is currently facing, it could lead the kingdom to a civil war," Lord Stapleton said.

"Are you suggesting we launch an attack on Everness instead?" the Duke of Ryker asked in surprise. "How is that any less threatening to Aries?"

"Nobody is attacking Everness." I silenced them. "I am still undecided on the subject, and until I come to a decision, we won't discuss this further."

"It's a beautiful painting."

I turned to face Elara as she approached me in the hallway. I couldn't help but smile at the sight of her before looking back up at the portrait that hung on the wall.

"It's always been one of my favourites," I admitted.

"Are they your grandparents?" She stopped next to me, placing her hands behind her back.

"Yes. When they were young and newly married."

"How long were they married for?" Elara tilted her head as she inspected the painting.

"I believe it was almost thirty years before my grandfather passed away."

"I'm sorry I never got to meet him."

"I think he would have liked you very much." I gently bumped her shoulder with my own. The truth was I could hardly remember my grandfather. But it seemed like the right thing to say.

"Your grandmother is quite a treat, though."

"Ahh." I let out a chuckle. "I heard you got cornered by her the other day."

"I did and I'll admit I was quite intimidated. But she was actually very kind to me."

"She's been through a lot, having lost her husband and now her son." I often had to remind myself that I was not the only one grieving my father.

"She must have been a great queen." Elara looked back to the painting with a long sigh.

"You have something on your mind?" It was more of a statement than a question.

"There have been no arrangements for my meeting with the council to discuss the marital agreement."

I sucked in a breath. "Yes, the council has been focused on the current situation with Argon." I didn't want to tell her about the uncertainty among the council about the alliance. Much less did I want to tell her that I was behind most of it. That I knew I felt affection towards Elara, but at the same time, I was afraid of what an alliance could do to the both of us. And like Lord Burrow said, it might just give Aries the push he needed not only to come after my kingdom, but after Elara too. I could never forgive myself if something happened to her.

She hesitated for a moment before placing her hands on her hips. "Look, Cai, if you don't want to marry me, then why don't you simply tell me so I can leave?"

"I didn't say that I don't want to marry you, Elara."

"Well, you certainly didn't say that you do."

"It's not that simple." I shook my head. There were so many things she didn't know. So many secrets I was keeping from her.

"It used to be." Her jaw clenched as she tried to keep her voice from cracking, and a pain grew inside me. "There was a time, not too long ago, when we were just two kids in a forest. When you told me that my past didn't matter. And I came back for you. I came back for you that day despite my cowardice, my fears, despite all my better judgements. I came back because you begged me to give you a chance. And now I'm asking you to do the same. And I'm sorry if that's too much—"

"Elara." I gently took her hands, willing her eyes to meet mine. "That time has since passed. We are no longer two kids in the woods who get to run away from responsibility. And believe me, some days I want nothing more than to go back to that time. But the things we do affect everyone around us."

"You think I don't know that?"

"A lot has happened in the past few months. Things have changed."

"Well, how am I supposed to trust you, or help you or confide in you, when you don't share things with me? You don't tell me anything, Cai. I don't understand what you're so afraid of," she confessed, and it broke my heart.

"What do you want to know?"

She pressed her lips together. She'd been thinking about this. Her questions were formed long before I asked.

"The Myrgonite stone." She hesitated. "Is it real?"

"What?" I asked in surprise.

"The jewel stone in your grandmother's necklace, it's the same as the one in the dagger you gave me."

"Is it?"

"I held the dagger between our hands when you were dying," she let out a breath. "I told you to come back."

In the darkness of my mind that night, I had heard her calling out to me. It was as if she'd pulled me out of a deep sleep.

"I was trying to remind you," she said. "By reminiscing about the stories we shared with the dagger. I was trying to remind you what you had to fight for."

I clenched my jaw. "Elara, I'm grateful that you stayed with me that night, but I don't see where you are going with this."

"Lance believed …"

"You're going on what Lance said? Lance, who cannot stay sober for more than twenty-four hours. Lance, who hurt you and used you against me."

"Because he knew it was real." The realisation set in on her face. "That's why he was willing to go to all those lengths. The stone is real, isn't it? And it's hidden somewhere here in Norrandale. Lance told me that King Evrin's wife, Queen Riona, stole some of the stones and had them forged into magical objects."

"Elara."

"Don't lie to me, Cai." She pointed a finger at my face. "Don't you dare lie to me."

"I'm not trying to lie to you. I'm trying to protect you."

"I'll decide when I need protection." She pulled the dagger from the pocket in her dress. "How does it work?"

"I don't know," I confessed. "I don't even know if that is one of the three objects or if the necklace is or what kind of magic we're talking about. All I know is what my grandmother told me after I was crowned."

"Well, what did she say?"

I looked around, afraid someone might hear us. I pulled her into the nearest parlour and shut the door behind us.

"Most of it didn't even make sense, to be honest. She sat me down one evening with such a serious expression I was worried she would tell me she was dying of some kind of illness." I could vividly picture the two of us in my study, the flames from the fireplace casting a shadow across her face.

"Your father should have been the one to tell you this when the time was right," she'd said. *"It is unfortunate he never got the chance."*

I could never have expected what she was about to say.

"She briefly told me about the history of the Myrgonite stones and how it was Norrandale's duty to guard them since they became part of the kingdom. As king, I am responsible for protecting them and making sure no one ever finds out where they are or what our ancestors might have done with them."

"And what about the objects?"

"She doesn't know what they are. It doesn't seem like anyone does. The objects have vanished from history."

She looked down at the dagger and then back up at me. "But what if they didn't disappear?" Between assassins, peace treaties and marital alliances, I did not need another thing to worry about. But if there was a chance that these objects were more than myth and they were possibly here in Mistwood Palace, I could not ignore it.

"Where are the Myrgonite stones?"

"My grandmother gave me a map and then forced me to burn it so that no one would be able to use it. The secret is only to be known by the kings of Norrandale."

I took her hand and led her to the door. "Come on, I want to show you something."

Elara remained quiet as I asked the groom to saddle up two horses for us and then ordered him not to tell anyone of our visit to the stables. I couldn't decide who was more confused, the young stable boy or Elara. She appeared hesitant and unsure of herself and yet there was curiosity in her eyes. The guards would be in a state by the time we got back but this wasn't exactly the type of outing where you could invite everyone along. Not even those that I trusted with my life — the more they knew, the more dangerous it was for them.

We rode for a few hours, further away from the palace. The grassy fields became hills and the hills became mountains. Elara kept her horse closely behind mine. Cold air swept across the stones and into the deep valley that lay nestled between the mountains. I didn't make a habit of coming here often, for more reasons than one. While most of the kingdom of Norrandale felt warm and inviting, these mountain ranges seemed to whisper a warning. The place was ancient and there was a haunting atmosphere. I ignored the shiver that ran down my spine. Elara looked like she sensed it too. She continued to follow me as we dismounted, and I led her inside one of the nearby caves.

"The Myrgonite stones were discovered by King Evrin's men, who built the mine. They closed it just as quick, however, to keep anyone from finding it. The only way to get there now is through these caves."

It was pitch black. I lit one of the torches with a knife and some flint, and held out my hand for her to take. She didn't hesitate, grabbing it as I led her through the narrow tunnels. I'd half expected Elara to make some kind of joke by now, at the very least, but she was stunned into silence, perhaps from nerves, I wasn't sure.

I eventually stopped and placed the torch in the nearest holder on the wall. The world around us lit up, the light reflecting off a thousand Myrgonite jewels embedded into the walls and the ceiling, completely undisturbed, as if they'd been resting for a thousand years, sleeping ... waiting.

I watched Elara's jaw slowly drop when she took in Norrandale's greatest secret.

"That's a lot more than I was expecting."

I shrugged almost sheepishly.

"And the entire mountain range is filled with these caves?"

She looked up once more, to where the stones stuck out from the cave ceiling like a canopy of stars. "If these things are worth what everyone says they are, then you could feed a whole kingdom."

I saw the wheels turning in her head. "Except the moment it's revealed that Norrandale is in possession of these stones, you are going to have every kingdom on the continent trying to conquer us. And that's not even to mention the complication of the magical objects."

"Do you think anyone could use the stones to make more objects?"

"I don't know. We don't even know what kind of magic was used and if it still exists. Unless the smith who did it documented it somewhere. But it's probably not impossible."

"This is a lot to take in."

"I don't know how to protect you *and* my people *and,* well … this."

"Protect me? Cai, if what you say is true, we have to do everything in our power to make sure no one ever finds out about this. If it gets into the wrong hands …"

"I was naive enough to believe that the peace treaty with Argon meant the end of it, an end to the fighting and the violence. But now King Aries has been sending spies into Norrandale and after the whole ordeal with Lance …" I trailed off, leaning back against one of the cave walls.

"This is why you were so upset that I'd left Lance in charge after everything that happened? You're afraid he's going to try and come after it again if he finds out the truth?"

I nodded slowly.

"I can't believe I've been so ignorant."

"What does that make me? If my grandmother hadn't told me, I never would have found out about all of this. I would have only believed them to be stories like everyone else."

"I guess that's kind of the point."

I sent a small smile her way and Elara surprised me by taking my hand again as we emerged from the mouth of the mountain. The forest and hills beyond were ready to greet us with an autumn breeze and insects buzzing, while our horses grazed in the distance.

"Cai, tell me I'm not the only one who thinks the stones look astoundingly similar to the ones in the necklace and the dagger?"

The first time I'd been to the cave, I was so overwhelmed by what I'd discovered that I did not bother to think beyond it. The stones used in those two objects were small and delicate with a rosy hue, evident especially when in direct sunlight.

"It could be possible. But I don't know." I didn't want to believe it. The only thing worse than having to protect a mine full of jewels from the world was having the magical objects those jewels were forged into identified by the wrong people.

"There is something else," I added.

"Why do I have a feeling that I'm not going to like what you're about to say?" She picked up her horse's reins. I took hold of her hips to aid in lifting her on to the horse's back. She grinned, as we both knew she did not need my help.

"I think there's a good reason the objects have remained undiscovered for so long. Though my grandmother isn't certain about what or where the objects are, she gave me a serious warning. The danger of the objects lies in the fact that they possess an ancient magic which no one knows how to control. While it may give you protection and great power, especially for one who has possession of all three objects at the same time, in order to balance the scales, it will take away from you too."

I mounted my horse and we proceeded at a brisk walk until we reached the trail that led back into the woods.

"In what sense will it take away from you?"

"I'm not sure. But I have a feeling that the more power you use, the higher the price will be. Like I said, we have no understanding of the magic. It can be very unpredictable."

Elara swallowed hard. "If the dagger is one of the objects, and I'm not saying it is, but if it's one of the objects …" I watched her mentally wrestle with everything she'd learned.

"Cai, I wished for your life when I was holding the dagger that night."

"I know." And as much as I wanted to say I wished she hadn't, it would have been a lie. I wasn't ready to die. "But as you said, we have no proof the dagger is one of the objects."

We continued walking the horses, with no rush to get back to the palace. Once we'd left the mountain ranges behind us, I felt the eerie feeling depart, and something more like comfort replaced it. Something I only felt when I was with Elara. The moment I stepped back through those doors, not only would I have to deal with my guards, who probably thought I'd gone missing, but I'd be bombarded with my royal duties and responsibilities when the only thing I really wanted to do was sleep. It felt as though I hadn't slept in a week.

"I'm worried about you, Cai," Elara said suddenly, as if she'd been reading my mind.

"I'm fine. There have just been so many things that require my attention."

"Which is why I'm worried," she continued. "You're not sleeping, you're hardly eating. You're carrying too much on your shoulders."

"I hadn't realised you'd been paying such close attention to me."

"Cai, I'm serious." She put her horse in front of me, forcing me to halt. "I may not be the best queen, but I know more than you think. Which is why I don't understand you not confiding in me with all this tension between Norrandale and Argon."

My horse had taken the stop as an opportunity to eat grass and I lightly tugged on its reins, guiding us past Elara.

"You have enough to worry about in your own kingdom as it is. My complaining won't help."

"This isn't about complaining," she replied gently. "You have so many around you that would literally give their lives for your comfort."

I shook my head. "I should be a better king than that. I should be able to handle my responsibilities."

"I know you think the best thing is doing all of this on your own. Trust me, I know that better than anyone." She hesitated for a moment and shifted her gaze away from me and to the forest around us. "But knowing what I know now, I don't believe a person is made to rule alone. You don't *have* to do all this alone."

"This is so much bigger than all of us." Not even I knew what exactly I was referring to.

She met my gaze with a worried look in her eyes.

"I know."

Chapter 19

Elara

My mind was racing.

Not only was there a cave full of Myrgonite stones in the mountains of Norrandale, but if the stones existed then it meant there was a possibility that the three "magical objects" of Queen Riona existed as well.

Lance was right. For all his idiocy and malice, he was right about the jewels. I barely knew what to think.

No wonder Cai was having sleepless nights. No wonder Norrandale was under constant threat. If someone were to discover and abuse them, the effects could be disastrous. Part of me was thrilled that Cai had finally decided to confide in me about something. But more than that, a new fear had etched itself on my chest. How on earth were we going to keep this secret protected? And even worse, what if we couldn't?

Cai and I arrived back at the palace a few hours later. It was Jack who ran up to our horses, his face filled with concern. "Your Majesties—"

But the expression on Cai's face told him that it wasn't the time. And Jack knew better than to press the matter.

"Sorry to have made you worry, Jack." Cai dismounted before walking over to lend me a hand. "I promise it was important."

"Of course." Jack bowed his head.

"Any news on our runaway assassin?" Cai asked. A groom ran over to take the horses from us.

"I'm afraid not. But they're searching everywhere. We'll find him soon, Your Majesty."

"Thank you, Jack."

I was surprised when Cai took my hand as he led me back inside the palace, but I didn't dare let go. The hallways were quiet, with few members of the court around. "Where do you think everyone is?" I asked him.

"I wonder. Possibly outside, enjoying what's left of the good weather."

"Do you have duties to attend to now?" I wanted to spend more time with him, wanted to talk about how we were going to approach the future with the information I'd learned. More than anything, I just wanted Cai's company.

"I'm afraid so."

I tried not to let him see my disappointed expression.

"But I will see you tonight at dinner." He squeezed my hand, and my heart fluttered.

The sound of female laughter came from down the hallway. "It sounds like somebody is having fun," I remarked.

"It sounds like Gwen and her friends."

When I first arrived, I was quickly intimidated by Lady Gwen and her close relationship with Cai. But the more time I'd spent at the palace, the more I saw the love they shared with each other was truly of the sibling kind.

Cai and I peeked around the door into one of the drawing rooms. Sure enough, Gwen and her friends were seated at a round table, playing cards being shuffled between them. I was relieved to find that Lady Meredette was nowhere to be seen.

Gwen's jumped up at my presence. "Your Majesty." Everyone stood up from the table and curtsied to Cai. "Queen Elara." Gwen's eyes lit up and she smiled at me. Her eager expression pleasantly surprised me. "I was actually looking for you, but Lady Anesta said she couldn't find you anywhere."

"My apologies, Gwen, I'm afraid I stole Elara away this morning," Cai said before I had a chance to reply.

Some of the women eyed the way Cai's hand was holding mine. I quickly stepped into the room.

"I'm at your disposal, Lady Gwen."

"We're playing a game of cards, and I was wondering if you would like to join us, Your Majesty."

I was flattered. Growing up among men and boys, I didn't always have the luxury of female friendships. It was nice to have my company wanted. On the other hand, it was absolutely terrifying. They would all expect me to act like a perfect queen, these young women of noble birth who had been raised in court their whole lives.

Suppressing my nerves, I looked back at Cai, who gave me a smile and mouthed "See you later", before departing from the drawing room.

I took a seat at the table and one of the women started shuffling the cards again. I was embarrassed to admit that I didn't really know any card games.

"What are you playing?"

"Queen of hearts."

"I've never heard of that," I confessed, biting the inside of my cheek.

"That's because we made it up, Your Majesty," Gwen said with a grin.

"Please call me Elara. I can't have any of my friends calling me by my title." It was bold of me to assume Gwen would even want to be my friend. But she seemed so kind and genuine and clever. She was the esteemed lady I could never be.

"I'd be honoured to." We turned our attention back to the cards and I focused on sitting up straight.

"So, how does the game work?"

Gwen proceeded to explain the rules to me very patiently. The main idea was to avoid the queen of hearts card that was hidden among all the other cards. You could exchange cards with other players and the one who held the queen of hearts at the end of the game lost. Everyone would play until there was only one person left. It took me a few rounds to fully grasp the rules but then it quickly became rather enjoyable.

"So, Lady Haisly, how is your courtship with Lord Flit going?" Gwen asked as she handed out a card to each of us. I turned it over. Seven of spades. There was a small breath of relief.

Lady Haisly blushed. "He sends me letters almost every day." Some of the other ladies around the table "ooo'd" with girlish excitement. "Some of them are just kind words and sometimes he sends me verse." Lady Haisly was clearly smitten.

Though I'd never been one to be seduced by poetry, I could understand her excitement. It must have been nice to have someone care so much. When you returned their affections, of course.

"Can we expect a proposal soon?" Lady Romy asked.

"He talks about the future all the time," Haisly confirmed. "I'd like to think he's planning to propose." I was almost jealous of her giddiness. Of the fact that she could happily marry who she pleased. That she didn't have a whole kingdom dependent on her marriage.

"You're so lucky." Gwen sighed. "I am never getting married."

"Don't be so negative," Romy said. "You just haven't met the right person." She looked down at her cards with a slight frown.

"If one more person says that I'm going to throw a vase at them," Gwen grumbled.

"At least you're not alone. My parents would love to arrange a marriage for me and I'm running out of excuses," Lady Romy complained.

"There's always Lord Thatcher." Haisly smirked and exchanged a card with Gwen.

"Last I heard, he was still interested in Lady Celia," Romy responded.

"Let's not talk about my brother in that manner, if you please." Gwen groaned. "I don't want to lose my appetite before dinner."

"Sorry, Gwen, but surely you must know that your brother is attractive and there's a reason he's so popular among women."

Gwen sent a look of disapproval in Romy's direction. "As far as I'm concerned, he's the most annoying person on earth."

"Can't be worse than my brother," I muttered, without thinking, and they looked towards me.

"I've heard quite a lot about His Highness," Lady Haisly said while Gwen's eyes focused on her cards.

"And none of it good, I'm assuming." Lance had a reputation, after all.

"At least you didn't have to grow up with him," Gwen muttered, still undecided on which card to exchange.

"That's true." I forced a chuckle. They might have heard about his drinking and frivolous parties, but I could never tell them who Lance really was, what he did to me and Cai.

"Don't you think Lord Thatcher is handsome, Your Majesty?" Lady Romy asked.

"Mmh." I tilted my head to the side, wanting to give an honest answer without making Gwen uncomfortable.

"He's not *bad*-looking."

"That's a very diplomatic response," Gwen said. "Though I suppose you prefer Cai's features."

I felt the heat crawling up my neck. Of course Cai was handsome. Anyone could agree he was good-looking. But having to admit it out loud made me squirm like a shy young girl.

"His Majesty is blessed with good genetics." I was suddenly very focused on the cards in front of me. Luckily no queen of hearts yet.

"Don't avoid the question." Gwen tauntingly bumped my shoulder. "We all know you're practically swooning."

I gave her a look but let out a chuckle, nonetheless. The girls giggled behind their cards.

Was this what I'd been missing out on my whole life? I was enjoying myself and their company so much more than I'd thought I would. The group of them were so inviting and we could joke about silly things. For an hour, I didn't need to worry about the politics of my kingdom or when the next council meeting would be. I could laugh about nonsensical things, my biggest concern the pack of cards in front of me and whether they contained a very specific queen.

"No but do you know what's really been bothering me?" Haisly changed the subject. "Why is no one talking about Lady Marlowe's dress from the other night?"

Chapter 20

Cai

"Can I borrow you for a moment?"

Elara looked up from the book she was reading to where I was standing in the doorway of the library.

"I believe it's grammatically correct to ask if you *may* borrow me and not if you can."

I pressed my lips into a line to keep from grinning. "Look at you, telling a king how to speak."

"Well." She shrugged. "If anyone ever was going to tell a king how to speak, you and I both know it would be me."

"I suppose that's true." I stared at her for another moment, leaning my head against the doorframe.

"Care to join me for a stroll?"

She sighed, looking up as if she was deep in thought. "You know, I'd love to, but this book I'm reading suddenly just got very interesting." She held it up for me to see.

"I thought you didn't like to read?" I crossed my arms.

"You're right. This book is terrible. I've read the same sentence

209

twenty times now." She tossed the book, and I chuckled as she climbed over the edge of the settee in a manner very unlike the queen she was.

With her arm linked in mine, I led her out to the gardens. My guards followed and I had to ask them to stay back to give me and the Queen of Everness some privacy. Elara's expression changed at this request, but she remained quiet at my side.

The weather wasn't exactly desirable. The sun remained hidden while the clouds covered the skyline in a blanket of grey. They gathered in the distance, accompanied by strong winds, foretelling a storm that was likely to arrive. Winter lurked around the corner.

We finally reached the ivy-covered wall, where I felt for the door. After I shoved it with my shoulder once or twice, it finally opened.

Elara took hold of my hand so that I could guide her inside, preventing the skirts of her dress tripping her over the tall grass and wildflowers.

"I see you still haven't gotten a gardener in here."

"It will definitely look a lot better once it's cleaned up. I can't decide if I should involve my mother in the process — the garden is her heart after all — or if I should surprise her."

"Either way there is a lot of work to be done."

I placed my hands on my hips as I took a look around. If I had any interest in horticulture I might have taken on the task myself. But I was likely to do more damage than good. "I do like being the only person who knows about it, though. I might keep it like that for a while." A place I could go to be alone, to find a little peace amid all the chaos.

"One of the only two people," Elara reminded me. She picked one of the flowers and twirled it between her fingers.

"So, are you going to tell me why you dragged me all the way out here, or is that a secret too?" Her mouth curved into a teasing smile.

Looking away, I scratched the back of my neck. "I figured it was time we talk about our situation."

"Our situation?" Elara didn't seem impressed by my choice of words.

"Well, yes?" I had thought she had wanted this discussion to take place for a while now.

She sighed. "All right, what do you want to discuss?"

The sky above grew darker, the smell of rain in the air.

I stated the obvious. "You need to marry me to strengthen your claim to the Evernean throne."

"Yes?" Her tone was uncertain.

"And I need to marry you for soldiers to better protect my kingdom against Argon, if we should go to war." There had been no discussion about the alliance since the last council meeting, and my noblemen would probably have my head if they knew what I was about to do.

She crossed her arms. "Are you proposing, Cai?"

"You didn't let me finish."

"Good, because if that is your idea of a proposal, I am really rethinking my choices."

Where did she find the capability for humour at a time like this? My palms were sweating. I could feel my pulse in my throat.

"This alliance could have a negative impact on Norrandale if Everness is on the brink of a civil war. The same goes for Everness should Argon attack. Your kingdom isn't the strongest it's ever been and sending soldiers to Argon could sink Everness into greater poverty."

"I suppose you're right," Elara confirmed.

"You have a knack for wanting to run away from everything and everyone all the time."

"What?" She seemed more confused at the boldness of my statement rather than arguing against my words.

"And I give people the benefit of the doubt when I shouldn't," I admitted. "And you have very little experience of being a queen."

Elara had a crease between her brows from frowning.

"Well, there is no need to twist the knife," she said under her breath. A gust of wind, cold and intrusive, blew the surrounding fallen leaves into the air.

"I spend too much time away from home. You used to be a criminal. There's been a lot of secrets and betrayal between us. Not to mention your family."

"Is there a point to this or are you just making a list of reasons we shouldn't be together? Because if that's the case, you making a list in the first place should also be a part of it."

She was annoyed, but I couldn't stop myself now. "I have things that haunt me. We have lied to each other, verbally insulted each other, almost tried to kill each other."

"Don't forget you tied me to a tree." She couldn't help but bring it up.

"The truth is, neither of us really knows what we're doing, and this could end in disaster."

Elara's expression stilled, and she bit her lip, knowing I was right but not wanting to acknowledge the truth.

"Our union could be the future for our people—" I sucked in a breath — "or the end of our kingdoms."

She swallowed hard.

"But the truth is, none of those things matter because I'm completely and irrevocably in love with you, Elara."

She met my eyes, and a raindrop fell onto her cheek. "What?" It wasn't much more than a whisper. Her expression shifted from annoyance to surprise.

"I love you so hopelessly beyond my control. I loved you when you held a knife to my throat and when you came back for me during the rebellion. I loved you when I thought you were a princess and when I found out you were a bandit. I loved you when I believed you to be engaged to someone else, and I'll probably still love you even if you don't want anything to do with me."

She tilted her head, face softening. "Cai."

"I heard you," I said, stepping closer and placing my hands on her cheeks as the rain began to pour. She didn't move away, she only sucked in a breath.

"What?"

"I heard you the night you asked me to stay." The night I almost died.

"I don't understand, I ... you—"

"You told me that I couldn't leave. When death was knocking at the door, you pulled me back and begged me to stay. I came back because of you. I know I have a family and a kingdom that needs me, and while those things matter, it was your voice, Elara. Only you."

She pressed her forehead to mine. I felt the locks of her hair against my skin. "You came back."

"I came back." I pressed a kiss to her head, which tasted of sweet rain, and she placed her hands around my wrists.

"If that's what it takes to keep you, I would fight death again." I wasn't sure if she confessed it more to herself or to me.

"Maybe you and I are better off when we're fighting together." Under the dark clouds, raindrops fell from the heavens and washed the earth. "Will you marry me, Elara?" I said, softly, into the autumn storm.

She pulled back and looked up at me, her eyes wild with firelight once more. Her lips formed a smile.

I hovered my mouth next to her ear. "Marry me, Elara."

Her hands were on my arms.

I pressed a kiss to her jaw.

"I'll marry you, Cai," she said, before kissing me.

Chapter 21

Elara

We were gathered in the throne room, a fire brimming with warmth in the hearth. I hid a yawn behind my palm, hoping that I would soon be able to take a nap, especially after the lunch we'd just had. It was an effort to pay attention to the conversation around me.

Across the room, Cai was in conversation with Thatcher. We hadn't told anyone about the engagement yet. Cai needed to make an announcement to his council while being certain all the correct protocol was followed before the news became public.

Upon meeting my eyes, Cai pressed his lips into a line to keep from smiling. He almost succeeded, the corners of his mouth turning up slightly.

He looked happier than he had in days. He looked almost relieved. I should be relieved. I'd got exactly what I came for … and yet.

"You know, I've never been to Everness before, but I have thought about travelling there." Gwen pulled me back to the conversation. I'd seen plenty of her around the palace, but apart from our card game the other day, there had been little opportunity for us to spend time in each other's company.

"The beaches aren't nearly as beautiful as here in Norrandale," I admitted. "It's mostly just rocks and cliffs. But the forest certainly has some quality attributes."

"Why would anyone want to be in a forest?" one of Gwen's friends cut in, before she remembered she was addressing a queen. "Especially when one can bide in a palace like this, Your Majesty."

"Rumour has it that Everness's forests are filled with magic." A few eyes widened and I held back a smirk. "But those are just rumours. The towns, however, are lovely to visit during the festive seasons."

"Perhaps I'll be able to make the trip one day," Gwen said, and her tone reminded me of how small her world must have been. She'd grown up in and around court, never left her kingdom and likely didn't often frolic in magical forests. The last one was probably for the best. I certainly didn't spend my adolescence scavenging in the forest for food for the mere pleasure of it.

The doors to the throne room burst open, making me jump. A group of men stormed inside, armed and clearly not invited. Someone let out a scream.

Their armour differed from anything I'd seen before. They were certainly not from Norrandale or Everness. Argon perhaps? My eyes flew to Cai as he reached for the nearest sword, from one of the courtiers. Behind me, a voice shouted to protect the King, as the men attacked whoever was nearest to the door. How had they managed to get inside the palace?

I looked towards the fire poker next to the hearth. It wasn't much of a weapon, but it could do enough damage if used correctly. I grabbed it — it was better than nothing.

Gwen and her friends huddled together while the palace guards tried to move everyone to safety.

"Follow me, Your Majesty." One of Jack's guards ushered me towards the back corridor that led out of the throne room.

Everything was happening too fast. More screams came from the room behind us. I felt the heat rising in my neck. I was angered at my slow response thus far. My mind raced, trying to focus on what was happening. Who were they? Why were they here? Then I realised I was going the wrong way. Where was Cai? I needed to go back to find Cai. I couldn't lose him. Not again.

More anger followed. Anger that I'd been so quick to run away. I'd run into the middle of a rebel uprising to save him. Had I become so frightened of my own shadow that I would now abandon him in his own palace?

"We need to go back. What about the King?" I stopped dead, causing the poor guard to almost bump into me. My voice was filled with panic.

"The King will be safe," he assured me, in the middle of the dark hallway. I looked to his face, and I was sure I could see fear. With a roar, one of the attackers stormed down the corridor. He brought his right hand up, his sword's sharp edge gleaming wickedly.

"Watch out!" I stepped back, giving him the space he needed to defend himself, but the guard was too slow, and I watched in horror as he was run through.

Without breaking stride, the attacker retracted his bloody sword, shouldering the helpless guard aside. The guard plunged to the stone floor, and in a second the soldier was past him. Our eyes met. Was he Argonian? He had to be. I'd never seen anyone who hailed from there before, but something in my gut warned me he was Argonian through and through.

He reached for my arms, and I tripped back over the hem of my long dress. We fell, him on top of me, and I gasped as the air was knocked out of my lungs.

"Elara!" I heard my name being called in the far distance. It was Cai's voice. He was looking for me. I wanted to scream. Nothing came out.

Overcome with fear that screamed at me to survive, I grasped around desperately, reaching for anything I could use. My fingers found the dead palace guard's helmet. The Argonian shifted, trying to get to his knees. His weight was still in his arms when the guard's helmet found the side of his head and he crumpled onto his side, dazed. It gave me the time I needed to scramble out from under him.

There was a clang beneath me as I accidentally stepped on the poker. The Argonian was recovering fast. I threw the now useless helmet at him and missed. His eyes gleamed with hatred. In a moment, he was on his heels. I grabbed for the poker and began swinging the sharp end towards him.

He lunged, his face filled with rage. The poker completed its swing and the sharp metal point sank deep into his stomach. His sword dropped to the floor. He grabbed at the poker wildly, trying to pull it out. I looked at his bloodstained hands as they encircled the poker. I couldn't stop the fear inside me. Couldn't stop myself as I pushed that poker deeper and deeper. The life slowly drained out of him. I pushed deeper still, until the metal point reappeared on the other side of his torso. He dropped to his knees. My heart was beating in my throat while I held back a cry. Blood blossomed, staining everything a deep red.

I didn't want to stand there any longer, didn't want to wait and see what would happen.

"Elara!" My name was called again, and the panic in Cai's voice pushed me to run towards the sound. I didn't turn around. Didn't look back as a large red pool flowed across the floor. I practically ran into Cai at the end of the corridor.

My eyes immediately scanned for signs of fatal wounds. He pulled me in to him. "You're okay."

Cai attempted to reassure me, and I wondered how he could be so calm and collected when I was beyond frantic.

"What happened? Is everyone safe?"

"Everything is under control." He sighed. "For now."

I woke up to my body covered in cold sweat, the sheets stuck to my skin. I practically fell out of bed as I scrambled to get free, to feel like I could breathe again.

The only image stuck in my mind was that of the Argonian soldier and the poker as I drove it through him again … and again … and again. The red stain blooming, growing, flowing.

I shuddered.

Wiping the hair away from my face, I stumbled over to the nearest window and shoved it open. The night air felt cold against my skin.

The vivid pictures stuck in my mind, made me feel sick.

I had to force myself to think of something else.

Anything else.

And so, without trying, in my mind's eye, I saw Cai. He told me that the war between Norrandale and Argon still haunted his dreams at times. I could only imagine how much more difficult that must have made everything. After what happened in the throne room, it was confirmed that the armed men were from Argon. No one knew how they'd managed to find their way into the palace, but all of them were killed or arrested. What were King Aries' intentions in sending a group of his soldiers into Mistwood Palace? If he'd hoped to assassinate Cai, wouldn't he have done something more subtle? I'd heard that Alastor had sustained some injuries during the fight, but Anesta reassured me it was nothing too serious. The entire rest of the day, the atmosphere was tense and dreary. Every person in the palace appeared to be walking on eggshells.

I didn't want to wake Cai. But I also knew better than to think I was going to fall asleep again.

There were two guards stationed outside my door. Usually, they would be further down the hall, but after what had happened today, it would seem that security in the palace had increased.

"Everything all right, Your Majesty?" one of them asked.

I tightened my robe over my nightshift. "Yes, thank you. All is well."

I proceeded to tiptoe down the hallway until I realised, after a few steps, that they were following me. Of course, they were only obeying orders, but I wouldn't have them see me sneaking into Cai's room in the middle of the night. No one needed to be gossiping about that sort of thing. And I was not naive enough to believe the servants and guards didn't gossip. Kings and queens hardly truly had secrets.

I gave them a determined look over my shoulder, which they seemed to understand. Sneaking silently through the hallways, I was thankful that Cai's chambers were close to my rooms. The last thing I needed was to run into more people. Even if it was the middle of the night, someone always seemed to be awake at court.

I nodded shyly at Cai's guards, who thankfully recognised me, though pretended they didn't see anything as I rounded the last corner.

I was surprised to see Cai's door slightly open, allowing the light from inside the room to stream out.

As I got closer, I realised there were voices coming from inside the room. One of them was distinctly Cai's.

"Too many people have already been hurt. Today was too close."

"Luckily most of the court members are uninjured, although I heard a few guards didn't make it." The other voice was Thatcher's.

"It seems like King Aries doesn't know where to draw the line. If he's willing to do all this, then who knows what else he's up to? And as long as his attempts keep failing, how long before he marches on Norrandale?"

"It's growing more unsafe at court by the day. How did they even get in?"

"I don't know. We have to consider the possibility that there's a traitor in the palace who knew security had decreased in number because of the group Jack sent to look for the assassin who poisoned me."

I heard something being poured, which I assumed was wine.

"Whatever the council decides, that decision will have to be made soon," Cai said, after a moment of silence.

"What about Elara?" Thatcher asked, and my ears pricked up at the sound of my name. I leaned as close to the door as possible without making my presence known.

"Everness has agreed to an alliance, but they might feel less obliged to accept a royal wedding if it immediately thrusts them into a full war with Argon."

"I'm sure Elara will stand by you."

I tried not to smile at Thatcher's faith in me.

"Elara is a new queen who has yet to establish a strong rule. Everness

221

needs a royal alliance as much as Norrandale, but they could refuse to send their men into war with us."

"She is still queen, and she still has the final say." Thatcher tried to reassure him, but I understood where Cai's hesitancy came from. It was one thing to make the alliance with the possibility of aiding in war. But the chances were increasing, and I doubted just as much as Cai that the people of Everness would be eager to give up a few thousand men after everything the kingdom had recently been through.

"It's so bizarre to me, though. You get back from your journey in Everness, where you were supposed to meet your future bride, and instead the kingdom had rebelled, and you were on the rebels' side. Not only that, but one of the rebels then became the new queen," Thatcher said, almost in disbelief.

"You make it sound to be what it's not."

"Which is?"

"I didn't side with the rebels because I wanted to end the Evernean monarchy for Norrandale's sake," Cai replied.

"Right, you sided with them because you liked the girl."

Heat rose in my face.

"And need I remind you that you cannot breathe a word of this to anyone?"

Had Cai really told Thatcher everything about my past?

"I know, I know. I won't tell a soul. But how lucky for you that one of the first things she does as queen is ask for your hand in marriage."

"But as we have already established, it's more complicated than that."

"Cai, if you don't marry the damn girl, then I will."

"Thatcher, come on, be realistic for once in your life. Even if I marry Elara, which I plan to do, it won't change the fact that she grew up a commoner."

It took a moment for me to register what I'd heard.

A commoner. He'd called me a commoner.

Thatcher said something but I didn't want to listen any further. Was that really what Cai thought of me? Was all the hesitancy about the engagement just excuses he made up? Cai had said that my past didn't matter. That he didn't care about my family or that I was once the masked bandit. Was I naive to believe him?

Maybe he was right. I had no proper education or upbringing. I didn't really know what I was doing as Queen. But if Cai truly believed I wasn't good enough for him, then why did he ask me to marry him?

I hurried back to my rooms and found my guards, waiting in angst and appearing relieved at my quick return. I couldn't think. I was overwhelmed by a wave of emotions I did not want to acknowledge.

"Wake Lady Anesta," I instructed one of them. "Tell her to come to my chambers immediately." He nodded before running off without further question.

"This just arrived for you, Your Majesty." The other guard handed me a letter. A message in the middle of the night usually wasn't a good sign.

I closed the doors to my room silently, instead of slamming them like I wanted to, and took a deep breath. With slightly trembling hands, I opened the letter. It was from Lance. The council and aristocracy had grown restless in my absence and inability to secure an alliance. They were considering alternative options, which only meant they would begin looking for ways to get rid of me.

It was the last thing I wanted but perhaps the very thing I needed to hear. I had to remain focused now. So, as calmly as possible, I began to dress myself in riding attire.

I was halfway through tying my braid when Anesta burst into the room. "What happened? What's wrong?" She seemed half surprised that no one was lying dead on the floor, as if she expected the worst.

"Start packing my things and tell Rhen to ready the horses."

Chapter 22

Cai

I tucked in my shirt without much care as I hurried to Elara's room the next morning. After everything that had happened yesterday, I wanted to make sure she was all right. I would never forget the fear in her eyes as she beheld the blood on her hands from killing the Argonian soldier. I wish I could have protected her from it.

There were two guards stationed outside her door. Their expressions grew nervous as I approached.

"Your Majesty." One of them corrected his posture and fisted his hands at his sides.

"Is Elara still in her chambers?"

The guard cleared his throat, taking too long to respond.

"No, Your Majesty. She's asked that we give you this." The other guard said.

He handed me a white envelope with my name written in Elara's handwriting.

Something about the guard's expression told me the contents of the letter could only be less than desirable.

Dear Cai,

I'm sorry to have left without a goodbye. Though you know
I was never really good at them anyway. I have things to take
care of back in Everness. My kingdom needs me now. Please
send my apologies and love to Cordelia.

Love, Elara

I scrunched up the letter, which still smelled of her, and hurried out
of the room.

"Jack!" My shout echoed through the palace hallways.

"Jack!" I called out again as I made my way towards the training
area, where he was most likely to be.

I didn't know if it was the panicked tone of my voice or perhaps
just coincidental proximity that made him appear before me suddenly.

"Yes, Your Majesty." He blew out a breath, giving away that he'd
been running.

"It's Elara, she's gone." I was out of breath myself, though the
origin was more likely panic.

"Gone?" Jack frowned, and I pressed the crumpled piece of paper
to his chest.

"She left me this."

He quickly read through the letter before looking back up at me.
"Your Majesty?"

"Something's not right." I gulped.

"Because she needed to go back to Everness or—"

"Because she wouldn't have just left like that without saying
anything," I said. "Not unless something was wrong."

"Are you sure she truly didn't just have to go home, Your Majesty?
Things aren't exactly going well in Everness."

I shook my head. "She gave no indication of coming back or any future meeting between us. She wouldn't do that unless something happened. Something that made her run." Like a bird always looking to escape the cage of her reality.

"Maybe with everything happening with Argon, she's just trying to protect herself. This court hasn't exactly been the safest of places."

"Ready the horses, we're going to Everness," I ordered., ignoring his comment.

"Everness?" he questioned. "With all due respect, is that the wisest thing to do right now? You need to be protected now more than ever, Your Majesty."

"Aries isn't interested in overthrowing my kingdom just yet. If he was then he would have sent an army yesterday, not just a few rogue spies. This is personal. I killed his brother. He wants to hit me where it hurts, and I have my guesses that he knows about Elara too by now, and if he doesn't, he's going to find out soon. As long as she is alone, she is a target."

"You think Aries will come for her in Everness?"

"I'm counting on it."

"Well." Thatcher folded his hands together. "This has all gotten very interesting." He leaned back in one of the chairs in the sitting area of my rooms while I readied myself for the journey ahead. The servants were in a bustle, the palace full of whispers about the sudden departure of the Queen of Everness.

"The longer Elara is alone there, the more danger she is in. Aries is going to come for me by chasing and threatening her." Though no one knew of the engagement, it was clear there had been a security breach in the palace. If Aries' spies could get me poisoned and attacked, it was certain that Elara wasn't safe. Jack was doing everything in his power to find the culprit, but that kind of thing could take a long time. I would never be at ease when I couldn't be certain she was out of danger.

"You've always been so noble, Cai."

Although I appreciated his compliment, now was not the time. "Focus," I said, tying my belt in a hurry. "Are you coming with me or not?" With all the chaos that had seemed to ensue since I'd been crowned, there was a feeling of comfort at the thought that I still had my oldest friend by my side. It was the familiarity of him that gave me the delusion we were still two kids running amuck.

"You think I would miss out on an adventure like this? I'm afraid you don't know me at all."

I was slightly relieved, though I wouldn't admit it to Thatcher. He loved spending time at court, and we'd never travelled this far together before.

"I'll take that as a yes, then." I grabbed my jacket, motioning for Thatch to follow me. We headed out the door and to the stables, where the horses were being readied for the journey.

"You must love her a lot if you're willing to fight for her like this."

I stopped in my tracks for a moment. "Haven't you ever cared for someone enough that you were willing to give up everything, just to see them safe and content? Even if it didn't always make sense? In fact, most of the time it doesn't make sense."

Thatcher seemed to think for a moment. "Can't say I have. Though *you* might want to look into it, because you sound like a raving lunatic."

I shook my head, thankful for his humorous attempt to cheer me up.

"If I may ask … ?"

"We both know you're going to ask anyway, regardless of my response."

"True."

The halls were busy with plenty of servants but many of the courtiers had chosen to stay in their chambers. I couldn't blame them after what had happened yesterday. I was terrified myself.

"Well, the thing is," Thatcher started. "I was just wondering, since the two of you are not officially engaged, what kind of message this would send out to the people, to Argon too?"

I bit my lip. Nothing was official yet. But Thatcher was my best friend.

"I'm telling you the same thing I told Jack — with the number of spies Aries has in my palace, news would have certainly reached him about Elara. Fiancée or not, he's coming after her."

"Because you killed his brother?"

"Aries wants revenge. Revenge for his brother. Revenge that he couldn't conquer Norrandale." More likely he was probably after Norrandale's biggest secret.

"I guess you're right."

I changed the subject. "Will you be packed in time? We're almost leaving."

"I have my charm and wit." He shrugged. "What more do I need?"

"Don't know," I replied as we reached the stables. "Everness can get pretty cold, you might want to take a blanket."

"Don't worry. I had my servants pack the moment I heard you were leaving."

"Wait up!" Both our heads turned in the direction of the voice calling out. Dressed in her riding attire, Gwen came running with a small bag over her shoulder. "Don't leave without me."

"You're not coming," Thatcher said in disbelief when she came to a stop next to him. She huffed, out of breath, dropping her hands to her knees.

"Oh yes I am," Gwen argued, causing him to raise his blond eyebrows at her.

"What makes you think we're letting you come along on our boys' trip?"

"Don't be a pig." She hit his shoulder.

"Mother will kill you if she finds out," Thatcher persisted.

"Mother doesn't have to know." She bent down to retie one of her boot laces. I looked to where Jack fastened the last of his belongings to his horse. Cordelia stood by his side, ready to bid him farewell. She would come to Everness a few days after us, bringing the rest of my guards. They had yet to return from their search for the assassin.

"She's going to find out eventually and you know it. And if she doesn't kill you, she's going to kill Cai for not forbidding you to come." Thatcher placed his hand on my shoulder. "Think of poor little Cai, Gwennie."

"Well, then, I guess it's a good thing that Cai is king and doesn't have to obey the likes of anyone." Lace tied, she straightened herself, tossing her hair over her shoulder.

"It could get dangerous," I warned her. "Are you certain that you want to come along?" It wasn't a lie. I had no way of guaranteeing her safety on this trip.

"I won't get in your way, I promise. But I'll drive myself mad if I have to stay in this damned place any longer." She looked at the palace walls with dismay.

Thatcher and I stared at her in silence, waiting for more of an explanation.

"You guys can come and go as you please. Cai, you've been gone more in the past few years than you've been home. I love Norrandale but I need to see what's beyond the palace walls every now and then."

Gwen was very hard-headed once she'd set her mind on something. I called for the stable boy to saddle another horse.

"Fine, but if you get killed, it's not my fault." Thatcher crossed his arms. Gwen ignored him and moved towards the stable boy, gathering her horse's tack.

"I may be a lady, but I can still kick both your arses," she replied over her shoulder.

Chapter 23

Elara

I stepped out of the carriage, the gravel of the front drive crunching, and burst through the front doors of the palace.

"Your Majesty, welcome home." The palace guard practically tripped over himself in surprise. My return was not announced or expected.

"Where's Lance?" I barked out the question.

"He was last seen in the library, I believe, Your Majesty." The guard didn't sound very sure of himself, or perhaps he was just clearly aware of my mood.

The soles of my boots sounded over the clean tiled floors. I hadn't bothered with a dress or any accessories when I left. It wasn't as if anybody was going to see me. What did I need to look formal for anyway? The journey from Norrandale was long and I wanted to be comfortable.

The palace was quiet, all the servants going about their daily routines. I could hear the guards training outside, through the open windows, while inside a maid busied herself with her duties. Perhaps I hadn't given Lance enough credit. Despite his past, which could only be described as selfish and borderline psychotic, the palace was still standing, nobody was trying to break down the doors in protest, and everyone seemed to be alive and well — things were in place. He'd been regent before when King Magnus took ill, and I was opposed to his rule back then. But there was still a form of order. Lance knew how to handle people. Something I'd never had much skill with.

My boots continued stomping as I headed towards the library. I wondered how my sudden departure from the kingdom to pursue an alliance had been received. Releasing Lance from prison would have raised a few eyebrows. I was too focused on surviving to put much thought into any of it. Had it been a mistake to go to Norrandale? Back then, it seemed like a risk I needed to take, but now I was back empty-handed and with the knowledge that Cai believed I wouldn't live up to the great legacy of all the queens of Norrandale.

Lance looked up from a book when I entered the library. "Elara?" There was an expression of slight surprise on his face but no trace of disappointment or distaste. "I didn't know you'd be arriving today." I didn't know what state I'd expected to find him in — raving drunk, surrounded by women maybe. But no, he'd been calmly sitting and reading.

How could everything and everyone be so well and happy when it felt as though my world was falling apart? How was I going to tell him I'd failed? The last thing I was looking for was Lance's approval. But it felt too shameful to admit that I couldn't do the single thing that might have saved my claim to the throne. And the only person I had to blame was myself. I was stupid for believing I could do this. Stupid for thinking I could make any kind of a difference. The politics of our situation was too complicated. All of this was too complicated.

"Are you all right?" Lance dared to ask. "You look a little pale."

Pale was the very least of my concerns. I'd managed to hold every piece of myself together all the way from Norrandale. But months of pain and anguish and fear had built up into something horrible.

And I broke.

Tears started streaming down my face. Lance's expression grew to discomfort, as if he was not quite sure what to do. Which was why he surprised me when he stood up, after a moment, to come over and wrap his arms around me in a brotherly fashion.

It was strange, perhaps even wrong considering our past. I didn't want him to see my pain. But right then, he was the only person there. And I needed it. Despite my instincts screaming at me, I needed just to be held.

In the end, I suppose, we were all only human.

And so, I let him hold me. But only for a second or two before I pulled away, clearing my throat.

"Should I call for some tea?" he asked, looking uncomfortable, but I shook my head, taking a seat in one of the library chairs. Lance sat across from me, reclining comfortably. The only person I knew who always seemed to be at ease.

"Do you want to tell me what happened?"

"What do you care?" I sniffed. He may have been my brother, but he was certainly not my friend. He was half the reason I was in this mess.

"I care because if you lose the crown, then you and I are screwed, little sister."

And there was the Lance I knew. The one who would only help as long as it entertained his own selfish goals.

"The matters here in Everness need my attention. I haven't managed to secure the alliance yet. We'd certainly create a reputation in this family if we both manage to lose our crown in the first year of our reign."

"I didn't lose my crown," Lance scoffed. "I abdicated. The only reason I was imprisoned was because you and your spitefulness like to hold a grudge."

"Maybe it was payback for everything you put me through trying to get that necklace." I glared at him, the hug from a moment ago already forgotten.

"I didn't know you back then. What did it matter if we were related?"

"You don't know me now," I retorted.

"I've seen you cry." He smirked.

"And if you tell a single soul, I will have you beheaded."

"Speaking of necks, whatever happened to that precious necklace?" I was surprised it had taken him so long to bring it up. Though I had no doubt he didn't mind my absence from the palace as it had given him enough time to turn the place upside down looking for the jewel.

"Did you honestly believe for a single moment that I would tell you?"

"It's only a matter of time before I find it."

"Let it go, Lance," I insisted. "It's a childhood fantasy, and the necklace is nothing more than a decorative accessory."

He squinted. "Then why did Cai resist telling me until I started to bargain with you?"

"Jealous that I actually have someone who cares about me?" I spat out, before thinking better of it. But my words only managed to create a pang in my own chest. He remained silent for a moment, looking at me as if he was trying to read my mind.

"Did you and Cai have a disagreement?" he ventured.

"No," I responded, too quickly. "King Aries sent men to attack the palace. Not an army but enough to cause damage. It was terrifying."

"You look as though you've come off fairly unscathed."

"I killed a man." That shut Lance up temporarily. "And ..." I paused. "Cai thinks I'm a commoner and he's worried I won't be the queen that his kingdom needs."

"What do you mean? Cai's known for a long time that you're the heir to the throne."

"He still believes that my upbringing is going to affect the way I rule." I rubbed my eyes. "I don't have the energy to deal with all of this now."

"And worst of all, for the both of us, you're still not married."

Had I been closer, I would have smacked the back of his head.

"Well." I tilted my head slightly.

"Well, what?" Lance asked, eyebrow raised.

"Technically Cai did ask me to marry him."

"Then why don't I see a ring on your finger?"

"He asked but it's not been announced or confirmed with the council. Nothing has been signed."

Lance groaned, rubbing his eyes with his palms. "Need I remind you what is at stake here?"

"I know. But I don't want to think about Cai right now. I need to focus on our next move."

Lance gave me a look that suggested I was too focused on my personal feelings rather than my duties. Not that he was exactly the example of duty. "Our?"

"Like you said, if we don't do something, then you and I might as well be carted off to the slaughterhouse."

He sighed and took a flask out of his pocket. I snatched it away before he could react. Lance looked at me with disgust.

"And no more drinking. I need you sober and focused." Was I truly going to rely on his help from now on?

"I'm really starting not to like you."

"Any news from Eloisa?" I contemplated taking a sip from the flask. "No."

"Lance, how can you not know where she is? She's still the princess of Everness, and need I remind you, also has a claim to this throne."

"Eloisa may have a claim by blood, but I can promise you she will never sit on the throne."

I was taken aback by how serious he appeared. "What are you talking about?"

Lance sighed again and bit the inside of his cheek. I cringed at the realisation that this was a habit we shared.

"Ever since we were young, she's had these … episodes. A lot of the time she seems normal, but then all of a sudden, she'll just …" He sighed. "I don't know. She's my sister but I wouldn't exactly call her mentally stable."

"You mean she's insane and now you've lost her?" How was it possible that matters were only getting worse by the second?

"When everything happened with Arthur, I sent her away with guards for protection," he said defensively.

"But?"

"But they came back and told me that she'd somehow managed to escape them, and now she isn't anywhere to be found."

I closed my eyes, the feeling of a headache starting to develop.

237

"Have you sent men to look for her?"

"Of course I have. What kind of a monster do you think I am?"

The expression on my face convinced him that he didn't really want me to answer the question. "Well, I've sent Ray to go and find her, so hopefully he comes back with some good news."

I returned to my rooms tired from travelling.

Anesta offered to unpack my things before helping me get ready for dinner, but I told her to take the rest of the afternoon for herself. The last thing I wanted was company. And besides, I hadn't become so high and mighty that I couldn't unpack a few trunks of clothes. I used to live in the woods.

A hot bath would have been nice, but I wasn't going to call on the servants now. I really just needed to be alone.

My room was clean, but it smelled slightly musty, so I opened a window to let in some fresh air. The scent of pine trees filled my nostrils. The queen's chambers were some of the finest rooms in the palace. No expense was spared when it came to the décor and furniture. Deep reds and gold flowed into patterns that decorated the chairs and silken sheets.

Though, in all the time I'd slept there, I'd never ventured to look through the things I'd inherited from my mother. Could never quite bring myself to. I grew up without her and spent my whole life without a single object or memory to accompany me. And looking through her things seemed to be asking to miss something I never had.

But I suddenly found myself curious so I strolled over to the nearest drawer and pulled it open.

Glittering pieces of jewellery stared up at me as if they'd waited years to see the daylight again. I picked up an earring and looked towards the mirror. It was large and decorative but not exactly suited for my face. I would look like a child playing dress up.

The next drawer held small bottles of perfume and oils, but most of the scent had evaporated over time. There was a golden hand-held mirror. The glass was grimy and stained, but the artistry of the object was delicate and beautiful. It was, unfortunately, cracked, so I put it back gently.

I also found a hair clip with a small hidden blade, which made me smile for some reason. When looking at her portrait and thinking back to stories I'd heard as a child, it was hard to imagine the gentle Queen Estella taking this out and stabbing someone with it.

A vivid image flashed into my mind of the Argonian soldier and the poker. The seeping blood. The sound as it pierced his flesh. A hint of anxiety and nausea washed over me. I placed the hair clip back before finally deciding to call for some tea.

I was surprised to open my chamber doors and find Rhen standing there with the tea tray. "Decided to resign your duties, have you?" I left the door open and walked over to one of the chairs near the fireplace. "Not that I think you're incapable, but I never imagined you'd want to be a maid."

"I wanted to make sure you were okay." He gave me a soft smile and handed me the cup of hot tea. Rhen wasn't in his official uniform and his white shirt hung loose over his shoulders. The expression on his face said everything. To hell with protocol for today.

"I'm fine." I took a sip of the tea, and Rhen took a seat on one of the other chairs.

"You don't have to pretend, you know," he said earnestly. "You don't have to be fine all the time."

I tried to muster a smile.

"Have you spoken to Lance?"

"When I arrived, yes. The council will probably gather tomorrow." I already dreaded it.

"The other reason I'm here."

"Of course." I sighed. "What else would we talk about?"

"Don't imagine I enjoy talking about this any more than you do," he said.

"No?" I feigned surprise. "Because it really seems like you do."

Rhen shook his head, his mouth curving into a smile. "I need to warn you that the council meeting tomorrow is not going to be pretty. The tensions are high, and people are scared. And they haven't even found out about Argon."

I tried to concentrate on his words, but a cold gust blew in from the window and I shivered.

Without breaking the conversation, Rhen stood up and started making a fire in the fireplace. "If the alliance doesn't pan out with Norrandale—" he had the courtesy not to mention Cai's name — "then we need to look at possibilities of other alliances. If not an Evernean lord, then further outside Everness's borders."

"You mean kings from the continent?"

He nodded. "But things like that can take a very long time. Something we don't really have."

"Whatever I have to do, I'm not marrying Edgar."

"Don't worry. We'll make certain the Darwicks don't get to you."

The fire burned brightly and slowly filled the room with heat.

"They know about my past."

"The Darwicks won't lay a hand on you." Rhen looked me dead in the eye. "I'll make sure of it."

And I believed him.

* * *

The long night didn't bring any rest or peace. I rolled around endlessly in my bed.

Dawn approached, the sun rising over the Evernean hills in the distance. I waited until the guards changed shifts at dawn before sneaking down to the stables.

A yawning stable boy offered to saddle up my horse, but I refused, wanting to do it myself. I took my time riding through the woods on the outskirts of the palace. It had been a long time since I'd been in the forest entirely alone. But all seemed quiet and at peace, as if even the trees could feel sympathy towards me.

I didn't want to think about the council and my fight for my birthright. But I realised I wasn't going to keep my mind from repeatedly wandering there until I came up with a possible solution.

An alliance with Norrandale certainly had its repercussions. There was the possibility of a full-on war — one which Everness wasn't prepared for despite the size of our army. And if I didn't marry Cai, the Darwicks could forever blackmail me into doing their bidding. I couldn't have Edgar sitting on the throne with me, having to watch my back for the rest of my life. The people loved the Darwicks. They were wealthy and well known, and the council would be more than happy to approve.

But I …

I loved Cai.

The thought alone nearly knocked me off my horse. Maybe that's why I left at the first sign of trouble. Because subconsciously I was looking for a reason to leave. It didn't remove the hurt I felt about what Cai had said. But running seemed easier than to risk losing him. Running always seemed easier after everyone I'd already lost.

The sun was perched in the middle of the sky by the time I finally took proper note of my surroundings and pulled myself out of my thoughts. A branch snapped somewhere behind me.

I was no longer alone in the forest.

In fact, I was being followed.

Leaving my horse to graze where she pleased, I watched the small group of guards from my hiding spot in the trees above. They were resting, having lunch. I didn't know if Rhen realised that I was aware of their presence or not. But I appreciated them staying far enough behind that it still gave me the illusion of my solitude. Perhaps he already understood something I was only beginning to learn myself.

I continued sticking to the outskirts of the woods, staying far away from the centre and whatever creatures and magic lurked beneath its moss-covered ground. I didn't care if it was all potentially legend and myth. I wasn't going to find out.

The night was cold and the clothing and provisions I'd brought along with me were few. I huddled closer to the fire while rubbing my hands and scolded myself for becoming accustomed to the luxuries of the palace. I wondered if my guards were feeling warm. I wasn't sure if I should let them know that I was aware of their presence. Maybe it would be better if they thought they hadn't been detected.

A few days into my journey, I stopped on the outskirts of Fairfrith camp. A place that I used to call home and was now too scared to enter. It wouldn't feel right without Uncle Arthur or Ray there. No matter what I wanted to hope or believe, this place was no longer my home.

The camp was smaller, less crowded — most, I suspected, having moved back to nearby towns and villages. There were fewer tents and fires than there used to be surrounding the huts. The air was quiet. A few kids were playing with stick swords in the distance. They were being watched by one of the women, who hung up clothes to dry. It was hard to imagine that a little further beyond the trees there was a small cabin that used to host a girl. The bandit turned queen.

Chapter 24

Cai

The journey felt long and tedious, while a tense atmosphere lingered between members of our party. Thatcher tried to lighten the mood with occasional humour, but it was of little use. We didn't stop to rest often, pushing to get there as soon as possible and only adding to everyone's tiredness and irritability. Even Gwen was too exhausted to talk. Alastor and Jack led our party safely across the border and into Everness.

When we finally arrived at the palace, it took a moment for the guards to realise we were royal visitors. Everyone seemed to scramble, unprepared. It was Lady Anesta who finally came out to greet us.

I didn't ask where Lance was, nor did I particularly care to see him.

Anesta told me that Elara had gone out riding and Rhen spotted her before she left. He'd gone after her, but they hadn't returned. It had been a few days.

I forced myself not to imagine the worst. I didn't even want to consider the possibility that Aries might have already reached her.

The Evernean Forest was a monstrosity of tall, dark trees and slopes, and she could have gone in any direction.

I needed to rest, to eat and sleep, but I wouldn't be able to do any of those things until I'd confirmed Elara's safety. I asked if we could borrow some of the palace horses, allowing ours to rest. I took Jack and a few guards with me, leaving the rest of our travelling party to get settled at the palace, all while trying not to think about the political storm that would surely follow my sudden arrival. I simply didn't have the time or energy for protocol and hoped Lady Anesta would be able to smooth over the worst of it until I returned to the palace.

"Any idea where she might have gone?" Jack asked me once we'd left the grounds.

"If she's upset or something's wrong, she is likely to go to a place where she feels at ease and peaceful."

"That could narrow it down to a few places."

"That's also assuming I really know anything about her," I replied.

"Don't worry, Your Majesty. I'm sure we'll find them."

Jack was a good tracker. If we stuck to the main routes through the forest, combined with visiting some of the places Elara might have gone, we stood a chance of getting to her.

I found her sitting alone by the lake.

The one we'd visited during our travel to Woodsbrook. It had taken quite some time to track her and her guards (who kept quite a distance), but Elara could be predictable in some ways. The sky was covered in clouds and a breeze began to form. Elara's arms were wrapped around herself, and I wondered if she was cold.

I dismounted and tied my horse to the nearest tree before

rubbing my eyes. I was beyond tired, and yet still I had to hold myself back from running to Elara and thanking the heavens that she was safe and unharmed.

If she'd heard me behind her, she made no effort to show it. Elara stared out into the lake as if answers to all the questions could be found beneath the surface of the water.

"You know, some would say it's dangerous for a queen to be out here alone."

She jumped at the sound of my voice. She really must have been so deep in thought that she had no idea I was there.

"Sorry, I didn't mean to frighten you."

She only looked at me for a moment. If she was surprised, she made no effort to show it. The breeze ruffled her hair. She was so beautiful. Her eyes scolded me before she shifted her gaze back to the water, which rippled in the last of the sunlight.

"What are you doing here, Cai?"

"I came back for you." The five simple words that meant nothing and everything all at once.

"You've got much to worry about in Norrandale. You should be there, on your throne."

"No," I replied, before taking a seat next to her on the ground. "I should be wherever you are."

"Don't," she said, too quickly. "Just don't."

"Elara, please listen."

"No, Cai. You listen." She finally turned to face me. "I overheard you talking with Thatcher."

"What do you mean?"

"You told him about where I come from and what kind of upbringing I had. At least now I know the real reason you waited so long to agree to the alliance." Her expression was so full of hurt, and I hated that I was the cause of it.

"That's not what it was about. I was trying to protect you, Lara. You have to believe me."

"Like the time you were trying to 'protect' me by not telling me I was the heir to the throne?" Lara's tone was cold, and it was as if I could physically feel the wall she had placed between us.

"It wasn't my place," I said. "No matter how much I wanted to."

She looked away, refusing to meet my gaze.

"What do you think would have happened if I'd told you? First of all, you wouldn't have believed me. And secondly, I thought back then that you wanted a different life, that you hated the monarchy. I believed that you wanted to leave that life and Everness behind to go and live somewhere else. And I believed you would do it if given the chance, regardless of what you thought of me. So imagine my surprise when you showed up at the palace that day of the rebellion? And even more so when you decided to take the throne after Lance got imprisoned, or abdicated, whatever you want to call it."

"I came for you because I cared, you idiot," she cried out. "I came back because I couldn't stand the thought of you dying." Elara shook her head. "And when Lance told me the truth, yes, at first, I didn't want to believe him. But I hoped that after everything we'd all been through, I might be able to do something good. I might be able to make a difference instead of just running away like I always do." She sighed deeply. "But it looks like I just traded one cage for another, shinier, one."

"You're the only person that can put you in a cage, Elara."

Her look told me that she didn't quite believe me.

"Yes, this royal life comes with its limits and consequences. It's a lot more responsibility than anyone is really willing to sign up for."

I placed my hand on top of hers. She didn't move away like I had expected. "But it's only terrible if you go through it alone."

"Do you really think I'm a terrible queen? That I'm nothing more than a common girl with a crown?" Elara said, after a few moments of agonising silence.

"I think the world of you, Elara." And it was the truth. "But being queen of Norrandale will bring so much more danger to your life." The kind of danger she'd wanted to escape from when she was still a bandit. Elara had always wanted a simple life, but it no longer seemed like a possibility for either of us.

"The thing is, I don't think I'm that afraid anymore." She stared out to the water. "Or maybe I'm just too tired to be afraid."

She finally looked back at me and then shook her head as if attempting to pull herself together. "We should start thinking about heading back. As much as I would like to, I can't stay out here for ever."

"How are things faring with the council? I can't imagine they are very good if you sneaked out of the palace to be here alone."

Elara shrugged. "I needed time to think. Besides, I'm not alone. Rhen and his guards have been keeping an eye on me."

I sucked in a breath. "I thought we could make the announcement of our engagement." Elara raised an eyebrow. "But once we do, Aries will do everything in his power to come after you too."

"Is that why you came back here?"

"You've seen what Aries is capable of. He doesn't care about rules or law or peace. And now that he knows about you and the possible alliance, Everness has also become Argon's enemy. With all due respect to Rhen and the royal guard, I couldn't leave you here to fend for yourself."

"I'm a big girl, Cai," she replied kindly, though her expression suggested understanding of my concern.

"Everness has already faced so much with a rebellion and a new monarch. Do you believe it's ready for a war too?"

"Is anyone ever truly ready for war?"

"Aries always seems to be." I turned my gaze over the still waters. "Won't our kingdoms at least have a better chance if we stand together?"

"Maybe. Wars cost more than human lives. It will be expensive to fund."

She squeezed my hand, and I squeezed back. "We're not doing this for our own sake, Cai. We're doing this because we have to, for the protection of everyone. Aries is coming whether we want him to or not and we need to protect our kingdoms. If Norrandale falls, Everness is next."

She was right.

Aries *was* coming.

"We should get back to the palace. It's not safe out here."

Her face softened and her mouth turned into a slight smile. "Have you forgotten you're in the presence of the Masked Bandit? You're safer with me than anywhere else."

"Of course." I stood up and held my hands out to her. "Forgive my insolence, my lady."

Trying to hide a smile, she took my hands, and I pulled her into an embrace.

Chapter 25

Elara

"You need to sleep," Cai said when we returned to the palace with my guards trailing behind. "You look exhausted." He was right. I hadn't had a proper sleep in what felt like for ever. And by the looks of it, neither had he.

"You're one to talk," I mumbled. "When was the last time you looked in a mirror?"

Cai chuckled. "Come on, I'll take you up to your chambers."

"How very gentlemanly of you," I replied, eyelids drooping. With my arm linked through Cai's, I leaned all the more into him. Not that he seemed to mind.

"Well, *I am* nothing if not a gentleman." I could practically hear the smile in his voice.

"Humph," I snorted. "Some gentleman you are. You practically kidnapped me after we'd first met."

"Are you ever going to let me forget that?"

"I wouldn't hold my breath if I were you."

Cai let out a laugh. It was good to hear him laugh again. We took the stairs in comfortable silence. But with every step, it became more of a battle to keep my eyes open. I faltered, yawning. My guards stood at the end of the hallway as I'd insisted, and they no longer spend their entire shift right outside my doors.

Mostly because I didn't want them to hear me having nightmares and possibly screaming myself awake.

Cai led me to my chambers. When we reached the doors and he turned to leave, I took hold of his arm.

"Don't go." It was barely above a whisper. I didn't know exactly what I was asking. Only that I didn't want to be alone.

He lingered on the threshold a moment longer before stepping inside my room and closing the door.

One of the servants had lit a fire, giving the room some light and warmth.

Cai sat on the bed while I made my way to the washroom.

I splashed my face with some cold water and took all the pins out of my hair, longing to slip out of my clothes and let sleep take me. I put on a clean shift and covered it with a nightdress which wasn't necessary, but the extra layer added some warmth.

When I stepped back into the room, Cai was lying on the bed with his legs dangling off the side, his boots discarded on the floor. His eyes were closed, and he looked so peaceful, but I could tell from his breathing that he wasn't quite asleep yet.

He felt my presence and lazily opened an eye, giving me half a smile. I picked up my brush from the dressing table and started to pull it through my hair, suddenly very aware that the two of us were alone in my room.

"Was this your mother's room?"

"Yes." I cleared my throat. "I moved in here after I was crowned."

"Did you redecorate it?" He was now propped up on his elbows.

"No," I said, looking around the room. "It's pretty much exactly as my mother had left it, apart from my clothes." I hadn't even thought about redoing any of the décor in the palace. There always seemed to be something more important to worry about.

"I haven't gone into my father's rooms since he died."

I stopped brushing my hair. Cai didn't wait for me to respond. He sat up, elbows resting on his thighs.

"When they told me he'd passed away in his sleep, I disappeared into the woods, not wanting anyone at court to see me fall apart. And when I returned to Mistwood, I could never bring myself to go back into those rooms again. After I was crowned, I continued to stay in my old chambers and had his closed off. Some days I walk past them and contemplate going inside. But I never do."

"Why?" I asked softly.

Cai had a far-off expression, sadness lingering in his eyes. "I think being there, where he died, and seeing all his things would make it too real. I never felt ready to face it."

I'd never known my parents and thus their passing caused no sense of a void in my life. Even though I'd mourned Uncle Arthur, the only father figure I'd ever known, he'd never been affectionate or told me that he loved me. But Cai and his father had been close. They'd shared a bond that I'd never known or experienced. And Cai was thrown into the deep waters of ruling a kingdom without being ready. That I could empathise with.

But Cai had a legacy to live up to and a secret that could destroy his kingdom. The weight on his shoulders had to be immense.

I walked over to him and stood between his legs. "I am so sorry, Cai."

He wrapped his arms around my waist and pressed his head to my stomach. I'd never been a particularly comforting person, but it was all I could offer him in that moment.

"I'm sorry you had to lose him. And I'm sorry for everything else that we're facing."

My fingers curled into his hair as I held him.

"What if I'm not good enough?" he said, after a few moments. "What if I can't protect them all?"

"Look at me." I took his face into my hands and forced him to look up. "You're good enough to me."

His eyes told me that he didn't quite believe me.

"You care more about your people and your kingdom than anyone, and that's what makes you a good king. You're the leader they need."

"I faced Aries' army on the battlefield once," he said, with a haunted expression. "I don't know if I can do it again."

I brushed my thumb across his cheek.

"If we have to do it, then we'll do it together."

He continued to look up at me, chin resting against my torso. The room was silent apart from our breathing and the crackling from the fireplace.

I bent down to kiss him, and in an instant Cai pulled me tight against him. My hands moved to his strong shoulders.

Cai coaxed my lips apart and I let out a sigh. I wanted to be closer still.

His hands slid down the back of my nightdress and lifted me onto the bed so that I was straddling him.

Suddenly wide awake, I couldn't help but think back to the library at Mistwood and how he'd made me feel things I'd never felt before.

Cai had managed to create a need in me. A need for a certain kind of intimacy and closeness that I had yet to experience.

Breathing became a second priority as his mouth possessed my own.

Cai's hands slid up my back and began to undo my nightdress.

I was filled with both apprehension and eagerness at the possibility of what was to come. My skin felt flush as heat that had nothing to do with the temperature in the room settled over me.

The King of Norrandale took his time removing my nightdress, as if he wanted to savour the moment. The heavy material dropped to the floor, and I was left in only my white shift, much like the one I'd worn on the night we first met.

His hands slid over the curves of my body, exploring me in a way he hadn't before. I pulled at his shirt, and he helped me lift it up over his head. I allowed my hands to graze over the muscles of his torso, admiring the strength of him. He wrapped his arms around me and turned us so that he could lower me onto the bed.

I grasped his upper arms as the mattress sank beneath our weight. Cai's hand slowly slid up my leg until it reached under my shift, and I shivered. His mouth placed soft kisses on my jawline and down my neck, all the way to my collarbone.

I clutched at him with greedy hands, wrapping my legs around him, and Cai breathed out my name with a trace of desperation.

He rested his forehead against me.

"I long for you in ways I haven't longed for anyone. In ways I will never long for anyone else again." His voice broke through the darkness of the room as the embers of the fire began to dull.

I trailed my hands up to his face. "You have me."

My heart beat wildly and I wondered if he could hear it.

His hands were at my hips, my shift bunched up between his fingers. His eyes stared deeply into mine as if he hoped to read my mind.

"Don't say it if you don't mean it. I want all of you, Elara, most of all your heart."

"I mean it." I pulled his mouth back to mine. Cai deepened the kiss, stating all his intentions as his mouth moved over mine.

He gently moved between my legs, and I trembled beneath him.

Whatever composure I might have possessed was long gone. Cai's movements were careful, yet urgent, igniting a fire I wasn't sure could ever be put out.

My hands were everywhere, his hair, his neck, and digging into his back, needing something to hold on to.

Cai's teeth grazed my neck before he continued to press long, ravishing kisses to my bare skin. No longer was there a wall or any sort of distance between us. I could not tell where I ended and he began as the two of us merged together, our souls intertwined. Nothing would ever be the same again.

The last of the flames in the hearth sizzled through my veins, coursing through my entire body. And for him, I would burn.

Cai's hands clung to me as if I were something precious and fragile. I arched against him, holding on to him as if I were holding on to dear life itself.

"I think you'll be the death of me," he murmured against my lips, in a low, deep voice, and it was my undoing.

"We have a big day ahead of us tomorrow. A serious meeting will need to be held regarding our state of affairs with Argon," Cai said, much later, sitting up in bed.

"What do I care about Argon?" I said into the pillow, with my eyes closed. "It's not as if we're married or anything."

Cai pinched my side, and I jerked while suppressing a laugh.

"It appears I'll just have to marry you whether I want to or not. You're so in love with me, who knows what you might do to yourself if I refuse."

I kicked his leg in response and received an "ow" in return.

"Some fiancé you are." I turned around and sat up against the headboard, pulling one of the pillows to my chest.

"I'm sorry, is there someone else you'd rather marry?" he joked, but it was enough to make me hesitate.

"Do you remember the Darwicks? When we stayed at their estate?"

"I remember drinking too much wine and not kissing you when I should have."

I had to refrain from grinning, keeping my mind on the important matter at hand.

"Somehow Darwick managed to find out about my past and he's now using it as leverage to try and manipulate me into marrying Edgar."

Cai was quiet for a moment. "And the only way to prevent that from happening was if you secured an alliance with a king. To become too powerful for them to risk threatening you."

I took the liberty of taking his hand in mine. "If I only wanted a king, I could have gone to anyone." I lightly bumped his shoulder. "You know I hear King Aries is quite a looker."

Cai scrunched his brow. "Why are you telling me this now?"

"Because I'm trying to be open and honest. And honestly, I'm more afraid of the Darwicks than I would like to admit. That family holds a lot of power in this kingdom."

Cai seemed to gather his thoughts for a moment. "So, Edgar isn't really your type, huh?"

I laughed softly at the unexpected comment as my eyelids drooped. "Don't even get me started."

He put his arm around me, and I rested my head on his shoulder. "Don't worry, Elara. We'll figure all of this out together."

I drifted off as he placed a kiss on my hair.

Breakfast was never particularly exciting. It was a time for Rhen or Anesta to brief me on everything I needed to do for the day. It was a time to fuel my body with breakfast foods because the guilt crept up on me for having more than others. It had never been a time for pleasantries and social gathering. Until this morning.

The whole lot of us were seated at the table, all trying to avoid eye contact. The silence hanging in the air was almost unbearable.

Lance downed one drink after the other while I resisted the urge to knock the cup out of his hand before he made a fool of either of us. Although, with every passing second, the need for something stronger than orange juice increased.

Cai looked too stressed to eat, while Gwen and Thatcher were constantly at each other, bickering and insulting in a sibling manner. Anesta sat quiet and invisible, watching the spectacle.

Thatcher finally turned his attention to the rest of the table. "Now that we're all reunited, what are our plans for the day?"

"You've all had long journeys," Lance replied. "Perhaps a day of rest is in order." I was surprised by his hospitality. But then I remembered it was the wine talking.

"Sounds like a plan to me." Gwen let out a yawn. "I'd like to explore the palace grounds if you don't mind, Your Majesty." She looked at me for approval.

"Be my guest, Lady Gwen."

"Thank you." Gwen appeared excited at the prospect of exploration. "You wouldn't happen to have an archery range, would you? I'd hate to lose all my skills while away from home."

"Unfortunately not," Lance replied for me. "Besides, my sister isn't much of an archer. But I assume you know this."

I should have expected this kind of behaviour from Lance, but I didn't exactly need a reminder of my embarrassing attempt at archery in Norrandale.

"It must run in the family," I cut back at him.

"There isn't much to entertain outside, I'm afraid," Lance continued, ignoring me. "But the dungeons are particularly lovely since we recently redecorated."

Now he sent a look my way and I was ready to throw my fork at him.

Gwen stopped us by returning to the subject. "What about the stables? I bet you have some fine horses, Your Majesty?"

Lance surprised us all by saying, "Perhaps I could give you a tour."

My eyes widened, but then again, of course Lance would say something to create more tension. Gwen didn't appear very eager to accept the offer. Lance had been to Norrandale before, so he'd met Gwen and Thatcher a few years ago but I was not surprised that Gwen hadn't taken a liking to him. Few people did.

"Absolutely not," Cai interjected. I couldn't blame him. He had even less reason to trust Lance than I did. He probably still carried a scar or two from the night Lance and his guards beat him at Woodsbrook Manor. It was the last time the two of them had seen each other and the tension was obvious. "Lady Anesta can escort you."

Lance's expression revealed nothing at Cai's words.

I shifted my gaze to him. "I need to gather the council, if you could help me."

Lance replied with a sigh. "If I must."

I stared at him for a moment and wondered, again, how we were related.

"Well." Thatcher clapped his hands. "That leaves you and me, Cai. What do you say we give the old training yard a go, see if Evernean steel hits the same?"

Lance snorted before trying to cover it up with a cough, and I sent a scowl his way.

"Maybe later." Cai's eyes bored into his plate, and Thatcher frowned but didn't say anything else. The dining hall descended into silence once more.

Lance let out another loud sigh and leaned back in his chair, cup in hand. "Aren't family meals just lovely?"

I remained in the council room after the meeting.

Though the engagement was official, treaties and documents were still to be drawn up. There was hesitance about the alliance when the possibility of war came into the picture, but we spent our time coming up with possible solutions and tactics. It would be long before we were ready for battle, should it come down to it, but at the very least there were plans.

The tension during the meeting was evident with every conversation and I wanted nothing more than for Cai to hold my hand. But I needed to appear like the strong and courageous queen they so desired. While not everyone was entirely on board with the marriage, the general agreement seemed to be that this was in the best interests of the Evernean kingdom.

A royal wedding gave the people something to celebrate and the hope of an heir.

Argon had not declared war on Norrandale *yet*, and the council hoped that an alignment between Norrandale and Everness would dissuade Aries from escalating the situation further. But armies might still need to be prepared until the threat diminished. And nothing was entirely set in stone until someone said "I do". I reminded myself that the day wasn't over and that I probably had more tasks to attend to, but I couldn't help lingering a little. The thought twisted and turned in my head, and yet, I still found myself struggling to believe it. I was going to marry Cai. Cai and I would be married. Together. For ever.

There was a sudden knock but I didn't look away from the window. Didn't want to be pulled away from my thoughts just yet. "Come in."

The door creaked and someone entered. I couldn't keep a smile from forming at the familiar scent of him. Though it quickly turned to a frown when the usual smell of Cai's fragrance became clouded with a hint of smokiness. I turned to face him, only to be met by Thatcher's intense gaze.

I practically jumped at the surprise of him standing so close behind me.

"Thatcher?" I sucked in a breath and took a step back.

His brow scrunched. "Who did you think it was, Your Majesty?" When I remained silent, his expression turned to a smirk before he said, "Ahh, you thought I was Cai? How very disappointed you must be."

I immediately felt heat creeping up my neck, embarrassed. "Was there something you wanted to tell me?" I cleared my throat.

"Yes, actually, Your Majesty, I came to inform you that there's been an urgent letter from your friend, and I thought you would like to know what it says."

"What friend?"

"What did the messenger say?" He pressed his fingers to his brow, trying to remember. "Ray, I believe it was."

Ray?

If Ray had news, it could only be about one thing.

"The messenger said it must go directly into the hands of the Queen." He took a folded paper out from behind his back. "And I assured him I would place it in your hands myself."

I was so anxious and eager to find out what the content of the letter was that I didn't care to ask why Thatcher was receiving my mail for me. I simply made to grab it.

With urgency, I ripped off the wax seal and unfolded the note with Ray's handwriting.

I found her …

He didn't say where she was, only that he was on his way back to Levernia.

I rushed past Thatcher and threw open the door. He stood in surprise, still holding an imaginary letter in his hand.

I hurried through the hallways in the hope of finding Cai. I had to tell him that Ray had finally tracked Eloisa down. I peeked into the library, where I found Jack browsing through the books.

"Have you seen Cai?" He flinched for a second as if caught doing something he wasn't supposed to do, but I honestly didn't mind him borrowing some of the books and I hoped he knew that. It wasn't like I was going to read them anyway.

"No, I haven't, Your Majesty. Is something wrong?"

"Thankfully, no. I just need to tell him something."

"I see." He nodded and assumed an upright stance, his hands hanging uncomfortably at his sides.

I lingered in the doorway. "Jack, can I ask you something and will you promise to answer me honestly?"

He scanned left and right, confirming that we were indeed alone in the library. "Yes, Your Majesty?"

"Do you think Cai is all right? With everything happening surrounding Argon and the engagement, I've grown worried about him. He doesn't seem quite himself."

"I think …" Jack took a breath. "I think he's worried."

"What do you think is bothering him so much?" I knew Cai had plenty on his mind. We all did. But I was missing pieces of the puzzle.

"Everything, Your Majesty."

Cai had told me the haunting tales about the war with Argon, his eyes glazed over as he stared into the distance, awakening the demons in his memories. His face told stories of bloodied steel against steel. And yet I couldn't help but feel that I hadn't heard all there was to it. Jack was there with him the whole time. I stepped into the library, closing the door behind me.

"Jack, what really happened on the battlefield that day?"

He let out a long sigh so devastating that I almost regretted asking him, but I needed to know.

"Cai met an Argonian girl. A blacksmith's daughter, I think."

"What?" I blurted out, too loudly. Of all the things in the world that I could have expected Jack to say, this wasn't it.

"They met by accident in the woods one day. Cai had gone for a ride and fell off his horse. She was collecting mushrooms or something of the sort. At first, she didn't know who he was. He'd hurt his ankle, and she took him back to her father's house to help him."

Jack let his finger trace one of the spines of a library book before pulling his hand back, jaw clenched. "When he told me what had happened and that he wanted to see her again, I warned him against it. It was a very bad idea for more reasons than one. Even if she was nice, if she found out he was the Norrandish prince, she could always turn and betray him in one way or another. After all, she was still Argonian. My duty above all else is to protect Cai. And it was simply too risky."

"But?" I urged him on.

"But Cai had already made up his mind and saw her again anyway. I'm not sure if he was truly in love with her or if she was just a friend or something to distract him from the chaos of war. I don't know if he ever told her the truth about who he really was."

"Do you think it was partly because he was trying to get over his heartbreak with Delany?" I asked.

Jack shook his head. "No, Your Majesty. Cai was always fond of Delany, but it was only because he knew he had to marry her. I don't believe he ever truly loved her. Not in the way you're meant to. I daresay he was practically relieved the day she told him that she was going to marry his cousin."

I couldn't help the hint of jealousy that pricked up in the back of my mind.

"One day, the girl didn't show up at their meeting place. He knew something was wrong. So he sent scouts to the village. But Argonian soldiers found them and hell broke loose, fighting and fire and innocent people getting in the way. Cai had never meant for it to happen."

Jack stalked towards the windows, gazing out as he recalled the memory. "The king of Argon's younger brother, Dexus, was fighting at the front then. His guards caught Cai, beat him and dragged him to the village centre. It turned out that one of Dexus' spies had followed Cai and found out about the Argonian girl. They'd caught her, and killed her there in front of him."

I felt the sharp intake of my breath at his words. "Were you and Alastor there when it happened?"

Jack nodded slowly. "I can still see it, and the pictures in my mind make me sick to my stomach, even to this day. Cai tried to fight, of course, but we were injured and outmanned. We didn't stand a chance. It was brutal and awful."

My stomach lurched at the thought of it all. At the idea of what Cai had had to bear. My hand grasped some of the fabric of my skirt as I went to stand next to Jack.

"After she was dead, they beat us until we were unconscious. When we came to, their mutilated bodies surrounded us. We were lucky a group of Cai's soldiers had discovered us and saved us. It was war, after all. Alastor and I buried her. Cai killed Dexus on the battle-field. Drove his sword right through him. Not that it would change anything. After that, he never mentioned a word about it again, and Alastor and I knew better than to bring it up. Something changed inside Cai that day."

"What do you mean?" I crossed my arms, hugging myself.

"The Cai you know isn't the one I went to battle with. He became solely focused on being a good soldier and now a good king, the perfect king. He ... he changed."

"Back in Everness, he told me that he was in love with me. Do you think he lied?" I couldn't help but wonder out loud.

Jack's eyes slowly receded from that faraway place and turned towards me.

"I think Cai was completely unprepared for you. You took him by surprise, and despite his better judgement, he liked you more than he wanted to."

"That's not answering my question." I raised my brow.

"No, I don't think he lied, Your Majesty," Jack admitted, and I felt some sense of relief. "I think—" He hesitated for a moment. "I think Cai would marry you in a heartbeat if he wasn't so afraid."

"Look, Jack." I sighed. "I know I don't exactly have a good reputation or a track record to accommodate it. But my intention was never to hurt Cai, not even in Everness. Lie to him, yes. Steal from him, yes, and occasionally want to murder him because he made me so bloody mad."

Jack released a knowing smile at my words.

"But I never wanted to hurt him."

"I know that. Cai isn't afraid of you hurting him. He's afraid of you getting hurt. He killed Aries' younger brother and Aries is going to want to retaliate, and he'll use you to get back at Cai."

"What was her name?" I asked.

"I don't know." Jack didn't meet my gaze. "Cai never told me."

I took a deep breath, trying to comprehend everything I'd just been told. "I'm sorry about what happened. I wish I could erase the pain he went through, that all of you went through. But," I added, "I'm not an Argonian girl who needs to be saved. And I'm not going to spend the rest of my life fearing a stranger across the ocean."

"You and I know that, Your Majesty," Jack replied. "But I wouldn't bet on changing Cai's mind."

"The treaty still needs to be written and signed. Cai can change his mind about this alliance."

"Cai loves you," Jack said earnestly.

Cai loved me and I loved him. It was as simple and as complicated as that.

Chapter 26

Cai

Though it was still the early hours of the morning, the sun burned hot and bright. The sweat made my shirt to cling to my body. I looked over to where Elara sat astride her mare. Her hunting attire reminded me of our time at Fairfrith camp. A time now lost and long gone with the wind.

When Elara had suggested a hunting trip, I wasn't convinced it was a good idea. We would be far away from the palace, while leaving Lance in charge once again. And although Elara seemed content with the arrangement, I didn't trust him.

Yet she seemed so excited at the prospect of spending a few days in the woods that I would have said yes to anything when she looked at me with those pleading eyes. I suspected she knew just as much.

"You're lagging behind," she called over her shoulder. "At this pace, we're not going to catch anything, *Your Majesty*." Her tone of voice was flirtatious, teasing as she used my title.

"Just admiring the horse's flanks." I made the same joke as I had in Norrandale, and she let out a laugh.

"Do you know where you're going?" I asked, urging my horse forwards so that I could be next to her, our small group of guards riding behind us. Jack and Rhen were in conversation with Cordelia (who'd arrived a few days prior), and Alastor was his usual quiet self.

"Of course I do," she scoffed, as if I'd just asked the most ridiculous question.

"Just checking, Your Majesty."

The weather of the morning changed, and the afternoon grew dark and cold. We caught a few pheasants but nothing of merit, and after a few more hours of riding, we finally set up camp for the evening.

"Everything in order, Your Majesty?" Jack checked up on me again for the umpteenth time in the last hour.

"Please, Jack. Take a seat." I gestured to the log on the other side of the fire.

"I hardly think—" he began, but I interrupted him.

"I royally command you to. Now sit, have something to drink. I doubt Argonian soldiers are just going to jump out of nowhere. You've scanned the surrounding area at least seventeen times now."

"I can't drink while I'm keeping watch." Jack took a seat, though his posture remained tense.

"Then at least have something to eat."

He kept his eyes on the trees above, hand on the hilt of his sword.

"Jack."

He met my gaze.

"It's not your fault."

"I beg your pardon, Majesty?"

"It's not your fault I was poisoned and it's not your fault the Argonian spies broke into the palace that day." And I meant every word. Jack hadn't been the same since we'd left for Everness, and while

267

I appreciated his commitment and efforts to keep me safe, I needed him to let go of the burden he now carried like a second skin. I could tell how much he blamed himself, and I hated it.

Everything in his expression told me that he didn't believe me.

"You've always done your job as you should have. You've always kept my protection as your main priority, Jack, and I still trust you with my life."

He shook his head with a trace of sorrow. "I failed at my job. My single most important duty is to protect you, and I have failed."

"I am still alive. And as long as I'm alive, I want you to remain head of my guard. Even if we do our best, there are things outside our control." Jack had seen me at my best and at my very worst. We'd been through hell together.

"One day I'll make it up to you. I promise."

I was about to respond when Elara's voice rose up behind me. "Do you mind if I join you?"

Jack jumped up and out of his seat. "Please do. I think I'll take a walk around camp again, make sure all is well." He cleared his throat and scurried off.

"I didn't mean to interrupt anything," she said, taking a seat next to me.

"You didn't interrupt."

The cool evening prompted Elara to press up against me. She rubbed her hands together and sucked in a breath. I took her right hand and held it between my own, attempting to create warmth. Elara gave me a smile before looking back at the burning fire.

"How did we find ourselves back in the Evernean Forest in the middle of the night?"

"What do you mean?"

"The night I found you guys while running for my life," she reminded me.

"Ah yes, the night you won't ever let me forget because of that damned tree."

With a chuckle, she nudged my shoulder. "It's still the best night of your life."

"How so?"

"Because it's the night you met me."

I pressed a kiss behind her ear and whispered into her hair, "How could I forget?"

Elara squeezed my hand, and I would have given anything in heaven or on earth to be alone with her in that moment. One day, I told myself. One day we could watch the stars together without the worry of alliances and wars and our duties as monarchs.

We rose with the sun, packing up our small campsite and readying the horses.

"Good morning." Elara braided the last part of her hair before reaching for her horse's saddle.

"Here." Looking for an excuse to touch her, I helped her onto the horse.

"Thank you." She put on her riding gloves. "Hopefully we have better luck with the hunt today."

We had no such luck.

No animal appeared. As if the forest was watching us, protecting its own from our bows and arrows. Not that I minded too much. It was a good distraction from everything that awaited us once we returned.

Speaking of which …

"How do you think things are faring at the palace?" I asked Elara.

"What do you mean?"

"We left Lance, Thatcher and Gwen there unattended," I remarked, as if they were small children in constant need of being watched. Maybe they were.

"True," she admitted. "We'd be lucky to return and find they hadn't destroyed the place yet. Why did we leave them there alone again?"

"Because none of them wanted to go hunting," I answered.

"Right. I'm sure it will be fine regardless. It's a big palace — they'll stay out of each other's way."

"I should think so." Knowing the three of them, she was probably right, and we would be lucky if they hadn't burned the place down.

Suddenly Elara's mare stopped, and it was only when I noticed her grip on the reins that I realised she was the one who had halted the horse.

"Is something wrong?"

"Do you hear something?"

Our guards drew their swords, our hunting party quiet.

I even halted my breathing until finally, very faintly in the distance, there was a sound. It wasn't easily distinguishable, nor could I decipher what exactly the sound was, only the direction it was coming from.

Jack and Alastor moved their horses in front of ours.

"Stay back, Your Majesties," Jack ordered while looking ahead.

Something was coming our way.

We all seemed to hold our breath in anticipation until something broke through the leaves.

A man on a horse came cantering towards us.

The surprise was in it being a familiar man.

"Ray?" Elara said in shock, and his horse reared at the sight of all of us ready to strike him down.

"Whoa." Ray held on to the horse, calming it. It looked like he hadn't slept, as if he'd been riding through the night.

"Ray, are you all right?" Elara said.

He heaved. "What are you all doing here?"

"Hunting," Rhen responded. "What are you doing here?"

"He's found her." Elara didn't give Ray a chance to reply. "He's found Princess Eloisa."

"Where?" I couldn't help but ask.

"She's in Argon," Ray answered.

Rhen suggested we return to the palace, and we all agreed. With the news of Eloisa, sooner was better than later. But we were more than a day's ride away. We'd have to cut our trip shorter somehow, so Rhen took the lead, changing our route.

Of all the places I'd expected Princess Eloisa to be, Argon wasn't one of them. Ray had got lucky in his search. After speaking to the palace soldiers who lost her, he interviewed people in nearby villages and eventually someone said they'd seen her get onto a ship. I looked towards Elara, her face etched with worry.

"Do you think Her Highness simply got on the ship or was made to get onto the ship?" Jack asked, pulling me away from my thoughts.

"I don't know. With the number of spies Aries has doing his bidding, I can't say I'm surprised he found her and brought her under his 'protection' or whatever he's going to call it."

"Aries will most likely try and use her as some form of bargaining chip against us," Elara commented. I hadn't realised she was listening to our conversation. She'd never met her sister, so it wasn't like there was any form of attachment between them apart from their blood.

But Aries liked to have every possible weapon at his disposal. He would use anyone he could.

"Could you find out anything else about King Aries' army?" I'd never particularly liked Ray, especially because anyone could tell he was in love with Elara. But we were beyond juvenile jealousy at this point.

"Nothing of real value. I wasn't really welcome there, and I'd only managed to find out about Princess Eloisa staying in the palace by word of mouth. I didn't see her."

"Then how we do we even know she's truly there and they are not just rumours?"

"She's there," Elara said with certainty. "She has to be."

We set up camp as the sun began to set, the shadows of the forest merging into night. I brushed down my horse, needing my hands to do something. I was on edge, my stomach in a twist. It felt as though danger lurked behind every tree and that it would only be a matter of time before Aries finally caught up to us.

My eyes searched for Elara in the camp's firelight. She was perched on a nearby fallen log, the dagger I'd gifted her in her hands. She turned it carefully, inspecting the weapon as if it held some deeply guarded secret.

My horse gave a small neigh as it gobbled up every blade of grass it could find. I petted the animal's neck gently.

When I looked back up, Ray was seated next to Elara. I tried not to take note of the proximity between them, or the prick of unwanted jealousy it caused within me. Ray had been her closest friend since childhood, and I knew how important he was to her. But I also saw the way Ray looked at Elara.

"I can't believe you actually found her," I heard Elara say. "I mean, I knew you could do it but ..." She sighed. "Argon, of all places."

"I was just as surprised when I found out."

"I'd just assumed she was hiding somewhere in Everness, possibly out in the country and away from all the trouble at court. But this is going to be a lot more complicated than I thought, especially with King Aries coming after Norrandale."

"I heard Cai killed Aries' younger brother in battle." My heartbeat increased at Ray's words and at the horrid memories it brought up.

"It's about more than that. Aries is after something else."

"What do you mean?"

Elara hesitated and I feared what she would say. Whether she would betray my trust by telling Ray about Norrandale's biggest secret.

She wouldn't do it, I told myself.

"Norrandale has some very valuable land that could make King Aries even more powerful."

A breath of relief escaped me.

"It always seems to be about power with these people."

"I'm one of these people now, in case you forgot, Ray."

"No, you're not. You're not like them, Lara. How long are you going to pretend?"

"Pretend?" Her voice rose a little. "You think I'm just pretending? This is my life now. This is who I am, and if you can't accept that …" She shook her head. "Then you're not the same person I grew up with."

"If anyone's changed then it's you. You used to hate these people and now you're trying to marry a king."

"I'm going to marry a king," she insisted.

"Don't marry him, Lara."

I stiffened but resisted the urge to intervene.

"Why not?" She was clearly annoyed.

"Because you don't need him or his kingdom. You are strong enough to rule on your own." He placed his hand atop hers, and my fist clenched at my side.

"You know nothing of this world," she said, more softly now. "If I don't marry him then I won't survive my reign."

"But are you really willing to spend the rest of your life with someone that you don't love?"

Elara looked away and I swallowed hard. Even though she'd said that she would marry me and that she cared for me, Elara had never told me that she loved me. I couldn't blame her. Love was something that took time to grow.

"I know you better than anyone else," Ray persisted. "And I know this isn't going to make you happy."

"You're right," Elara said after a few seconds, and I thought my heart stopped. "I have changed. No matter how much I miss the girl I used to be, I don't think there's any way back to her now."

She removed her hand from Ray's and stood up. "I'm going to marry him. And nothing will change that."

We packed up our little camp and continued our journey back to the palace the next morning. It was early enough that the sun had yet to rise properly. Hues of orange and red surrounded us, while many fallen leaves coated the forest floor.

I wondered what the Evernean Forest would look like in the height of winter. If Aries did plan on attacking Norrandale, I hoped he would wait until spring. The only thing worse than sending an army out was to send them out in the middle of winter. They'd be marching to their deaths.

"How much further until we reach the palace?" Cordelia asked.

None of us had a chance to reply before an arrow came flying out of the trees and straight into Ray's chest.

It happened so quickly, Elara's scream, Ray's body falling to the ground. The guards screamed something. More arrows flew.

I was off my horse before I knew it, running towards Elara.

She was crouched over Ray's body, holding on to him as if it would save his life.

"Elara, we need to go."

"No!" she cried and pulled out of my grasp, her eyes welling with tears.

"I'm sorry but we can't save him." I had to make a choice, no matter how broken Elara's heart was. Her life was more important. And as for Ray … Ray was gone.

She was near hysterical as I pulled her away.

With every second, more armed men emerged from the woods, clad in Argonian armour and symbols. The sight of them seemed to bring her back to some sense of reality. Swords clashed, men cried out in pain, our guards prioritising our protection. I pulled my sword from its sheath, shielding Elara.

Except, when I reached for her, she wasn't behind me anymore. I swerved to see her jumping onto the nearest horse and kicking it into motion.

"Elara, wait!" I called as she galloped away. One of the Argonians came at me before Jack stepped in his way, giving me enough time to mount one of the other horses and set off after her. She couldn't be too far ahead. The trees and branches went by in a blur, the horse's hoofs echoing off the pathway.

My worry intensified with the realisation that I wasn't catching up to her, and so I eventually slowed the horse into a trot. I listened for any sound that could hint at which direction she went in.

A few seconds later, the familiar sound of her scream sent me barrelling forwards. It wasn't long before I realised why.

A white mist started creeping up like it was being exhaled by the trees. *Damn.* With our shortcut, I hadn't thought about how close we were to the centre of the forest. The last time, Elara made the group of us run for our lives when we got this close.

I had to find her before she got hurt.

My horse was tempted to turn away from the haze, but I pushed it onwards, until the mist surrounded us.

The forest was quiet in the middle of the mist.

I woke up alone on the leafy forest floor, with my horse gone. The mist itself was so thick and heavy that I could barely see around myself.

I exhaled with a cough, wondering what kind of mist it was. Based on the myth Elara had told me, it trapped men in this part of the woods until they died. I'd never seen anything like this in my life, and while my instincts warned me to be terrified, I wasn't dead yet.

"Lara!" Calling out her name seemed like the sensible thing to do, but there was no response.

I had no idea which direction I'd come from, and I was starting to understand all the more why she had warned us against the mist during our previous visit to Everness. One truly had no sense of direction. I couldn't see the sky to tell where the sun was and get my bearings.

I shifted my position, my limbs sore from what I suspected was falling off my horse.

I froze at the sound of a growl. Though I couldn't see anything, I could sense something coming towards me.

Fingers digging into the ground, I quickly pushed myself into a standing position.

As the growl grew louder, a wolf emerged from the mist. It looked similar to the one I'd encountered the day we entered Everness for the first time, but this one was larger, deadlier. This was no normal wolf. This was a beast of the forest.

A male scream erupted in the distance, causing both of us to look in that direction, before the wolf turned its attention back to me.

I stood my ground while the wolf continued its approach. It sniffed the air. There was blood on my hand. I must have scraped it when I fell. My mind felt fuzzy and disoriented.

The wolf looked into my eyes as if it was searching for something. As if it was more than just animal. And then, to my surprise, it walked away, disappearing into the mist as if it had never been there at all.

I blew out a breath.

Elara.

I called out her name but there was no response. Only the vastness of the thick mist and the echo of my voice. And so I ran. Surely it couldn't last for ever. It had to end. There had to be a way out. "Elara!"

I ran until my legs started to ache, the mist creating its own maze. It was blinding, consuming. Something ran into me, knocking the air out of my chest. My arms reached forwards instinctively. She smelled sweet. Elara jerked in surprise.

"Cai."

"Are you hurt?"

"No." She let out a breath. "I don't know which way is out."

I didn't care. In that moment, I only cared that she was unharmed. Holding her by the shoulders, I breathed heavily. Too much had happened in too little time.

"I thought I'd lost you."

She met my gaze, her eyes filled with fear. "I'm sorry. I didn't …
I couldn't—" She struggled to find the words.

"We need to find a way out." Later, I told myself. Later there
would be time to process and discuss everything, but first we needed
to get out alive. I took hold of her hand and turned, going back in
the direction I'd come from. Or at least, what I thought was the
direction I'd come from.

We walked in silence, her hand in mine. It may have only been a
few minutes, but it felt like hours had passed. The mist finally began
to fade, and we stepped back into the light of the forest.

"We're out." Elara's tone suggested she almost didn't believe it. She
continued looking around her, as if half expecting the fog to creep up
on us again. "I didn't think we were going to get out."

"I knew we would." I didn't want to tell her that I was starting
to have my own doubts for a while back there. I looked around the
high trees and green branches. There was a path not too far off. "Any
idea where we are?"

"More or less. I think I might be able to find my way back." She
let go of me and started making her way towards where she thought
the road would be.

I stopped in my tracks behind her. "Elara, I'm really sorry
about Ray."

"I don't want to talk about it."

It might have been a coincidence, or it might have been the fact
that she helped save my life with a price she wasn't willing to pay.
I didn't want to think too much about it, but I couldn't help my
eyes from boring holes into her pocket, which I knew carried the
dagger I'd gifted her.

Chapter 27

Elara

Cai and I were taking a morning stroll through the hallways when Anesta crossed our path. "Your Majesties, Cordelia and I are having tea out on the terrace, since the weather is so nice today. You should join us."

"I'd love to, but I actually need to go and see Jack about something, he's probably been looking for me." He gave me a warm smile. "If you ladies will excuse me."

Cai apologised and hurried off as I linked arms with Anesta. "Tea sounds lovely." There was still a hollow feeling in my chest after the events of the past few days. I knew talking about it would probably help but despite spending the morning with Cai, it was like I couldn't get the words out. Perhaps some time with my female friends was the kind of distraction I needed.

A table had been set on the terrace with fine porcelain and sweet treats to accompany the tea. Though I wasn't hungry, my mouth practically drooled at the sight of the caramel truffles and lemon cream pies. I sat down next to Cordelia while a servant filled my cup. She'd

279

only arrived in Everness sometime after the others and despite her joining on the hunt, it felt like we hadn't had much time to catch up.

The palace grounds were busy with servants running about and a few guards doing their rounds.

"Don't tell me you're sitting out here with the hopes of seeing the soldiers train," I teased.

"Of course not," Anesta scoffed. "Unless we happen to see them around somewhere." She looked over her shoulder as she said it, allowing me and Cordelia to chuckle.

"Easy for you to laugh," she retorted with a smile. "You're both in happy relationships." I thought about it for a moment and realised she was right. Cai and I were in a good place. I could only hope it would last.

"Lord Thatcher is quite attractive," Cordelia remarked, and I remembered how he was flirting with Anesta that night at the ball in Norrandale.

"True, but Lord Thatcher has no intention of making serious commitments as far as I've heard," I responded honestly.

"It's always the pretty ones." Anesta sighed.

"What about Rhen?" I suggested, taking a sip of my tea. It was citrussy and I wasn't overly fond of the taste, but it immediately made me feel warmer.

"He's quite a few years older." Anesta shrugged. "I don't think he even takes note of me."

"I would be surprised to see my brother in a relationship," Cordelia responded.

"Why?" I asked.

"I don't know." She tilted her head to the side. "Rhen doesn't really do relationships. At least not publicly. He's always prioritised his duties. When we were young, it was looking after me. But I'm glad to see he makes a good soldier. I think he's happy now."

From experience, I knew what she said to be true. But that didn't mean there wasn't a maid secretly visiting his chambers at night. Not that it was any of my business, anyway.

"Don't worry, Anesta, we'll find you a rich husband," I joked. "You know the Duke of Dankershire is looking for a wife." I raised my eyebrows.

"The one you said wouldn't shut up about horses?"

"What's not to love about horses?"

She laughed and shook her head.

"We cannot just march into Argon." Cai dragged his fingers through his hair with frustration. "We'd only manage to breach the nearest villages, and it would take far too long to reach Myrador Stronghold with an army."

Alastor spoke up. "But we cannot simply wait for them to attack us."

I crossed my arms, glancing at the group of men as we stood in the map room.

"It's clear Aries knows you're both here in Levernia." Rhen referred to me and Cai. "Or he wouldn't have pulled that stunt in the woods the other day."

"If he's just planning to assassinate us, then why would he prepare such a large army?" I asked.

"Killing us would be a lot quicker and less effort. He might even get away with blaming someone else," Cai answered. "But we haven't exactly been that easy to get rid of and he knows it could most likely come down to marching onto a battlefield, a battle he wants to be certain he's going to win."

The words made me shudder. Was Aries out of his mind? Even risking the peace treaty to get rid of Cai. I understood that Cai had killed his younger brother, but still, was it worth getting thousands of others killed? Unless Aries knew something we'd rather he didn't.

I made eye contact with Cai. If Lance had found out by accident, what was preventing Aries from finding out too? He could have been after much more than just me and Cai.

"Are you suggesting it's safer to go back to Norrandale?"

"Not necessarily. Levernia is further away and better guarded. As long as we stay out of the forests," he added.

"But Norrandale is closer to Argon. How are we supposed to defend Norrandale should they decide to attack us?" Jack questioned.

"What if they find out you've gone to Norrandale and attack Levernia instead?" Rhen crossed his arms.

"They would still have to make it past the Evernean border or sail much further north to make it to the coast," Jack replied. The territory along the western coast of Everness didn't allow for many places where you could dock a ship. The tides and rocks were more likely to sink your entire fleet.

"They've already made it inside the kingdom," Rhen said.

"Well, the longer we wait, the more villages will get in the way as collateral damage, and I'm not having that," Cai spoke up.

"It's not like you can just waltz into King Aries' palace and change his mind," Jack commented.

"What if we could?" I said suddenly, and all heads turned in my direction. "Aries hasn't sent out an army yet. The attacks have been in small, calculated groups. Now that we know Eloisa is with him, we can go to Myrador Stronghold with the excuse of getting my sister and renewing the alliance agreements."

"With all due respect," Jack cut in. "This isn't exactly very safe. Especially considering the man has already made several attempts on your life."

"True, but they were all here or in Norrandale," Cai responded. "He can hardly kill all of us in his own court. There are too many diplomats and representatives present from other kingdoms. It's too risky for him. Aries is a bastard, but he's not that stupid."

"The only way we're going to beat him is if we play the game the same way he does. And that doesn't mean playing fairly."

"So what do you plan to do when you get there, Your Majesty?" Rhen asked. "Slit his throat?"

"I haven't thought that far," I admitted. "But I think it's better to be on the offence rather than the defence. It's the only way we might get the upper hand."

"Do you think there is any part of Aries that would be willing to negotiate?" Alastor said, after minutes of silence from his side.

"Considering how many times he's already violated the peace treaty, I would hardly hold my breath." Cai inspected the map again. "Showing up at Aries' court uninvited might throw him off guard just enough for us to come up with a more solid plan."

We spent a few days preparing for the sea voyage that would take us across the ocean to Argon. Gwen and Thatcher remained in Everness for the time being. I was going to miss Gwen's company but every person who came along to Argon was at risk.

With every hour bringing us closer to the borders of our enemy, I wrestled with the nerves inside me.

"Have you ever been on a ship before?" Cai asked when we reached the docks. We'd decided to sail straight from Everness rather than waste time travelling through Norrandale, even if its border was closer to Argon. But Levernia was far away from the sea and we had to travel all the way to Woodsbrook, one of the few places that actually had a harbour.

"What makes you think I've never been on a ship before?" I asked, watching as the sailors loaded our luggage.

"You're very pale."

I clenched my jaw. "I'll be fine."

"This was your idea, remember?"

Of course I remembered, but that didn't mean I'd thought it through when I said it.

"If we die because of a sea storm, I'm coming back to haunt you."

Cai took my hand, leading me up to the deck. "Don't worry. I'll make sure you don't fall overboard."

"Very funny," I muttered, though grateful he was holding on to me. I hated the feeling of the ground constantly moving beneath my feet. How did sailors and fishermen do this for a living?

I didn't go below deck much during our journey. The spaces were too dark and confined and reminded me of the prison cell in Everness. Thankfully, I didn't get seasick, though I didn't have much of an appetite either.

"Are you still all right?" Cai made a habit of constantly checking on my welfare.

I nodded, resting my arms on the ship's handrail while I stared into the horizon.

"I'm fine."

He remained standing next to me. "I didn't think I'd be going back to Argon this soon," Cai admitted. "Maybe I hoped I wouldn't have to go back ever."

I thought about what awaited us once we reached the shore.

"Cai, how much did you know about Eloisa?" I finally brought up the topic that had been bothering me all this time.

"Not much." He looked intrigued at my question. "Apparently, she kept to herself a lot, though I didn't hear anything scandalous. Why?"

"Lance finally admitted why she was so separated from society, why no one ever really saw her. According to him, she has these ... episodes."

"Episodes?"

"I'm not exactly sure what happens to her, but Lance described them as a kind of fit. They come and go. Sometimes she's fine and normal, and other times she's screaming for no reason. I think she's ill."

"And this is the princess Lance wanted to marry me off to?"

"I think Everness hoped it would be a marriage on paper. I don't think it was intended for you to find out. Regardless, who knows what state we'll find her in."

He was silent for a long time. "Why didn't you tell me Ray had found her?"

I bit my lip. "I was going to, as soon as I'd heard, actually."

"What stopped you?"

"I ran into Jack while looking for you." I squeezed the wooden railing of the ship, looking over to where Jack was sitting with Cordelia, sharing lunch. Jack had insisted she stay behind, and Cordelia had insisted he was being overprotective for no reason. "I told him I was worried about you and, well—"

"Well, what?"

I shook my head. "I don't want you to be mad at him."

"Why would I be mad? What did he say?"

After another moment of hesitation, I said, "He told me the story of the girl in Argon."

Cai's eyes widened and his face lost all colour.

"You were already so stressed with everything going on, and I didn't want to upset you more. I know I should have said something sooner, but the right time never came around."

He looked down into the water with a deep sigh. "War asks more of us than we can afford," Cai said. "We've all lost someone."

And I knew what he meant. Knew we'd yet to talk about Ray and what happened in the forest. I couldn't bring myself to say his name out loud. Couldn't admit that I didn't know how to grieve my oldest friend. Not when everyone needed me to be strong now more than ever. Not when everyone needed a queen they could count on.

Tears welled up in my eyes and I pushed them back. Cai pulled me into his embrace so he could wrap his arms around me from behind.

"Whatever happens, promise me you'll stay alive," he said.

"As long as you promise the same."

He only pulled me closer in response.

War could take what it wanted from me, but it could not take him.

Argon was a land of sand and heat. The fields close to the rivers boasted lush grass and tall palm trees. Within the main city, an oasis of water and greenery burst up and out of the dust. Myrador Stronghold was unlike anything I'd ever seen before. We waited outside in the palace courtyard, in a slightly awkward fashion. This was hardly protocol, though I supposed things were done differently in Argon. Waiting gave us ample opportunity to stare at the soldiers in the training yard, not too far off.

The soldiers weren't in their armour or uniforms. Instead, the sun glinted off their naked backs, their only covering a garment around the waist. Each soldier's legs and arms appeared to be stronger and bigger than the one next him.

"You could just slather them in honey and call it dessert," Anesta said next to me, probably not having intended to say it out loud.

"Anesta." I bumped her with my elbow as Cordelia's eyes widened.

"Look at them." Anesta didn't shift her gaze. "Have you ever seen any other men like them?"

"They're just showing off," Jack muttered, and Cai's face carried a look of distaste.

"Right, because they knew we were coming and wanted to impress us." Cordelia snorted.

"You could always join them," I teased, and all heads turned towards me. "I'm sure none of the ladies would complain to see you remove that much clothing."

"Your Majesty!" Rhen dared to scold me, but Cai tried to hide a smile. Amid the group's inappropriate staring, a servant arrived, informing us the King was ready to see our party.

The interior of Aries' palace was little different to the exterior. Thick sandstone pillars supported high ceilings, allowing for large open windows. The floors were marble, while the entire palace was full of fountains. Had I not been so nervous, the sound of all the trickling water might have calmed me. As we made our way to the throne room, I noticed how many people were inside the palace. Did they all live here? There were more soldiers, standing guard, as well as the nobles.

The women's attire looked very different from the kind of fashion I was used to. Some of them wore dresses that barely had any sleeves, with belts pulling the material together at their waist. It was simple, yet elegant. Others wore long skirts with tops that had puffy sleeves and barely covered their stomachs.

The throne room had no wall on one side. Instead, it led out onto a large balcony that overlooked the city.

And at the far end, King Aries reclined atop a sandstone throne.

Chapter 28

Cai

King Aries wore a deep smirk.

His malicious expression alone made me want to punch him in the face.

"Prince Cai." He rolled his shoulders back and reclined on his throne, which was covered with animal pelts. "We finally meet again."

"It's King Cai, actually," Jack corrected him.

"Oh, that's right." He took a sip of whatever was in his golden cup. I sensed the hidden glare behind his gaze. "I'd forgotten you were crowned."

Liar.

He hadn't forgotten anything. He was simply looking for a way to verbally diminish me.

"This is Linus and Theuses. They're diplomats from the kingdoms of Cedia and Briarstead. We were just discussing some upcoming social events. There's to be a banquet soon. How ideal that it coincides with your visit."

The two men bowed their heads in greeting, followed by a "Your Majesty".

Aries' silver eyes shifted to Elara, and I tensed at the way they roamed her body.

"Well, aren't you going to introduce me, King Cai?" Even with the correct title, he managed to mock me.

I instinctively reached for her hand, and she laced her fingers with mine.

"Aries, this is Elara, Queen of Everness."

He tilted his head. "You know I heard a tall tale that the two of you were engaged."

Elara's hand stiffened in mine.

"But you can never be sure these days with all the rumours going about. It's so difficult to know what is fact and what is fiction."

"It certainly is," she replied.

"But then I thought that there was no way the two of you could be so foolish. Everness and Norrandale aligning? One might even call it an act of aggression against Argon. I'm sure the other kingdoms on the continent wouldn't be able to ignore it either." He looked to the diplomats for confirmation.

Linus, a tall man with long grey hair that had been neatly tied, chose to reply. "Cedia would definitely take an interest if Everness and Norrandale were to be united. Even if it was merely for the sake of considering new alliances." What he didn't say was that if Everness and Norrandale united, they would become a slightly bigger threat to some of the kingdoms on the continent.

This was a reckless game, and we were all playing with our very worst intentions.

"If one should be so lucky as to find an ally, one must certainly protect it. Trust is such a rare thing these days," Theuses added.

"Very true words there." Aries snapped his fingers and a servant showed up with a tray of wine. The servant offered to pour but Aries took the jug, ready to pour himself. He was mid-act when he looked up and met all our stares.

"Forgive me, would anyone else like anything to drink?" Our group remained silent. "This visit is most unexpected, but pleasant nonetheless."

"Surely you must know why we are here," Elara said confidently. Aries gave her a look of challenge.

"I've heard my sister resides in your court. I've come to collect her."

"And you decided to bring the King of Norrandale with you?"

"Cai was visiting my court. And since there is a peace treaty between Argon and Norrandale, it seemed like the perfect opportunity to revise the agreement. Two birds with one stone and all." Her smile was decadent but fake.

"I must admit, the resemblance is quite eerie." He rubbed his mouth. "I've heard many stories about the lost heir of Everness. It's lovely to finally meet you in person."

"If my sister has been here for the past few months, then surely by now you know of her illness and therefore I think it would be best if she were to return to Everness with me."

Aries scanned all of us slowly. "You want to take Eloisa with you."

"I think now that things have settled in Everness, it would be better for her to be home with her family."

"Ah yes, how is Prince Lance? He must have been the shortest ruling king in the history of the kingdom." He let out a laugh. "I heard he's quite fond of the bottle."

I sensed Elara bite the inside of her cheek to prevent herself from saying something she would later come to regret. "He's just fine."

Aries clapped his hands together, making Cordelia jump. "Shall we all have dinner together this evening?"

"Thank you for your hospitality, but I think we're all quite tired from our journey and would prefer to take dinner in our chambers." The last thing I wanted was to share a dinner table with this man, but I knew I wouldn't be able to avoid it for ever.

His eagle eyes swayed back to Elara, and he stood up from his throne, holding out a hand. "Would you like me to take you to your sister?"

Elara stepped forwards but didn't take his hand. He must have noticed me about to follow because he pointed in the opposite direction.

"I'll have my servants take you to your chambers." He looked to Linus and Theuses. "We can continue our conversation later." Two servants stood ready to guide us and I clenched a fist at my side. I didn't want Elara alone with Aries, but I also didn't want to cause a fight within the first few minutes of our arrival.

I sent a look Rhen's way and he gave a small nod, following a distance behind the two of them. At least there would be someone to keep an eye on her. I followed the servants to my rooms.

Chapter 29

Elara

King Aries looked younger than I had expected. Still, he had to be at least a decade older than Cai. I wasn't sure why I'd thought he would be further along in age. Maybe because everyone appeared so threatened by him all the time. Not to say I was entirely at ease. Every time his silver eyes looked at me, it felt as though he was staring right through my very being. Like he could tell all my secrets from one simple glance.

I followed behind him, trying to keep as much distance between us as possible.

I half expected Aries to make small talk but thankfully he remained quiet, strolling on. He was so much taller than me, and his hair was short and neat.

I walked after him until we stopped in front of a bedroom door.

He opened it and stepped to the side, allowing me to look inside. I didn't have to walk into the room to see her.

Princess Eloisa sat on a comfortable chair, looking out the window. Her back was turned to me, but Eloisa's side profile was enough to make me feel as though I were looking in a mirror. It was eerie, and I felt a twinge in my gut.

I expected her to look up at the sound of us, but she didn't move, only staring into the distance. It didn't even look like she was blinking.

"How long has she been like this?" I asked Aries.

"Since the day after she arrived here. We have servants take care of her and she eats a little, but other than that, she's catatonic."

"She hasn't had any outbursts?" The kingdom of Argon knowing about Princess Eloisa's mentally ill state probably wasn't something we needed, but there was nothing to be done now.

"No, just staring into the distance, refusing to speak. It's like she can't even hear you."

"Eloisa?" I tried anyway, but there was no movement.

"Has she always been like this?" Aries asked.

"My brother tells me so." I shrugged.

"And no healer could find a cure?" How was I to know what kind of doctors and physicians Eloisa had seen throughout her life?

"Eloisa," I tried again. Still no response.

"I should probably get to my room. I'm quite tired after our journey." I stepped back in a hurry. This was all becoming very weird, very quickly.

"Of course. I hope our rooms are to your liking." Aries was smirking again, and it unnerved me. I really hoped coming here wouldn't be a mistake.

"This is a disaster." I dramatically fell back onto the bed of the guest bedroom I was occupying for the duration of our stay in Argon.

"I wouldn't call it a disaster just quite yet." The bed dipped as Cai took a seat next to me.

"Your optimism inspires me to be a better person, really," I said sarcastically and patted his leg.

Cai let out a chuckle before his face got serious. "Are you all right, though?"

"You mean with Eloisa?" I pulled myself up into a sitting position. "I'm not sure how I feel just yet."

"It must have been strange."

"I think Lance should be relieved to find out she's safe and unharmed at least."

"Well, I wouldn't say I have a particular care for Lance's feelings." He scooted back to lie down and I joined him. We were exhausted. It had been a long day.

"Unfortunately, Lance did a little too much damage just to be forgiven without consequence. Though I will admit his advice has been helpful at times. Even if he only cares to help me as long as he can get something out of it."

"What advice are you talking about?" Cai asked.

"I already told you: he said I should marry you."

"Yes, the one and only reason you're marrying me: because Lance said so."

"Ha." I pinched him softly. "Very funny."

Cai's brow creased. "Lance said that Eloisa managed to escape under the watch of her palace guards, right? And then someone saw her at the docks?"

"Yes," I said, not entirely sure where he was going with this.

"Do you think it's a coincidence she ended up here with Aries?" We'd had this conversation before, wondering just how Eloisa managed to fall right into the hands of our enemy. It was too convenient. Too coincidental.

295

"I'm rather sure Aries orchestrated it. But to what end?"

"He could've lured us here for many different reasons."

I shuddered, not wanting to admit that Aries could be so much smarter than me and that maybe there was a good reason people feared him.

"I think I need a break from being queen." I rubbed my tired eyes and then remembered I was probably smudging the kohl that Anesta had lined them with.

"We could always go away after the wedding." Cai wiggled his eyebrows, and I gave him a look.

"You know what I mean." I tried to ignore the heat crawling up my neck.

"Try and get a good night's rest, at least, and you'll already feel better by morning." He sat up.

"I'll feel better when this is over."

"That too." He placed a soft kiss on my cheek before saying goodnight.

I was on my way to breakfast the next morning with a rumbling stomach. Anesta hadn't spared any effort with my attire, though I'd begged her to keep it as simple as possible. I didn't feel like fancy dresses and glamorous accessories today. It was too hot anyway. It didn't feel like winter was approaching in this desert of a place.

As I walked down the halls, I found myself craving freshly squeezed orange juice, and then wanted to laugh at the realisation. How very spoiled and privileged I'd become.

Back in Camp Fairfrith, breakfast wasn't even always available, and here I was planning to satiate my hunger with a decadent breakfast spread.

"Good morning, Eloisa."

I froze at the sound of King Aries' voice behind me, combined with disbelief. Eloisa?

Had something happened last night after I saw her? Had she woken up from her episode and talked to Aries, so he now thought I was her?

He can only see the back of your head, I reminded myself. Or had he been lying and she hadn't been in that state since the day after she'd arrived?

I turned around and plastered a smile on my face. I'd pretended to be Eloisa before. How difficult could it be? My mind continued to remind me involuntarily that, the last time, things didn't exactly work out very well. But if something suspicious was going on, I wanted to find out.

"Morning." I swallowed audibly.

Aries approached confidently. He was dressed in a fine tunic, a large knife sheathed at his waist. I started to sense why everyone dressed the way they did in Argon. The sunbeams streaming in through the large open windows alerted me that it was going to be another scorcher of a day.

"Shall we go to breakfast together?" He extended his arm, and I hooked mine in the crook of his elbow.

Bad idea. Bad idea. Bad idea.

Too late to back out now.

If he did believe I was Eloisa, he might divulge information which could be of value to us.

Something inside me dreaded seeing her again, even though I knew I couldn't avoid Eloisa for the rest of my life. Her behaviour made me understand why Lance carried such a haunting expression when he talked about her. I believed Eloisa needed help. But this was something we could look into once we were all safely returned to Everness ... or Norrandale. Cai and I hadn't exactly discussed what would happen when all of this was over.

Aries slowed our pace, and my stomach dropped. I could just pretend I didn't hear him call me Eloisa. Elara, Eloisa, it all sounded very much alike.

"What are your plans for the day?" he asked, looking at me.

I avoided eye contact with all my might, afraid he might see through me before I could get anything out of him.

"I'm not sure. What are *your* plans for the day?"

He chuckled at the way I asked him. "I'll probably have to see Cai again. Try and figure out what exactly the idiot's plan is for thinking he could just march into my palace. He really isn't fit to be king. Argon should have taken over Norrandale a long time ago."

I had to bite back a bitter reply, forcing me to clear my throat.

"And why exactly is it so important to end Cai's reign again?" I posed the question with the sweetest, most innocent voice I could muster.

"It's nothing personal against Cai. Norrandale just has something that I want."

Which was exactly what I was worried about. If Aries had any inkling of Norrandale's secret, we were in so much bigger trouble than just a war.

"Oh?" I feigned casual interest.

We only took a few more steps before he shoved me against the nearest wall, that previously sheathed knife now against my throat.

"Now." He bit his lip, and I sucked in a breath of fear. "How about we stop pretending and you tell me what it is, exactly, that *you* want, Queen Elara?" He practically purred my name.

"If you knew it was me then why did you—?"

"I wanted to see if you were capable of lying. Now I will ask again — what do you want?"

I breathed slowly, wanting to keep as much composure as possible with the knife against my throat. I didn't want to show him my fear. So, I licked my lips and gave a smile. "Don't we all want the same thing on the same basic level?" He held my stare, and just to show him how much he didn't intimidate me, I pressed myself closer to the knife.

"Power."

"Is that why you're here?" He raised his chin in question.

"Don't be stupid." I returned to my innocent expression. "I'm just here for my sister."

"Hhmm." He stepped back, dropping the knife, but not giving me enough space to move. "You're playing a dangerous game, Queen."

"I've seen the depths of hell. I don't fear anything anymore."

"Do you honestly believe that even with your alliance, you and Cai can defeat the armies of Argon?"

I thought about how his soldiers trained, moving as one. Disciplined and powerful.

"Argon had agreed to the peace treaty because of what happened to the villages. If we didn't end the war, our own people would start turning against us. But I defeated Cai on the battlefield once and I can do it again."

"I don't need to defeat your armies," I said. "I just need to end you. An army, after all, without their king is as good as no army at all."

"You may be a good liar—" he tilted his head slightly — "but even I can see you're not a murderer."

His words ignited a fire inside my chest.

"Oh, I'll keep you alive. But by the time I'm done with you, you'll be begging for a merciful death." For Everness, for Cai, I would stop at nothing.

He sucked his teeth. "It would appear I chose the wrong sister."

I continued my death stare.

"Well, come along, then," he said nonchalantly while stepping back and holding his arm out to me again. "Breakfast is waiting."

I avoided all eye contact with Aries as we sat through breakfast. Cai tried to set up a meeting so they could revise the conditions of the peace treaty, but apparently Aries already had business elsewhere and so the meeting was pushed back until the next day. Part of me was relieved that I didn't have to see Aries for a whole day. It was one less conflict to worry about.

I needed to see Eloisa, but I didn't have the courage to go alone. So, I asked Cai to come with me.

"Prepare to be unsettled," I told him while knocking on the door. I wasn't sure why I knocked. Did I expect her to answer it?

"It's going to be fine."

A servant opened the door, to my surprise, but Aries did say they had people looking after her. The woman was old and plump, and she had a calmness about her.

"I'm here to see my sister," I informed her, and the servant stepped aside with a slight bow. She didn't even appear shocked at my striking resemblance to Eloisa.

I led Cai into the room after me. Eloisa was on her chair again, looking out the window. The servant went back to making the bed.

"Good morning, Eloisa." I took a seat opposite her and tried not to feel creeped out by the fact that I was practically staring into my own reflection. But she was much thinner and more pale, dark circles under her eyes. The bedroom was big and open, but furniture was scarce. No sharp objects lying around. No open windows.

"I'm not sure if Lance ever told you about me," I said.

Cai took a seat next to me.

"But I'm your sister, Elara."

She didn't move or look my way. I wasn't sure what I was expecting from her.

"This is Cai." I placed my hand on his forearm. "He's the king of Norrandale."

Silence continued to fill the room while I thought of what I could say next. I cleared my throat.

"Lance wants you to come back home." Maybe it would help if I reminded her of something familiar. "Your room is waiting for you back at the palace in Everness." I scooted forwards in my seat. "You're going to come home with me, okay?"

Nothing could have prepared me for her scream as she jumped up from her seat and came at me. Her momentum pushed my chair back, and she tackled me to the ground, clawing and screaming at me.

I tried to fight her off, but she was strong for someone so frail-looking. Cai and the servant pulled her off me. I sat up, catching my breath. The servant held her arms, whispering soothing things while she brushed her hair back with the palm of her hand. Cai helped me up.

"How often does that happen?" I asked the servant.

"Never," she replied. "I think it's best that you leave her be for a while." She didn't have to ask me twice. I didn't even care to look back as I walked out of the room, slightly shaken.

After spending some time exploring the palace grounds with Cordelia and Anesta, I returned to my chambers. I closed my bedroom door, taking out the clip that had been holding my hair in place. It was too hot for this dress. I started pulling at the lacings of my bodice.

"I must admit, that's the quickest a woman has ever started undressing in front of me. Which is saying a lot." I jumped at the sound of King Aries' voice. He was seated on a chair in the corner of the room, so still that I hadn't seen him as I came in.

"What are you doing in my rooms?" There was a sense of violation. Where was Rhen? Had he gone through my things? Was he looking for evidence of the Myrgonite stone? Was someone going through Cai's things as well?

"I thought we could have a chat, you and I," Aries said. He stood up from the chair. I quickly tightened my dress, thinking about all the ways I could escape this room should it come down to it.

"What more could you have to say that we didn't already establish this morning?"

He approached and I had to keep myself from recoiling. Every single one of my instincts wanted to put as much distance between me and him as possible. But I couldn't let him see that on my face. Couldn't let him believe for one moment that he had the upper hand.

"Well as you probably heard, I had business in town this morning," he started.

"Yes?"

"It also gave me time to think certain matters over."

I waited for him to continue, watching his every move with anticipation.

"And after some careful consideration, I believe you should accept my offer of marriage."

My mouth almost fell open but I clenched my jaw shut. His offer of marriage?

What was he talking about?

"I'm sorry, I don't think I heard you correctly," I responded.

"Oh, I think you heard me just fine." He was getting closer now.

"You cannot possibly be serious," I insisted.

"Why not? Everness and Argon united, no one would dare stand against us."

"You're only doing this because you want Cai off the throne, because you want to conquer Norrandale," I said, before I could think better of it.

"Can you blame a man for being ambitious?" He stopped in front of me, and if he dared to move any closer, I was going to pull out my dagger and let him know just what I thought of him. Consequences be damned.

"Is this because he killed your brother?" I asked. I didn't know if the subject would anger him and make things worse. I risked it.

"Dexus was family," he acknowledged. "But this isn't just about revenge."

"Then what is it about?" I stared into his eyes, daring him.

"I think you know." His smile was vicious, deadly. He was deadly.

"I'm not going to let you use me against Cai."

"Why?" He leaned his head down towards me. "Don't tell me you love the boy?" His tone was mocking, and I hated how he referred to Cai as a boy.

Yes. My mind told me to respond. *Say yes.*

"Don't fool yourself, Elara. I know where you come from, who you really are."

What did he mean by that? Was he talking about my life before becoming royalty? I didn't want to ask.

"People like you and me, we're not capable of love. You and I both know you'll ruin him."

His words were a punch to the gut, and I didn't want to believe him. But maybe they hit so deep because what he said wasn't unfamiliar to me. Subconsciously, I believed the same thing.

"Get out of my room," I said, through clenched teeth.

"Think it over, will you?" He brushed my chin with his fingers, and I jerked back.

"I'll see you at tonight's dance."

"Dance?"

"Don't you remember? I told you about the banquet when you arrived. There's to be dancing afterwards."

Trap. It must be some kind of trap.

"See you there," he said, before walking out of the room.

Chapter 30

Cai

An Argonian banquet held similarities to a Norrandish and Evernean one when you took into account the wine, the food and the loud chatter. But the atmosphere was unfamiliar and the air was humid. Even my attire was uncomfortable.

Instead of my usual breeches and jacket, I was dressed in a robe, held together by a golden waistband. I wouldn't have humiliated myself had it not been for Aries' insistence that we wear his "gifts" for the dance that was to be held after dinner. Elara had yet to grace the room with her presence and I found myself missing Thatcher's sense of humour to calm me down. I was on edge.

Linus and Theuses met my gaze from some distance away and they raised their glasses in greeting. They were dressed in the same style of clothes as I was and looked equally uncomfortable. Of course we fitted right in with the rest of the court, their robes all bright colours, following elegantly around the room to the music, which consisted of flutes, drums and old-fashioned lyres. Some of the guests clapped along to the beat.

"Are you all right, Cai?" Her voice came from behind me. I turned to face Elara.

Her clothes had been fashioned in Argonian style as well. The teal dress had a low neckline with golden leaves on the seams. The upper part of her hair had been braided out of her face and more golden leaves had been pinned to her head. I was momentarily speechless.

"Yeah." I cleared my throat. "All good." She came to stand next to me. "I just don't think I'm really in the mood for a party."

"I know what you mean."

I guided us to the nearest standing table. "We'll just show face for the sake of it and then leave as soon as we can." I gave her half a smile.

I reached for a cup of wine, but before I could bring it to my lips, Elara grabbed it away from me. "What are you—?"

She quickly took a sip.

My shoulders sagged. "Don't tell me you're testing if it's poisoned."

"I'm not going through that ordeal again."

Never mind what it might have cost her if it had actually been poisoned. She wiped the corner of her lips and handed me the cup back.

"And what about you? What if there was something wrong with it?"

She looked up at me from under long lashes. "I spent the majority of my teenage years trying to build immunity against poison, so I stand a much better chance than you."

I couldn't help but shake my head at her.

She remained standing close to me, staring out at the crowd, but I was only watching her.

"Are you nervous about the meeting with Aries tomorrow?" Elara said after a while, and I sighed.

"Who knows? Maybe something positive can come from it. Maybe we'll find a way to prevent a war."

"Do you really believe that or are you trying to remain optimistic?"

"I'm trying to remain idiotically optimistic, because if I don't, I feel like I'm going to lose my mind."

Her expression was tense, her eyes full of worry.

"What?"

She looked around at everyone before pulling me behind one of the large pillars. It gave us a little privacy from the crowd.

"I think Aries *knows*."

"Knows?"

"About the stones," she said in a hushed voice. Legends of the Myrgonite stones had been around almost as long as time, though I wondered what made Aries so sure that he would be willing to send out an army.

"What did he say?"

"This morning, on my way to breakfast, we ran into each other. The conversation led to Argon and Norrandale, and he said that he doesn't care about your reign as much as Norrandale has something he wants. What else could he mean?"

I leaned my head back against the pillar. "Even if Aries marches into Norrandale, it would take him for ever to find those caves up in the mountains."

"But is he ever going to stop unless he's dead?"

"Is that a suggestion?" I asked with slight surprise.

"No." She thought about it for a moment. "Maybe. I don't know."

I could tell by her fidgeting that she was nervous, agitated.

"Did he say anything else?"

Elara looked at me and then away again. "No."

The air around us was dense and hot, as it always seemed to be in this place.

"Let's get some fresh air."

Outside, the party was calmer, with fewer people, the music further away. The evening was still warm, but it felt easier to breathe.

Elara was gazing up at the stars as if she was looking for answers.

"What are you thinking about?"

"I never thought I would miss the forest this much." The world she'd grown up in was different from this one in every way. It was still a game of survival, but the rules had changed.

"I'm sorry about Arthur and Ray and everyone else you had to lose to get here," I blurted out.

"It's not your fault," she replied.

Arthur, no, but Ray …

"I don't want them to have died for nothing. Their sacrifices have put me in this place, and as much as I want to run away, I cannot let their deaths be in vain."

"Their deaths will never be in vain. They died for you and that's worth more than anything."

Her eyes softened. "I know there is a part of my life before you, but I'm afraid the more time we spend together, the less I seem to remember of it."

"Marry me."

The night was silent around my words.

She laughed after a moment. "I believe you already asked me, and I also believe that I already said yes."

"No." I took hold of her waist and gently pulled her in to me. "I mean tonight. Marry me tonight."

"Tonight?" she asked. "Here?"

"You can say no," I promised her.

"No, I mean …"

I raised an eyebrow at her.

Her eyes widened. "You just took me by surprise. How do you plan on doing it? You and I both know Aries wouldn't allow it out of spite."

"I don't think I need Aries' permission to make you my wife."

"Maybe not," she agreed. "But you certainly need a priest."

"Well …" I tilted my head slightly.

"Well, what?"

"Only for the legal part of it."

She pursed her lips. "The legal part is kind of important."

"We can sign a marriage contract when we get back home," I responded with nonchalance. "Marry me, Elara."

Her expression grew warm, and she nodded. "Okay."

We chuckled and I pressed my forehead to hers.

"I have to tell you something, though," she said, as if she'd just remembered whatever it was, and I supressed the urge to worry.

"Yes?"

"You know that marital agreement you signed at Woodsbrook Manor, that you thought was false?"

My eyes widened slightly.

"Well, turns out it's not really that false," Elara said, almost apologetically, and bit her lip.

I couldn't help but start to laugh. "Why didn't you ever tell me?"

"Because I didn't want to force you into an alliance or marrying me." She shrugged. "I wanted you to want it."

"Come on." I pressed a kiss to her lips and started leading her back inside.

"Oh, you mean like right now?"

Chapter 31

Elara

Marry me.

Was I really about to marry Cai?

We stepped back inside, where people were talking and dancing, completely unaware of us. "I need to find Anesta. I need to get changed." I was still holding Cai's hand.

"Why? You look perfect."

I looked down at my provocative neckline. "I'm not getting married in a dress like this. I'm still a queen." I smiled, as if he needed reminding. "Who's going to officiate?"

"Well, I was thinking Jack could do it."

"Great. You go find him and I'll find Anesta."

I searched through the crowd of bodies until I spotted Anesta, dancing with one of the Argonian men. If I hadn't known any better, I would think he was one of the young soldiers. Anesta was dressed up herself, looking elegant in her gold-trimmed gown.

I took hold of her arm. "I need to tell you something." The music was loud and blaring. "Can we please talk outside?"

"Sure." She nodded. Her partner seemed disappointed that I pulled her away, but I didn't care very much for him in that moment. I walked until there were fewer people around.

"What I'm about to tell you is quite serious, so please remain calm," I started.

With a gasp, she exclaimed, "You're with child?"

"What?" I looked down at my stomach and then back up at her again. "No! Cai and I are getting married in secret tonight."

"Oh, phew." She blew out a breath. "I don't know how I would have handled that."

"Why would you think I was with child?"

"Not important." She grabbed my arms in excitement. "You're getting married!"

She took a step back and clasped her hands together. "We have so much work to do."

Anesta meant what she said and took her job very seriously. She sat me down in front of my dressing table and proceeded to redo my hair and the makeup that had been applied earlier.

"It's a shame we didn't pack any white dresses." She placed her hands on her hips after digging through my trunk of clothes. "Do you want me to borrow an Argonian one?"

I shook my head. "I'd rather wear a dress of my own."

"Who's going to officiate?" she asked while helping me into one of my dark blue dresses. It had a square neckline, which I found the most flattering, and the sleeves flowed out from my elbows.

"Cai said he was going to ask Jack to do it."

"Oh, this is so exciting," she said, clapping her hands. I pressed my own to my sides — mostly to keep them from shaking. Why was

I so nervous? I'd wanted this alliance for what felt like for ever. But I knew I couldn't kid myself into believing it was merely about an alliance. I was about to marry Cai.

Married.

Me.

The masked bandit from Fairfrith camp who used to steal food from aristocrats and wear hand-me-down clothes.

You'll ruin him. Aries' words ran through my head. I tried to shake them out. I couldn't believe him. He was only trying to use me to his own advantage. But Cai was kind-hearted and caring and sweet. He looked out for me and trusted me. We made a good team.

We decided to meet on the palace rooftop that overlooked the city.

Downstairs, the party was still going in full force. Normally, guards would be stationed on the rooftop, but Rhen found out that they had been moved to stand guard at the dance.

Cai, Cordelia and Rhen were waiting by the time Anesta and I got there. I'd never seen Cai smile so broadly.

"Where's Jack?" I asked.

"He's on his way." We interlaced hands. "You're breathtaking," he whispered.

"This old thing?" I moved the skirts of my dress side to side with a grin before meeting Cai's eyes again. "This is really happening, isn't it?"

His expression remained unchanged. "Sure you don't want to run yet?"

"I think I'd like to stay."

Five minutes passed. Jack didn't show up.

"Do you think he's lost or something?" I asked no one in particular. The longer we waited the more nervous I was getting, and the more Aries' words crept inside my mind, no matter how hard I tried to push them out.

"I'll go and look for him. He probably took the wrong staircase or something."

Cordelia hurried off.

I let out a long breath.

"Nervous?" Cai asked with a grin.

"Should I be?" I teased back.

"I don't know. I have a pretty intimidating grandmother, as you mentioned."

"Have you met my family?" I snorted. "I have Lance and a sister who can't even speak to me."

"I'm assuming you're going to take her home?"

I nodded. "She'll be safest in Everness, I think. And then Lance can spend all his free time taking care of her."

"Do you think he'll ever settle down, get married?"

"I don't know. Somehow, I have trouble imagining him in this scenario." I gestured to the two of us standing there. "Do you think if you hadn't been enemies then maybe you would've grown up friends?"

"Perhaps when we were younger, but I doubt we would have been friends now."

"Ironic that he's going to be your brother-in-law."

"As you keep reminding me."

"The holidays are going to be chaotic, aren't they?" I wanted to laugh. The things we were talking about seemed so far-fetched. And yet, there I stood, about to get married.

Ten more minutes passed. No sign of Jack.

"Something's wrong. Where could he be?"

Cai was looking worried by now too. "We'd better go looking for him and Cordelia."

313

We turned to leave, my mind running through every possible worst-case scenario. Just as we reached the stairs, Jack came around the corner.

"We have to leave right now," he said, panic in his voice.

"Why? What's going on?" I asked, but he'd already started escorting us down the stairs. I pulled up the hems of my dress to keep from falling.

"I wasn't supposed to find out. It was an accident. I overheard someone talking."

"Find what out?" Cai questioned.

"Aries is dispatching an army tomorrow. They're going to march on Norrandale."

Chapter 32

Cai

The wind appeared to be brewing up a storm and I held on tighter to the ship's railing. We'd left as soon as Jack had told us what he'd overheard. It didn't give us much of a head start but it was better than nothing. The only thought on my mind was that we needed to get back to Norrandale as soon as possible. Worst of all, I didn't have any way of alerting anyone until we returned.

Elara walked up the stairs that led onto the deck and came to stand next to me.

"How is she doing?"

"She's sleeping, thankfully, so all is calm." It had been a mission to get not only ourselves out of the palace undetected but Eloisa as well. Elara had refused to leave her behind, which was understandable. We got lucky. Whatever state she was in, she was quiet and compliant.

"I'll have to find a way to get her safely to Everness, but one thing at a time, right?" She placed her hand atop mine, which was still clutching the railing.

"I don't think there's any other choice," I confessed.

"Are you scared?"

"Not so much for myself but for my kingdom, for the people I care about, yes." I looked over to her. Her expression was filled with distress. "Are you?"

"I'm terrified," she muttered softly. I wanted to console her. Wanted to wrap my arms around her and tell her that everything would be fine. But I couldn't do that. Couldn't make promises that I might not be able to keep.

She was biting the inside of her cheek again, as she did when she was deep in thought.

"What is it?"

"Well, I was just thinking. Norrandale doesn't have the strongest army at this stage, and by the time soldiers from Everness arrive, it could be too late."

This I knew only too well. This very thought was keeping me awake at night.

"What if we ..." She hesitated. "Do you think it would be possible to use the Myrgonite objects to help?"

"Elara." I sighed. "It's too dangerous."

"No, I know but—"

"Those damn Myrgonite stones are the reason Aries is coming after us. It would have been better if they never existed. They're more trouble than they're worth, and we're not even entirely sure what the objects are." We had our suspicions about the necklace and the dagger but no way to confirm it.

"But if we don't have a choice," she pressed on.

I turned my hand and laced her fingers with mine. "I'm not willing to pay the price for it." And that seemed to be the end of the conversation. She remained standing next to me and eventually leaned her head against my shoulder.

"I'm sorry I dragged us all the way there. We should never have gone."

"If we hadn't gone, we'd have had no way of knowing that Aries was coming. At least some chance is better than no chance at all."

She nodded slowly but didn't respond.

"You know, of all the ways I saw today panning out, this was not it." I attempted to lighten the mood.

"What do you mean?" Elara responded with slight confusion.

"We were about to get married last night, don't you remember?" I chuckled.

"Oh right." She'd clearly only been thinking about what lay ahead of us the moment we set foot back on Norrandish soil. "Well, a trip back home seems pretty realistic to me. Or did you intend to spend the whole of our honeymoon in Argon?"

"You have a point." I tried not to grimace. Words like honeymoon seemed so futile when we had a war on our hands.

She groaned and rubbed her eyes with her palms. "I can't wait to get back on solid land again. I hate that the floor is always moving beneath me."

"It helps if you stare out onto the horizon," I told her.

"I think I'm just going to have a lie-down. I didn't exactly get much sleep last night."

Neither had I, and I had a feeling I wouldn't be getting much sleep for the days to come either.

I couldn't describe my relief when land finally came into view. I might have been perfectly happy if I never had to leave Norrandale again.

"I'm going to secure us some horses," Jack said as we sailed into the docks. We weren't due home yet and we'd left in such a hurry that no proper arrangements were in place for our return.

"What about the village?" Elara asked. "This shore is nearest to Argon and most likely where Aries is going to station his ships. He'll demolish this place and everything else in his wake. We have to warn somebody."

She was right, but evacuating a village was easier said than done, especially when we needed to get to the palace as soon as possible.

"We'll stay," Cordelia offered, referring to herself and Anesta. "If you spare a few guards, then you can go ahead and we'll warn everybody here."

"Are you sure?" Elara asked, and Cordelia nodded.

"We'll be fine. You get to the palace, and Anesta and I will find you." It was the best option we had.

"What about Eloisa?" Elara looked back to the ship.

"We'll take care of her too," Anesta assured her.

Jack managed to secure horses for the four of us as well as the handful of palace guards we'd taken with us on the journey. I wished Alastor had been here, but I had asked him to stay in Everness. I needed someone to watch over Gwen and Thatcher while we were gone.

Nobody spoke much during our journey to the palace. There seemed to be the overwhelming threat of doom looming. My stomach was tied in knots. But I had to stay strong and certain. People were relying on me for their safety.

We were all exhausted by the time the palace came into view. The journey had been long and hard. We'd pushed ourselves and our horses to get to Mistwood as quickly as possible. Aries' soldiers had most likely reached the coast by now. Hopefully Anesta, Eloisa and

Cordelia got somewhere safe in time. When we finally reached the palace gates, there were no guards stationed on the walls or towers. Perhaps they were rotating shifts. But when we entered the courtyard, I knew my gut's warning had been right. It was deathly quiet, not a single soul in sight. No guards, no servants, no courtiers, nothing.

A crow landed on one of the roof ledges in the courtyard. It gave a loud shriek, breaking through the silence. I watched as it pecked at one of its black feathers. Something about the bird created an uneasy feeling in me. "Where is everybody?" Elara asked.

"Something's wrong." Rhen stated the obvious.

Jack dismounted and pulled out his sword. The rest of our party followed suit.

"Stay behind me, Your Majesty."

I obeyed as he led the group inside the castle, our guards surrounding me and Elara.

We crept through the hallways, all empty, anticipating something or someone jumping out at any minute. Where were the courtiers? My guards and my family? What the hell had happened?

We finally reached the throne room. I shouldn't have been surprised at the Argonian soldiers. I should have known better. And yet nothing could have prepared me for the sudden fight that broke out.

How did they get inside the palace? How was Aries always one step ahead of us?

If Argonian guards had taken hold of my home, then what had they done with everyone in the palace? I forced my train of thought away from all the gruesome possibilities my mind managed to conjure up. My sole focus was keeping Elara safe and getting out alive.

One of the Argonian soldiers broke through our small wall of guards and swung his sword towards my torso. I managed to block it and the next few swings after. He was so distracted trying to fight me, he didn't notice Jack coming for him from behind. With the soldier down, we nodded at each other and moved on.

I struck at the next soldier and the next, the fury at Aries building up more inside me with every passing second. I looked for Elara behind me, but she had Rhen on her side, defending her. Another soldier. Another. I was out of breath, trying to block the memories of killing one Argonian soldier after the other during the war.

The tiles in the throne room became slick with blood and I slipped, losing my sword in the process. I panicked and one of the soldiers saw this as his opportunity. He came at me. I pushed myself up, bracing for what was to come.

"Cai!" It was the last voice I thought I'd hear. I looked to my right where Thatcher stood in the doorway, pale but armed. He tossed me a sword just in time for me to defend myself and counterstrike. The soldier was young but unfathomably strong, and it was an effort to keep him from slicing through me. I searched for weak spots — areas he left vulnerable and exposed to being hit. When he raised his sword to come down at me, I struck his chest as quickly as I could. Blood seeped through his uniform before he dropped to the floor.

My heart beat so loudly I could hear it, overcome with an overwhelming need for survival. I had tunnel vision as I searched for the next attacker.

Thatcher rushed over to me, his own sword in hand.

"What the hell are you doing here?" I asked. He looked dishevelled and tired.

"I just arrived. I came back as soon as I heard Aries was coming with an army. It seems I got here just in time."

I looked around the room. There were so many dead bodies on the floor. Too many. Both Argonians and our guards. But Elara was still safe, and Rhen was fighting among our other guards. Only a few were still alive. I heaved.

Jack was on the floor. He'd taken a nasty hit to the leg, red colouring the breeches of his uniform.

"Jack!" I feared one of Aries' men would take advantage of his vulnerability before we could reach him.

Elara was next to me. She had blood on her chest.

"Are you hurt?"

She shook her head, but her pupils were dilated, her chest falling and rising quickly.

Thatcher hurried towards Jack with his arm stretched out. I was too busy fighting for my life to consider his words before. How did he know Aries had an army coming? There was no way the news could have reached him and have him make the journey here in time.

Jack took his hand so that Thatcher could pull him into a standing position. Instead, I watched as Thatcher drove his sword through Jack's body.

Chapter 33

Elara

Jack was dead.

And Thatcher had been the one to kill him.

Time had come to a standstill. We were all frozen with shock.

What was happening?

Cai's eyes were wide. He didn't move.

My first instinct was to lift my dagger and head straight for Thatcher. If not to kill him then to disarm him. My fist tightened around the handle and there was a taste of blood in my mouth.

One of Aries' guards had tried to kill me. Rhen was quick to step in to protect me. While the soldier was occupied trying to fight off Rhen, I took my dagger and stabbed him in the neck. His blood now coated my clothes, and I felt sick at the thought.

There were more of them now. It was as if they had multiplied somehow while most of our guards lay dead on the ground. At this rate we would be outnumbered within minutes. Outnumbered and dead.

Adrenaline rushed through my veins, finally shaking me out of it. I grabbed Cai's arm. I'd been betrayed enough in my life to know exactly what was about to go down. There was only one way we would make it out of here alive.

"We need to get out," I said under my breath.

Thatcher stepped away from Jack's corpse and let out a menacing laugh. "I'd been waiting a while to do that."

I wanted to scream as I watched Jack's blood cover the floor beneath his body.

"What the hell are you doing?" Rhen called out, about to step up to Thatcher, but I grabbed his arm and stopped him. Thatcher wasn't here in some foolishly heroic attempt to help us. In fact, I was willing to wager that Thatcher had been at Mistwood Palace for some time now.

Cai hadn't moved yet, hadn't said a word. He was staring at Jack, completely still. It was only a few seconds that passed but it felt like an eternity.

Rhen had his sword still. We needed to run. While the remainder of our guards were occupied. While we still had the chance. As much as I hated the idea of fleeing, of leaving Jack's body behind, I wasn't a trained fighter the way they were, and Cai and Rhen would only be able to hold out for so long before the Argonian soldiers surrounded us.

Thatcher made his way across the throne room, walking away from us. "I really hate to do this, Cai." Cai's eyes didn't move away from Jack. "I mean, I've known you for as long as I can remember." He stopped in front of the throne and turned around to face us again. "Which is also why I know you have no business being king. Really, you give me no choice but to do this. Someone has to stop you from running this kingdom to the ground."

I hadn't let go of Cai. Clutching his arm, I slowly took a step or two backwards.

Run. Run. Run.

"You must know that I took no pleasure in killing your family, but Aries made me an offer I couldn't refuse," Thatcher continued, and then he slowly sat down on the throne, like he was relishing every moment.

"Norrandale needs the strongest king possible, and it needs Argon as an ally. You were always too blind to see that. But now ..." He smirked. "Now we're going to change history and make Argon and Norrandale the most powerful kingdoms the world has seen."

"Cai, we need to leave now." I tried to shake him out of his daze, but he wouldn't budge.

"You should listen to her, Cai," Thatcher said. "You should run away as fast and as far as you can, because once Aries catches up with you, whatever pieces of you are left behind will be beyond recognition. So yes, I would run if I were you."

I didn't hesitate this time. I yanked Cai as hard as I could and pulled him out of the throne room with all my strength, Rhen swiftly in position behind us, making sure none of the Argonians caught up. I could still hear Thatcher laughing as we made our way out of the palace and into the courtyard where our horses stood.

"Get up," I said to Cai, forcing him onto his horse. There was no time for kind words or sympathies. We needed to get out alive first. Rhen mounted one of the horses and I climbed on another.

We kicked the horses into a gallop, rushing out of the courtyard and the gates. I could hear the Argonians coming out of the palace. They wouldn't be far behind us. We'd have to lose them in the woods. My horse huffed beneath me, hoofbeats loud on the path.

"Where to now?" Rhen shouted over the wind.

"Back home. Back to Everness."

THE END

Acknowledgements

Where to even begin? This book has been such a journey. I wrote the first chapter of this novel in late 2021, and to finally see it finished and out in the world means so much to me. It took late-night writing sessions after work, endless rewrites, many rejection letters and even contemplating giving up writing as a career to get here. It's hard to believe how far this story has come.

First, I would like to thank my mother, who listened patiently as I rambled on and on about the manuscript and the ideas I had in mind, for encouraging me to keep pursuing a professional career in writing and who was excited with me every step of the way as I got my first book deal.

To my dad, who took it upon himself to edit an entire draft of this book before I submitted it to publishers. Thank you for being so invested in my stories, for helping me improve my craft and for believing in me as an author.

Thank you to my connect group, Carina, Thomas, Mieke, Kelly, Simoné, Cari, Francois, Dom, Marcel and Camryn. I appreciate your constant prayers, especially when times were tough and deadlines were stressing me out. You are the most supportive people in the world, and

I see you as my second family. Thank you for always celebrating my work with me.

To Vera, Jordan, Juan-luc, Kyle and Marco. You have been in my life longer than you have not. We've grown up together and celebrated milestones with each other. I am so proud of all the things you have done and accomplished. You continue to inspire me to better myself. I value your friendship more than words can express. Even if you don't always read my books, ha ha.

To my editor, Jasmine. You are such a delight to work with. Thank you for always valuing my opinion and helping me get the best out of my work. I could never have done this without you. Thank you to Laurel and Hannah for their helpful comments and edits. Thank you, Sasha, for all the work you've done marketing my book. I've looked up to you as a writer for a long time and appreciate all the effort that has gone into promoting my novels.

To everyone else at Joffe Books, as always, I am so thankful that I get to work with such an amazing publisher. Everyone on the team is so wonderful and I'll forever be grateful to have such an amazing group of people working on my books.

Lastly, thank you to my readers. Thank you to those who have been patient for the last three years as I worked on making this book a better read. I hope you enjoyed the story and that it was worth the wait.

The Joffe Books Story

We began in 2014 when Jasper agreed to publish his mum's much-rejected romance novel and it became a bestseller.

Since then we've grown into the largest independent publisher in the UK. We're extremely proud to publish some of the very best writers in the world, including Joy Ellis, Faith Martin, Caro Ramsay, Helen Forrester, Simon Brett and Robert Goddard. Everyone at Joffe Books loves reading and we never forget that it all begins with the magic of an author telling a story.

We are proud to publish talented first-time authors, as well as established writers whose books we love introducing to a new generation of readers.

We won Trade Publisher of the Year at the Independent Publishing Awards in 2023. We have been shortlisted for Independent Publisher of the Year at the British Book Awards for the last four years, and were shortlisted for the Diversity and Inclusivity Award at the 2022 Independent Publishing Awards. In 2023 we were shortlisted for Publisher of the Year at the RNA Industry Awards.

We built this company with your help, and we love to hear from you, so please email us about absolutely anything bookish at: feedback@joffebooks.com.

If you want to receive free books every Friday and hear about all our new releases, join our mailing list: www.joffebooks.com/freebooks

And when you tell your friends about us, just remember: it's pronounced Joffe as in coffee or toffee!